D. M. Cayer is the pseudonym of a well-known writer of fiction, non-fiction, poetry and plays.

D. M. Cayer

Scarborough Fear

Where are you going? To Scarborough fair?
Parsley, sage, rosemary and thyme.
Remember me to a bonny lass there
For once she was a true lover of mine.

Futura
Macdonald & Co
London & Sydney

A Futura Book

First published in Great Britain in 1982 by
Macdonald & Co (Publishers) Ltd
London & Sydney

This Futura edition published in 1983

ISBN 0 7088 2364 5

Reproduced, printed and bound in Great Britain by
Hazell Watson & Viney Ltd, Aylesbury, Bucks

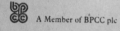
A Member of BPCC plc

Futura Publications
A Division of
Macdonald & Co (Publishers) Ltd
Maxwell House
74 Worship Street
London EC2A 2EN

for Owen Brookes

One

'So you see, you'll have to go,' my mother said.

I did see. There was no ignoring the tunnelled hump under the bedclothes that made a cloche over her broken plastered leg. Still, I couldn't help feeling suspicious, as if the whole thing might be a hoax and when I looked at my mother's face, with not a blonded hair astray, her cheeks very slightly flushed and her lips perfectly outlined in rowan, this year's autumn colour, I almost wondered if she had arranged the perfect fracture too.

'What about John?'

'He can't go, of course,' my mother said, embodying her attitudes to men in general and her brother in particular in one brief statement. Men were both too important to have their lives disturbed and too incompetent to be asked to deal with the real world. 'I don't know why you're making so much of this, darling. It's not as if you were doing much at the moment.'

'Yes,' I said, needled as she knew I would be. 'It was very thoughtful of Aunt Meg to die during my year's sabbatical.'

I knew at once I'd gone too far. The hurt came into her eyes and the carefully painted bottom lip trembled.

It was always the same. My mother stuck her little pins into me one after the other, until, like the bull stung by the bandilleros, I put my head down and charged. And then the sword went in deep, past my shoulder, through the delicate lung tissue and into the heart. The sword was her own pain, and my blood seemed to gush up and choke me even before I felt my heart turning to stone under its piercing blade. It had happened so often I wondered sometimes if any passer-by would ever be able to pull the sword out and return the stone to flesh that might feel again, and beat and do all the things hearts are supposed to do.

'She was my only sister.'

I almost sighed. The banal reply merely increased the cold pain in my chest. I wanted to say: 'You never saw her, never wrote except at Christmas, and if you had met you would have had nothing to say to each other.'

As if I had spoken, she went on: 'You might be a little more considerate, Paul. It's been a shock even though we didn't see much of each other. Blood's thicker than water, and coming just after breaking my leg—which was a shock to the system in itself ...'

'I'm sorry.'

My mother always called me by the masculine form of my name, thereby emphasising that it was my fault I wasn't a boy, except when she wanted to really scold when it was, 'Paula', with equal strength to both syllables to show I was just a girl, and therefore part of the lesser half of humankind.

My apology had appeased her, as it always did. 'Ring me when you get there and see what has to be done. I imagine they won't have cut off the phone yet. When will you go?'

It was a double edged remark, meaning that she'd had enough of me now, having achieved her objective, as well as being the simple practical enquiry it seemed.

'Tomorrow.'

'Good.' A hand began to stray towards the embossed silver glass on the bedside table. 'Bob said he'd drop in. How am I looking?'

'You're splendid Ma, as always.'

'Not too peaky?' The hand closed over the handle and drew the glass towards her. My heart, or rather my stomach since my heart was stone, turned to water with pity at the

8

liver spots and thickening veins. The spots were still faint. They could even pass as freckles in the summer, but I knew how she would watch them spread and deepen. Bob was her lover. He was dull but kind, and I alternately blessed and cursed him. Without a man somewhere her life was meaningless to her.

It wasn't her fault of course. Her childhood had made her what she was, as in turn mine, under her tutelage, had made me, or unmade me, as I often thought.

'I'll ring you,' I said, as I bent and kissed her cheek very lightly. The flavour and texture of her made—up skin had repelled and excited me for most of my twenty—eight years. My mother's face stared up at me, narrowed to the confines of the oval glass as if trapped there.

'How's Martin?'

'I don't know. All right, I expect.'

I felt her draw back from the questions that were forming, instinct telling her that I would snap at them and wound us both again. Besides, Bob was imminent and she wanted me gone before he arrived. She could always come back to it another time.

'Wrap up warmly, darling, and take plenty of woollies with you. You know how cold it can be up there.'

'I do, but you don't. You never go North of Oxford. Give my love to Bob.'

At the door I looked back, but I was already gone for her. She had composed herself to a picture of charming distress. I wondered if he would sit by the bed, holding her hand, or whether they would go further. I never knew about my mother and sex. I suppose children don't.

I let myself into my own studio flat with all the evening still ahead to be killed and no Martin but only the questions to go over and over, like an olive stone at a party you don't know how to get rid of. Where was the convenient plant pot I could ditch it in and would it merely split and sprout at once into a tree loaded with hard, bitter fruit? I remembered a poem we had read at school for a literature exam, about a girl who buried her lover's head in a pot under a sprig of basil and wept it into a bush.

She hadn't been responsible for her lover's death, though. Or had she? Weren't we always responsible? Well, Martin wasn't dead. He was alive and well and living in Earl's Court, but he was dead to me. I had killed him as effectively as if I'd driven over him and smashed him into the road with my wheels.

I made myself a cup of instant coffee. The granules floated to the top as I poured on the boiling water and made a swirling vortex that I wished I could fall into and be sucked down scalding and screaming. I saw my pigmy arms flailing and then vanishing in the burnt toffee whirlpool as I slopped in the milk. The books I hadn't opened for weeks reared an accusing pile beside the bedraggled pages of the thesis on social divisions in the Victorian novel that I had been given a sabattical to write. I made a cheese sandwich and ate an apple, with the television flickering meaningless, disjointed stills at me and the rest of the watching world.

Then I rang King's Cross for the times of trains. I would catch an early one. I almost began to be glad I had something I must do. Half a bottle of wine and two sleeping pills later, I was able to fall into a haunted doze that saw me through to a cold grey morning.

The station was like a turreted fortress or a prison against a tossed charcoal and wash sky. I sat myself in the belly of the train and let it haul me through the northern suburbs. The train I had chosen was the slow one straight through. We trailed through old railway towns, Grantham and Doncaster, still black with the smoke of steamers long since scrap, and on to York. I ate railway cake compounded of grit and sweet paste, with my paper cup of coffee. At lunchtime I had a miniature of whisky and a cotton waste and rubber sandwich decorated with red rings of tomato tasting of bile. I was glad I hadn't bothered with lunch in the restaurant car.

At York the train turned towards the coast. The wolds beyond the window were mud– and sludge–coloured under the low grey canopy. Here and there, sheep stared briefly at the train and then went back to nibble at turf bitten down to

the finger ends by the wind. I wondered what had possessed
Aunt Meg to live up here. Perhaps it was the sure knowledge
that her sister would never come calling.

Meg was the clever girl; Eileen, my mother, the pretty one.
Meg had been pleased by my scholarship to Cambridge and
sent me twenty pounds, even though I hadn't seen her for
years. I had met her eighteen months ago in the station buffet
at King's Cross. She was on her way to some conference and
asked if I could spare the time to see her. I was glad now that
I had.

Scarborough station was full of old world charm. As I
stepped through the glass doors I caught the first tang of the
sea and two gulls flung themselves shrieking and mewling
above my head. I would have the luxury of a taxi out to Aunt
Meg's cottage just this once. I wanted to get there before it
was dark, and already the short winter day which had hardly
seemed to get up was gathering towards its close.

'I can't take you to the door,' the driver said. 'There's a bit
of a path down to it. I'll set you down as close as I can.
Grand old girl,' he went on. 'Didn't use us much, had her old
bicycle. But sometimes I've taken her home when it was late
or she had a lot to carry.'

Aunt Meg suddenly took on more substance. There were
people here who saw her every day—friends, perhaps, who
would miss her. I should have to get in touch with them. They
might want to come to the funeral. Maybe there would be an
address book among her things, or a list of handy telephone
numbers. My mother had given me the name of the
undertakers and I would have to ring them at once.

'Here we are then,' the driver said, as he pulled up. I paid
him and got out my bag. A little white gate had the name
Bayview on it in weathered black lettering. 'It's just round the
bluff. You can't miss it. Here's my card in case you want a
taxi any time.'

I thanked him. He waved a salute and was off. I felt the
wind tug at me, and the desolation of the empty cliff road. I
clutched at the little oblong of white card as at a passport
back to civilisation. At least I had made it here before dark. I

11

opened the gate and set off down an asphalt path, with the smell of the sea growing stronger at every step. I rounded the bluff and almost caught my breath. I was facing out to sea and the wind hurled itself at my face. Between where grey sea and sky met, there was a strip of brilliant orange that was almost blinding. The cliff swept round in a great curve. I couldn't see the beach below, if indeed there was one, because Aunt Meg's cottage and the garden blocked it out.

The path became steps going down and then a path again, between shrubs. Then there was a hedge and beds of autumnally stricken plants with a small lawn, where fallen leaves had been raked into a tidy brown heap. Perhaps Aunt Meg had done it. She didn't sound the sort to employ a gardener.

'How will I get in?' I had remembered to ask my mother.

'Darling, you must use your initiative. Break a window,' she suggested, with all the conviction of someone who had never done such a thing in her life, but had read about it.

I put my bag down and pushed at the door. It was shut fast with the small round brass disc of a Yale lock. I stepped back and looked at the cottage. It reminded me of a favourite story about a witch called Cousin Blodwen, who had come to tidy up her cousin's home and life. Aunt Meg's was more of a bungalow than a cottage and it was far from unkempt, but somehow it brought the book vividly into my mind. I walked round the side to find a back door or a window not quite closed.

A verandah ran along the rear of the house. There was more lawn, with a white-painted garden seat looking towards the sea. The back door had a cat flap let into it, but that too was shut, and without Alice's shrinking potion it would have been useless to me. Then I saw the flower pot, trying to look unostentatious, lifted it and there was a key wrapped in a little transparent plastic bag. Alice in reverse should now be able to get out of the garden and into the house. I fitted it in the lock on the back door, and turned.

My first instinct was to switch on a light and flood the little house with the comfort of an electric glow. The sense of relief was enormous. Everything became possible. I marched to the front door, opened it and brought in my bag that was sitting disconsolately on the path. Then I toured from room to room, getting my bearings as my mother, with her perfect sense of cliché, would have put it. The house wasn't quite a proper bungalow: it had two bedrooms with cut—off corners under the eaves. One had obviously been Aunt Meg's. The other was a spare room, where I dumped my bag.

The telephone gave a lively ping when I picked up the receiver, and began to purr comfortingly. In the little kitchen the fridge still hummed. I found tea and a carton of Long Life milk and set about the first necessity of the English, taking possession in the tea ceremony. There were tins of soup and baked beans. I shouldn't go hungry. I found a tray and carried the tea things through into Aunt Meg's sitting room.

It was as if I had come to stay and had arrived while she was out. Any moment now she would come in and share the tea with me, her usually neat mouse—coloured hair, tinged here and there with grey, blown a little awry from cycling in the wind. I looked at my watch. It was four o'clock. I had better ring the undertakers.

Theale and Partners answered me in the unctuous tones of professional sympathy. I explained that I was enquiring about Miss Hackstead, representing her sister, my mother.

'The coroner's office has released the ah ... deceased, which means that the funeral can take place as convenient.'

I was completely taken aback and all at once very angry with my mother. She had said nothing to warn me that there was anything irregular about Aung Meg's death.

'There won't be any need for an inquest,' the silky professional voice reassured me. 'The post mortem showed a massive heart attack.'

I supposed I was meant to find this comforting, but suddenly I found myself unable to embark on the details of choosing between mahogany, oak or pine, and brass or steel handles. I would have to consult the rest of the family, I said, and would ring them tomorrow. Theale and Partners said they quite understood and I had a vision of the traditional thin, stooped, black–suited figure making motions of hand–washing. When I put the phone down it felt damp and chilly in the room, as if the sea or a foggy breath from it had crept under the door.

I thought I had better look for wood or coal and firelighters, and warm myself and the house, which seemed to be sinking into sadness, as if it too had just realised that Aunt Meg wasn't coming back. As I was searching for matches in the kitchen my eye took in the closed cat door. On impulse I opened it, and then the whole door, and stepped into the garden.

The smack of waves on rock face, and then the unfurling of water along a beach, followed by the grating noise as sand or little pebbles were drawn back by the seasucker fingers was very close. I was glad of the light spilling out of the kitchen door and window behind me. I felt a bit silly but I called into the now foggy darkness, 'Puss, puss!'

It was a great disadvantage not having a name to call but I tried again. I would have been glad of the company yet instinctively I felt that no one would come. I went indoors and shut out the night.

The blaze I coaxed into the sitting room fireplace cheered me again. I decided it was time to ring my mother.

'You never told me that Aunt Meg died suddenly,' I accused her.

'Didn't I, darling? Are you sure...? I know I meant to. You don't always listen.'

'You didn't tell me. Fortunately the post mortem showed it was a heart attack, so there won't be any further trouble.'

'I don't understand ...'

'Well, if there'd been traces of drugs or poison, there'd have had to be an inquest.'

'Poison!'

'She could have drunk something by accident. Anyway the undertakers want to know what sort of coffin, handles etc.'

'Can't you deal with it, Paul? I'm hardly well enough.'

'Shall I ring John about the date, or will you? He'll have to come, especially as you can't, and there'll have to be a notice in *The Times*.'

'You do what you think best, darling.'

'Then there's the matter of a will,' I went on, determined that she wasn't going to escape entirely.

'Yes. There ought to be one somewhere.'

'I'll look through her things tonight. It's probably at her bank. I'll ring the manager tomorrow if I can find out which one she used.' More and more I was beginning to wonder if my mother had really broken her leg. I hadn't realised there would be so much to do but she would have had to do it all when my father died and so must have known. I turned away from that line of thought. I was still mourning my father. I supposed I always would.

'I'm terribly grateful, Paul, and I'm glad you've got the phone for company. It sounds very lonely. So typical of Meg, thoughtless.'

Anyone who hadn't had a lifetime of my mother might have been shocked. I poured myself some more tea and guiltily took a biscuit from the Edwardian silver barrel which had been grandmother's. I knew, because my mother had never ceased to covet it.

There was a desk in one corner of the sitting room by a window that would give long light hours in summer and a view over the sea to anyone sitting at it to work. Every foot of wall that wasn't otherwise taken up was lined with shelves of books. I wouldn't be short of reading material but they could wait for my inspection. First, with almost a silent apology to Aunt Meg, I would look in her desk for a chequebook.

It was there in front of me, the end sticking tidily out of a pigeonhole, as soon as I lowered the flap. I began to go through the other compartments and then to look in the desk drawers, making a little pile of useful finds, which I carried over to the fire to examine. I sat down on the rug with them, glad of the warmth on my face and the comfort of live flames that sang quietly in the burning wood.

There was an engagement book, an address book, a photograph album and a series of small cheap jotters that seemed to contain notes on work in progress. The addresses, apart from my own and her brother's and sister's, meant nothing to me. I turned to the last pictures in the photograph album, carefully mounted, captioned and dated. A handsome ginger and white cat, tail erect, was labelled 'Tiger'. He figured in another snap, too, with a middle–aged man called 'L.W.' There were more of L.W., and then one of my aunt taken by him, unless Tiger was a photographer, labelled with the same date as the others and the initials 'M.H.'.

L.W. had black hair brushed smooth on his narrow head, and a smile which curved his rather wide mouth. The sun had been in his eyes, giving them a crinkled opacity almost as if he were blind. I turned back a thick page and found another of Aunt Meg's companions, this time a woman, photographed on the back lawn with the sea behind and captioned 'Mary'. Tiger, obviously not a cat to be left out of any picture he could get himself into, was winding, tail up, about her legs. The picture had been taken in the spring, several months before the others.

I went back to the address book and tried 'M' for Mary, but Aunt Meg had been very systematic, unlike me. If I had thumbed up 'M' in my own book it would have given Martin Alford. Going through all Aunt Meg's 'W' entries, I would probably find L.W. There was unlikely to be more than one, though there were probably several 'Marys'. I turned to the engagements.

All the little doings of her life were noted. Tiger went to the vet, her shoes went to the cobbler's, people came to tea, a Professor Kagashoni called from Tokyo, and every few days L.W. made an appearance. If I looked back to the year before last which was no doubt tidily stacked away somewhere I would find: 'Paula, King's Cross, 11.30.'. It gave me an uneasy feeling again; as if Aunt Meg hadn't really gone at all, but would put her key in the lock at any moment. I got up from the rug, stepped out of the charmed circle of the firelight and went to the windows.

There was nothing to be seen outside. It was as if the cottage was suspended in black aspic that might press in through the windows, imprisoning me in a glutinous tide until

I was nothing but a wisp of petrified moss at the heart of a black agate, with the bones of the house fossilised around me.

I had had these sensations all my life. The line between reality and the other was broken very easily for me. The tumbled leaves of a virginia creeper instantly, almost banally, became daubs of blood. Poets make images, metaphors out of such perceptions. I had no need to invent them and no cathartic outlet for them when they came. If I could have written or painted them out I had always believed I might be freed from them; but I had no talent, no medium to channel them into. The sensations lodged in my mind and putrified.

Since I had killed Martin's love it had become worse. I was raw all through, my whole body a thrumming nerve, a visionary who saw the real world dissolve and be transformed but without a god to cling to. Now I could only hold on and wait for the feeling to pass like an attack of giddiness, of perceptual vertigo.

Perhaps I loved Martin so much because he was perfectly at home in the real world. My mother would have said it fitted him like a glove. Not that she approved of him or our relationship. Her enquiry yesterday (was it only yesterday?) had been meant to draw out the information that we hadn't made it up. Martin was thought not good enough for the product of a Hackstead and a Cockburn, even though we both earned a living by lecturing at the same college.

His subject, education, was unacademic and faintly ungenteel. If he had even been one of those who used jargon to obscure the practical problems of teaching teachers to teach she would have thought better of him. As he merely inspired confidence in his students and brought out, without pretentiousness, any latent ability they might have for interesting a class of thirty–five grubby nine year olds in the improvement of their reading age, she despised him. He hadn't minded. He had loved me too much and only wanted to protect me against the worst of her barbs.

I was back on the rug now, with the world restored to its place, the curtains drawn and the tears falling into the fake fur pile. It was my inability to cope with what I called to myself 'the sex bit' that had driven him away in the end. I had watched him begin first to lose confidence in himself, then in me and finally in us. Inevitably he had turned to someone else.

Yet I had loved him physically, had wanted to touch him, kiss him, be held until the moment when, quite naturally, he would ask me to go to bed. Then the dead hand would fall on my body, my flesh would become ice and my heart a trapped, terrified animal hammering at my chest as he lay over me and entered me. Martin, the gentlest, most considerate of lovers, became for me a dominating, lustful animal, rearing over me and pounding his body into mine. My only sensations were pain, fear and resentment.

It was the last of these that stopped me seeking medical help of some kind. If we had been married or had a child, I might have been forced to. Martin tried every position, every form of coaxing and foreplay. I lay on my back and saw the top of his head, which normally could turn my bowels to water with tenderness, and felt his lips on my belly as I stared out with cold hostility wondering when it would be over and why anyone should have chosen such wallpaper.

I knew I would lose him. I saw his pain and I loved him desperately. But I didn't want to be changed, 'cured' as it would be called. I didn't want the violation of my personality and my flesh, to be made to conform. Why should a man enter my body like climbing a mountain just because it was there?

A piece of burning wood fell into the hearth showing a charcoal heart, sectioned like timber whose substance has been leeched away by the fungoid tentacles of dry rot, and frilled with a lace of ash that crumbled where it touched. I must stop thinking. I pulled the little pile of notebooks towards me.

Each had a rubber band tidily round it and a title on the front. Some were the names of local places like Filey, Staithes and Pickering. Others said: Sea, River, Trees. One was labelled 'Mrs Osmotherly' and contained several poems. The

18

most interesting to me was headed simply 'L.W.', but when I opened it, it held only one line: 'Is L. a Ganconer?' There was no answer in the notebook and none I could even begin to hazard to such an inscrutable question.

My absorption must have obscured the first tentative rattle of the door, but I heard the second. I got up noiselessly and went out into the small dark hall. Someone was trying to get in, trying a series of keys in the lock. I looked round for a weapon. There was an umbrella stand that housed, as well as an assortment of mostly broken umbrellas, a sturdy walking stick.

I seized it silently and moved to the front door. A faint shadow of light filtered through the panes above the door and through the uncurtained window. I put a finger on the light switch just inside the door, and a hand on the knob of the inner catch. At the same moment I turned the knob, threw open the door and flicked the switch.

There was a small shriek and the muffled figure on the porch almost fell backwards down the one step.

'*Oh*! Oh dear.'

I saw at once that I was taller and younger than the would—be intruder and felt foolish with my walking stick.

'Oh dear, I didn't know there was anyone here. I thought … I came to look for Tiger. He's run away. I was sure he'd come home.'

'Won't you come in? I'm Miss Hackstead's niece, Paula.'

'Oh. I'm Mary Dunscombe. I didn't want to disturb anyone. It's just Tiger. I took him home with me when, when …'

Though I couldn't see, I heard that she was on the edge of tears. 'Please come in if you can spare a moment. There are so many things I need to ask someone about Aunt Meg.'

'Well, if you're sure it isn't an intrusion and then perhaps I could go into the garden and call him.'

'Of course.' I drew her in and made her take off the mackintosh and headscarf she was swathed in. I saw at once that it was the same Mary as in the photograph. 'I'll make some more tea. Mine got cold while I was looking through a few things.'

I sat her down in the sitting room, added more logs and went into the kitchen. Mercifully, Aunt Meg had nothing against the convenience of an electric kettle, that blessing to those who live alone. All interest in a solitary cup of tea or coffee can evaporate with the faint steam of a kettle taking its time to come to the boil.

She looked like a small storm—battered bird crouched in the corner of the biggest armchair. Mary opted for milk but no sugar and refused a biscuit. 'Such a pretty barrel'. The firelight ran among the silver tracery of leaves and branches.

'It was my grandmother's. My mother always wanted it, but it was left to Meg.'

'And now it's yours.'

'Oh no. I don't expect so.'

'Oh, but it is,' she said, sitting up a little. 'It's all left to you. I witnessed the will. The house and everything.'

I was stunned. If I'd thought about it at all, I had expected some books, or a piece of jewelry, perhaps even a hundred pounds.

'It doesn't seem possible. I just can't get used to it.' Suddenly the tears began to trickle silently down her cheeks, which had reddened a little in the fire's heat.

'I hadn't realised until I got here that it had been so sudden.' I tried to find the right words, but knew there weren't any.

'I found her, you see. When I came over in the afternoon, the milk was still in the box just inside the gate at the top of the path, where the milkman leaves it. They don't like coming down the path. I knew something was wrong. Meg was so methodical, she would never have left the milk there until after lunch, let alone the post and *The Times*. However bad the weather, she always collected them in the morning.'

The tears flowed again, and I didn't know what to say to comfort her. Perhaps it would do her good to tell the story in her own time. I waited with what I hoped was an encouraging expression.

'When I got down here I saw the curtains were still closed. I knocked and there was no answer, so I used my key.' She

20

held up a bunch of assorted shapes and sizes. 'It always takes me some time to find which one it is. Meg used to laugh at me and say I should label them or put a different coloured cotton on each. She was lying just inside the hall. It was like a nightmare. I worry all the time that if I'd come earlier I might have been able to do something.'

'I don't think you should distress yourself with that. I understand it was a really massive heart attack. I doubt if anything could have been done.' I wasn't sure if this was true, but I was fairly certain it could never be proved either way, and I felt she should have the benefit of what little reassurance I could offer.

'We'd been friends for twenty years, ever since she came here.'

'Miss Dunscombe, what exactly did my aunt do?'

'She was a local historian and folklorist. You know Briggs' dictionary?' I didn't, but I nodded. 'She contributed a lot of Yorkshire material to that. And she wrote several things of her own. She was always in demand for conferences. She was such a marvellous speaker, she just bewitched an audience. I used to love to sit at the back and watch her take hold of them. Who would have thought she might be glamoured too.' She sighed a little. 'I should be going. You must have a lot to do, and I've kept you long enough. If I could just go into the garden and call Tiger.'

'Of course.' I got up. 'Perhaps you'd better go by yourself. A stranger might frighten him off. I expect you know your way better than I do.'

Mary Dunscombe stood up too. 'I don't think you'd frighten him. Cats always know whom they can trust. I'll just try a couple of times.'

I heard her voice, blanketed and reduced by the fog. In a minute or two she was back. 'No luck, I'm afraid.'

'Shall I ring you if he turns up?'

'Would you? I'd be so grateful. There's so little I can do and I've failed her in this one thing.'

'I don't think Aunt Meg would have seen it like that.'

'Yes, she would. She thought I was wet and so I am. Only

sometimes I've seen things only too clearly.'

I made no comment. The remark was as opaque to me as the strange line in the L.W. notebook. I helped her into her mackintosh. She peered up at me as she knotted the headscarf under a puckered chin. 'I don't know what you intend to do this evening, but it's as well not to wander around after dark. The police have warned against it.'

'I'm afraid I don't understand ...'

'There's a nasty character in the area.'

'What about you?'

'Oh, he wouldn't bother with me. He likes them young. I'll ring you tomorrow if I may.'

'Please do. I'd like to talk to you about the funeral.'

'Yes,' she sighed again. 'There's all that to be got through.'

The house seemed very empty when she had gone. I hadn't intended to go out again myself, but perversely, now that I had been warned against it, I began to feel shut in and longed to take a bus into the town and find a hotel bar where there would be people and light.

If indeed there was a bus ... Aunt Meg's bicycle should be somewhere about, but I hadn't ridden in years and I didn't fancy trying in the dark and the fog, which had condensed into a light drizzle by the time Mary Dunscombe had left. Perhaps I ought to hire a car tomorrow. Obviously I should have to stay until after the funeral. Tiger had to be found too. Mary would probably be glad to give him a home.

And then there was the cottage. If Mary was right and Aunt Meg hadn't altered her will at the last moment, the house was left to me. It would almost certainly have to be sold to pay the estate duty. I was sorry about that. It was like selling off a piece of Aunt Meg. But then, I wouldn't want to live up here. Or would I? What was there now to draw me back?

Well, there was the job I would have to go back to when my year's leave was over, with all the pain of daily encounters with Martin unless I applied for a post somewhere else. I ought to give them at least a year in return for my year off, which had come at just the right moment in the collapse of our relationship; though when I had applied for it I couldn't, of course, have foreseen that. It had all been fair weather then—or at least, nearly all. There had been just the small problem of my unresponsiveness, but we had thought that would sort itself out.

I had to stop myself retracing all the old ground, which was as painful to me as walking on knives. I got up and went to look at the books. There was a section on immediately local history and one on Yorkshire as a whole. There were guidebooks and maps brought back from holidays abroad, but most of the shelves were filled with books on folklore, some of which I judged must be antiques. *Pandemonium, or the Devil's Cloyster*, *The Discoverie of Witchcraft* and *Saducismus Triumphatus* were all there in conker–coloured leather–bound first editions. True to character, Aunt Meg had kept all her books in order, and although the sections weren't labelled, it was easy to pick out where mediaeval romance ended and witchcraft began, and to sort faery from psychical phenomena. There were tales from different countries all shelved together, collections of ballads and dictionaries.

On an impulse I took out one of these in a modern paperback edition and carried it back to the rug. *A Dictionary of Fairies*: it seemed a strange thing for adults to solemnly concern themselves with. The scholarly preface with its discussion of classification by motif soon put me right on that. I turned to the dictionary proper and began reading at random.

An unconscious echo must have directed me to the letter 'G'. Certainly I wasn't aware of looking for the strange word in Aunt Meg's notebook, but there it was: *Ganconer* or *Gean–cannah*, the Love–Talker. According to the entry, he appeared in lonesome valleys, made love to country maidens and then faded away, leaving them to pine to death. He also smoked a pipe like my father, but clay, not briar.

This final detail made me laugh. It seemed such a long way from flower fairies with butterfly wings on children's birthday cards. I had never considered a pipe–smoking fairy. Still there was Oberon. Perhaps if he appeared now he would smoke a slim panatella. His revenge had been adult and horrible enough, making Titania lust after a clownish monster. There had been nothing butterfly—winged about that.

Suddenly I felt exhausted. I needed a drink of something stronger than tea. I began opening every cupboard that might be doing duty as a hidden bar. In the old—fashioned walk—in pantry off the kitchen I found what I was looking for: rows of bottles, all neatly labelled and dated. Fortunately for me, Aunt Meg had made her own wine from fruits and flowers. I selected a bottle and took it, with a glass and a corkscrew, back to the sitting room. It was elderflower that when I drew the cork seemed to bring all the captive fragrance of a warm June evening to the little house wrapped in winter. I sipped and read on beside the fire ...

The flames had grown very tall and blue. They reached up from the fireplace and poured through the roof, roaring as if a great wind fanned them. But nothing was consumed. From my perch high above, I looked down on the cottage and the figure on the rug and knew they were safe from the chill columns of cobalt fire.

Then I saw a great wave gather itself out of the sea like a bunched fist, smashing down on the house to break over it and bury it forever in green foam and thrust it from its narrow shelf on the rock. The tall flames wavered for a moment and then steadied triumphantly, as the water poured down the transparent sides of the house over the edge of the lawn and torrented down the cliff, back to its natural place.

As if they had been waiting for this, and their protective purpose was now finished, the columns of ice fire began to shrink, humming towards the hearth, and I was drawn down with them back into the body on the rug ...

I woke stiff and chilled, with just wit enough to put a guard in front of the embers, before staggering up to bed. My body felt like a battleground through which armies had trampled. I fell at once into an exhausted sleep. From time to time I half—woke, hearing noises in the house that I was too dulled

24

to investigate.

At what must have been the darkest hour before the dawn I woke again, this time from a dream in which I was being crushed so vividly that I couldn't at once tell dream from reality. Something was lying close to me on the bed. I sat up in terror and groped for the bedside light. A huge orange and white cat had curled himself in to me as I slept. It must be Tiger. I almost laughed as I switched out the light again and lay down. His warmth seeped comfortingly through the bedclothes into my body as I fell asleep.

He was still there in the morning, or I might have thought he had been all part of my dream. I left him asleep and went down to make myself some breakfast. As it usually does, the light of day brought reassurance. My dreams faded. I looked forward to telephoning Mary Dunscombe with the good news of Tiger's return. Then I would go into town and deal with the practical matters of funeral and will. I felt reinvigorated.

While I champed on a dish of muesli, I looked through Aunt Meg's address book again in pursuit of L.W. He wasn't hard to find: Leonard Wallace, with address and telephone number. Then I looked again at Aunt Meg's recent engagements. They seemed to have met at least a couple of times a week. That argued that they were fairly close. No one else figured as much; Mary hardly at all but she might have been in the habit of dropping in without a formal appointment.

Should I call him and make myself known? The telephone began to ring on cue as I was turning the question over.

'He's come back,' I was able to tell Mary. 'I left the cat door open and he must have just walked in during the night and found a warm bed. He's still asleep.'

Mary was full of delighted relief. 'Should I come over and fetch him?'

'Why don't we let him stay here for a couple of days. Quite frankly, I like his company.'

'You're sure he won't be a nuisance?'

'Absolutely. Miss Dunscombe, there was something I wanted to ask you when you rang: Leonard Wallace ...'

'Yes?'

'Was he a great friend of Aunt Meg's? I mean, should I get in touch with him, let him know about the funeral and so on?'

'You must do whatever you think right. I'm glad Tiger's safe. Do ring me if there's anything I can help with, and ... and let me know the date.'

I didn't have time to answer. She had rung off. Obviously I had stepped on a very delicate area. Mary Dunscombe must have resented the intrusion of Leonard Wallace into Aunt Meg's life. Long friendships like theirs could take on all the attributes of marriage, even without any physical relationship. Mary might have been very jealous.

From the photograph it looked as if Leonard was considerably younger than my aunt. What had been the connection or indeed attraction between them? I reached again for the phone and dialled his number from my aunt's book, composing one of those 'You don't know me, *but* ... ' gambits in my head while it rang.

The voice was smooth, full and accentless.

'I'm very pleased to meet you although I wish the circumstances could have been different,' he said, when I had finished my prepared speech. 'Your aunt often spoke of you.'

'I have to come in to town today to go to the bank and make various arrangements. I wondered ...'

'Why don't we meet? Or better, have lunch. Let me give you lunch at the Royal. It's worth seeing for itself.'

'That's very kind.'

He gave me directions. 'At one? How shall we recognise each other?'

'Oh, I shall know you from your photograph. I'm medium height and sort of fair. There's nothing to describe really.'

He laughed. 'Then I'll know you at once.'

L.W. was certainly a charmer, at least on the phone, I decided as I put it down. First, though, I must get myself into town and deal with practical matters.

It was a nuisance having only a back door key. I was constantly afraid of locking myself out. Perhaps Mary Dunscombe had taken my aunt's key with her. I must remember to ask her.

There had been a bus timetable in the desk and I looked up a suitable bus. I regretted now having left my mini in London, but at the time I had felt unable to face the long drive. A tramp to the nearest stop and the cold wait while the sea wind plucked at me showed me just what a mistake I had made. I got off in the town centre and found Aunt Meg's bank.

The manager was fatherly and helpful. Yes, it was true as Mary Dunscombe had said; I was my aunt's chief heir, with small tokens for my mother, my Uncle John and a thousand pounds for the upkeep of Tiger, which I was bidden to see to. The manager was her executor. He foresaw no difficulties. As well as the house, my aunt had investments in the safety of a building society and a sizeable deposit account.

'About fifty or sixty thousand will be the total value I should say when you've sold the house. You will sell, I imagine?'

'I expect so.'

'There will be tax to pay but the deposit account would cover that. Perhaps you'll keep the cottage as a holiday home? I'm sure Scarborough would be pleased to have you as a regular visitor. You won't see us at our best now. In Summer we're very lively—without, I think, being vulgar.'

I smiled and said I would certainly think about it. The discovery that I was my aunt's heir had disturbed me. I supposed I would get used to the idea, but I just wished she had gone on staying alive to enjoy it herself. I could, I imagined, turn the money into some kind of annuity or buy myself a bigger flat; but I hadn't been thinking in terms of changing my life so radically, and I wasn't at all ready for it or sure I wanted to. One good thing was that I could certainly afford to hire a car while I was here. The manager was happy to advise me about a reputable firm and I equipped myself with a small, sturdy Volkswagen before going on to Theale's where everything was settled but the date. I had to consult my Uncle John first. Somehow I felt I couldn't face Aunt Meg's funeral without some family support.

By the time all that was over I needed a quiet drink and

was regretting that I had let myself in for lunch with a stranger, which was certain to require a lot of hard work to cope with a potentially embarrassing situation. What would we talk about? I was tempted to drive straight home and leave Leonard Wallace to wait in vain, but my upbringing wouldn't quite let me. 'Always see something through when once you've started it', was one of my mother's maxims, together with that one about lying on beds you've made, which sometimes caused me to leave my own bed unmade all day as a gesture of defiance.

The Royal was a curved sweep of white stone, pierced by elegant windows and steps up to glass doors: late Northern Regency. Inside was all marble and chandeliers fountaining light. The dining room was on the first floor. As I pushed open the door, the sun was flung directly into my eyes so that I was momentarily blinded. I peered about against the dazzle and saw that a tall black silhouette had risen against the crystal oblong of a far window. The sharp light behind obliterated all his features; yet I knew it must be Leonard Wallace.

I began to stammer something, but he put out a calming hand and shook mine, easing me into a chair sideways on to the window, so that neither of us should face the great reflecting glass of the sea which had struck the sight from my eyes as I entered. When they were acclimatised, I was able to look out without pain and take in the long curve of the bay to the south.

'It's certainly a stunning view.'

'If you look behind the other way, you get the castle and the lighthouse.'

I twisted my neck. 'I hadn't realised it was such a handsome town. No wonder Aunt Meg chose to live here.'

'She loved the sea.'

'Did she? I hardly knew her. I expect you knew her far better than I did. It seems such a waste now; not to have known her, I mean.'

'She felt she knew you. As I said, she often spoke about you. Now what will you eat? The fish is very good, of

28

course.' I thought the leek and potato soup looked warming, followed by *oeufs florentines*. Leonard Wallace chose local smoked trout, followed by equally local venison. I could sense that he was relieved when I insisted on red wine in spite of the *oeufs*. In truth, I felt it would have been bizarre to make him drink white with venison, and I could make up for the bloodlessness of my own choice by showing strength of character in my choice of wine. A part of me wanted very much to impress him.

He insisted on the wine being brought at once and two rich full glasses being poured as soon as he had satisfied himself that it was warm enough. He raised his glass and looked at me over the top of it, his wide mouth curving in the snapshot smile. 'Here's to our better acquaintance.'

I raised my own glass. I wouldn't blush or lower my eyes. I was used to men who used this moment to beat the woman down and establish their dominance. I looked full into his eyes and took a large pull at the rather gamey claret he had chosen; it tasted of blood and iron and was as smooth as drawing a silk scarf through a gold ring. 'Yes, indeed.'

'You should see something of the local sights while you're here. I wish I had a car. I'd love to take you around, but I don't drive.'

'I've just hired a car. If you could spare the time you could be the navigator. It does seem a pity as you say not to see what I can while I'm here.'

Part of me heard this statement with amazement. I seemed to have been suddenly split into two people, one of whom I recognised as my usual self. The other was a person I didn't recognise at all and over whom I had no control. She had spoken, and I was amazed. Suddenly I remembered my last night's dream: the dying fire … the columns of blue ice—flame … Perhaps when I had returned to my body, there had been someone else already in it; someone who had taken it over during my strange abdication and was only now letting her presence be known. The words she had spoken were some kind of open invitation to Leonard Wallace.

He was answering them now, taking her at her word,

accepting her offer while he looked deep into my eyes again as if he saw her in their depths and was looking down through me at her. 'You should see the Vale of Pickering, which was once an inland sea enclosed by the moors, and Whitby's only twenty miles away where the famous Hilda was abbess. I used to say Meg was rather like her. It was a joke we had. The ruins are well worth seeing, although they're not Hilda's, of course.'

'Are you interested in local history too?'

'Oh yes. We had many interests in common.'

I looked out at the bay, but the sunlight thrown back by the sea blinded me again so that I could see nothing but brilliant speckles of light in a solution of molten glass. I tried to focus on the cliff gardens falling away below the hotel, but the trees and shrubs seemed to have shrunk and lost substance and I saw them as the toy vegetation from a model railway layout. The occasional figures of people were diminished too and seemed suspended or moved as if wound up and running down.

Leonard Wallace was speaking, but I had missed what he had already said. Our first course had come and he was filleting his smoked trout. He raised his fork to make a point, pausing in a list of local places, Hutton Buscel, Goathland, Ravenscar, that sounded in my ears like the dark conjurings of an incantation: Asmodeus, Setebos, Moloch ... As I looked up from my soup plate, spoon halfway to my mouth, the prongs of his raised fork caught the light and blazed as if electrically charged. 'How's the soup?'

'Fine, fine,' I managed to get the spoon to my mouth. The soup was really rather good and reassuring. The world righted itself and I became aware of the sounds of other diners, of knives, forks and spoons on plates and subdued trickles of conversation.

'With a name like Cockburn you should have some good Scottish blood.'

'So should a Wallace.'

'Indeed I have. And on my mother's side. I'm a Highlander, so I have the second sight. Perhaps you have too.' He smiled, but I wasn't sure if he was joking.

'I don't think so.'

'People often don't know until something calls it up.'

'Did my aunt?'

'She always said she was an agnostic in such things, but I think I was beginning to convert her. I'm glad by the way that you've got yourself a car. It's a lonely way to Meg's and we have a very unpleasant character in the area.'

'So I've been told. I take it he attacks women on their own?'

He nodded and sipped his wine. 'He's a redcap.'

I didn't understand, but was unwilling to ask for an explanation. 'Another one with a deep hatred of women.'

'Perhaps.'

'What else can it be?'

'It could be simply the power of evil manifesting itself.'

'But why here?'

'Why not? What does it say in the good book about Satan going up and down seeking whom he might devour?' He was smiling again, so that once more I didn't know if it was a joke. Behind his actual words was a kind of menacing, yet at the same time patronising, eroticism. 'Scarborough isn't immune.'

'Do you really believe in evil as a force, a power?'

'Definitely.'

'You don't think his mother neglected him?'

'She may have done. They often do. But not many people commit murder because of it. There has to be an X–factor.'

'You don't think it's just the irreconcilability of men and women? That never the twain can meet? Men have to dominate.'

'Fortunately for the continuance of the human race, they meet very easily. Some women must like being dominated, if that's your thesis.'

'The mouse loves the cat?' It was my mouth that spoke, but the words and tone of voice, a heavy coquetry, belonged to that other.

A waitress in black dress with white apron and a tiara of

white cap on her neatly permed iron-grey hair whisked away our plates and brought the second course. The North will sport the last of those perms in the world and the last waitress with a bow in her hair.

Leonard Wallace sliced through his mattress of venison and let the blood run. He put a piece in his mouth. 'Very good. Why don't you try a bit? Those eggs look very pallid.'

'I don't much like meat, particularly underdone.'

'That's when it does you most good. Are you thinking about the pretty little deer with their doe's eyes?'

'A bit.'

'Blood is part of the nourishment of life, an essential part. Red wine is the blood of the grape.'

An echo remembered from the communion service set itself up in my head. I concentrated on my eggs and spinach. I was still having difficulty in controlling my speech, and there was the additional problem, for what I thought of as the real me, that I wasn't at all sure how seriously to take anything Leonard Wallace said.

I declined a pudding and opted for coffee, black with sugar, aware that I had to drive an unknown car along unfamiliar roads. I thanked Leonard Wallace for my lunch as we stood on the steps of the Royal. The light was like the blade of a sword cutting into my eyes, and a headache was settling itself comfortably behind them.

'Ring me when you want to see some of our local sights. If I don't hear in a day or two, I'll phone you. And you'll let me know the date of the funeral, won't you?' It's been nice to meet you at last. Your aunt first raised my expectations and they haven't been disappointed.'

There was no answer I could make to that, or to the top of his head inclining sardonically, I thought, over my hand. 'Can I give you a lift anywhere?'

'Thank you for the offer, but I've some shopping and things I must do.' Leonard Wallace gave a half–salute, half–wave and turned away towards the sea. I let in the clutch as carefully as I could in case he should turn and see me kangarooing in a strange car.

It was already falling dusk when I got back. I had stopped to buy a few things, notably some cod steak for Tiger. A fish treat might encourage him to stay home. He seemed pleased to see me and wound round my legs as he took me to the kitchen, where I found what looked and smelt like a fishpan, coated with the lime of many boilings, and dumped the steak in cold water. Tiger told me I had got it right by jumping on the draining—board and shrieking his impatience. 'You're rich,' I told him. 'We'll have to watch out for catnappers. You've got a thousand pounds on your head.'

When I had cooked and cooled his food and he had tucked his blunt muzzle slightly askew over the dish the better to chew, I made myself some tea and took it into the sitting room to drink while I telephoned my Uncle John and talked about dates and announcements.

'Have you found a will?'

'Yes. It was at the bank. The manager is the executor.'

'I expect she's left everything to one of her societies.'

'No, no she hasn't. It's rather embarrassing. She's left it to me.'

'Good. I'm glad she showed some sense of family in the end.'

Defensively I tried to think of something to counter his comment. When had either John or my mother shown much family feeling toward Meg? Perhaps she had sometimes been lonely or frightened up here by herself. They had made little effort to keep us all together. John was a retired civil servant, unmarried like Meg. Maybe he had envied her her still—active life of conferences and visiting Japanese professors. He was certainly more of an old woman than she had been. I saw her sitting opposite me in the pink plastic compartment of the station buffet with such clarity, she might have been an apparition evoked by my presence in her house. But I felt no fear of her. If ghosts walked, Aunt Meg would come to me for nothing but good.

Nevertheless I was glad that her only brother could and would come up all the way from Seaford and had even offered to deal with the notices in the papers. I put the receiver down in a spirit of forgiveness. Tomorrow I must begin to sort out Aunt Meg's clothes, a dismal task I would leave till daylight.

On impulse I picked up the book I had been reading last night when I had fallen asleep, and turned the pages until I came to 'R'. Leonard Wallace had said the 'unpleasant character' in the area was a 'redcap' and I had had only a mental image of the red–banded hat of a kind of military policeman which I knew wasn't right. Finding the word in the dictionary would prove that Leonard Wallace had shared my aunt's interest in folklore.

He was there all right: a malignant old man with large fiery eyes and a red cap whose colour came from his habit of redying it in human blood. Human strength was useless against him. Only a cross or scripture could make him vanish with a dismal howl.

Presumably Leonard Wallace had used the word metaphorically, to express his concept of someone who was a manifestation of the power of evil. That would fit with his being driven off by the traditional Christian symbols of book and crucifix. Wallace had also said that my aunt had been an agnostic, but that he had thought that he was beginning to make some impression on her before her death. His twice–weekly visits must have been to discuss this, and presumably other folklore questions.

From what I had seen of my aunt's work she had been a gatherer and sifter rather than a theoriser. An agnostic was by definition someone who didn't know, or who believed that certain things couldn't be known. It left the door open for doubt. Leonard Wallace on the other hand believed that he knew there was a force of evil. He had said nothing, however, about any power of good to oppose it. Maybe that was just assumed, like the two sides of a coin.

I had closed the book and put it down. Now I picked it up again. At one time people had decided their fates by opening the bible at random and picking a verse with a pin. Suppose I tried it with the dictionary? What would I get? I shut my eyes, opened the book and let my finger fall on it. Then I opened my eyes again.

My finger was resting on the first entry in the 'W' section at a word I had never read before: 'Waff'. According to the notes, it was the local term for what the Germans call a *Doppel gänger*, a wraith or double that gave warning of death. With typical Yorkshire hard-headedness, local tradition said that the waff could be driven off, and the doom averted, if you spoke to it severely. That made me laugh and I put the book down. Then I took it up and reread the entry.

I hadn't known that such creatures even existed in English folklore. Bizarre beliefs like this seemed to belong to the Black Forests of the Brothers Grimm or the feverish imaginings of an Anderson. Wasn't it always said that there were no peasants in England? I had imagined that where there weren't any folk, there couldn't be any lore, but this book was full of examples. Many of them came from the Celtic fringe, it was true, but the story I had just read had taken place twenty miles away in Whitby, which Leonard Wallace was going to take me to. A man from Guisborough had seen his waff when he went into a shop in Whitby and had told it 'Get thy ways, you'm,' just as my taxi-driver of the other night might have done.

My experience of being outside my own body, and of someone else being inside it with me, an other, an intruder with my face and shape, was akin to that. The other had receded deep within me, but I knew she was still there, waiting for her chance to speak through my mouth. Three days ago I would have laughed at such an idea, but now, although my natural scepticism kept trying to re-establish itself, I felt my half belief in her like a slight ache that is almost no more than a mild sensation but that you know will flare into pain if you move too quickly.

I began to turn the pages and read entry after entry while the wood fell into ash in the hearth and the room chilled. As I read, presences seemed to be all about me and the air full of their half-caught chatterings, whispered obscenities, high hard laughter. I knew that the other 'she' inside me could hear it and understand what they said. It was me they were mocking and they were in league with her against me.

The ring of the doorbell startled me, half—restoring my senses, but bringing a new feeling of terror with it. The walking stick was still in the hall, but I didn't want to open the door and stand exposed in the hall light. As I had done the night before I threw back the door and switched on the light at the same time. I was so relieved to see Mary Dunscombe I could have hugged the small bundled up parcel of her.

'I realised I still had both sets of keys, my dear. How silly of me not to have thought of it before.'

I persuaded her in, made up the fire and insisted that she have some tea. While I was making it, Tiger appeared at the catdoor and poured himself through it with a little chirrup. By the time I took the tray into the sitting room he was perched on Mary's lap, purring and looking very pleased with himself.

'You know Tiger's an heir in his own right?' I said. 'I've warned him to be careful of catnappers.'

'They'd have to be very quick to catch Tiger,' she said, and rubbed a bent forefinger up and down his throat. 'I've seen someone try, and they got more than they bargained for.'

There was a simplicity about Mary Dunscombe that made me feel more myself. No doubt it could be very irritating, and she had said herself that my more forceful aunt had found her 'wet' but the very commonplaceness of her steadied my mind, which had seemed to be in danger of veering off any normal course ever since I had come to Scarborough, as if I was caught in some emotional or psychic time—warp.

'I mustn't go away without giving you the keys,' she said, and I realised that they were merely an excuse and that she was probably lonely.

'You must miss Aunt Meg.'

'I suppose I shall get used to it, but it'll take a long time. What will you do about the cottage?'

'I haven't decided yet. The bank manager wants me to make it my holiday home.'

'Oh, do consider it, my dear. It would be something to look forward to, for me, I mean.'

For a moment I felt guilty. If she knew that other who had moved in with me, Mary Dunscombe mightn't be so eager to have me as a holiday neighbour. 'I keep meaning to ask you where exactly you live?'

'You must come and have supper before you go back to London. It's only ten minutes away if you walk briskly, on the other side of the main road into town. That's how I met Meg. We were waiting at the same bus stop. That was nearly twenty years ago.'

'Did you share my aunt's interest in local history and folklore?'

'No,' she laughed. 'I'm not clever enough. I sometimes wondered why she bothered with me, but she said I was good for her, that I kept her feet on the ground.'

'Miss Dunscombe ...'

'Please call me Mary. It doesn't make me feel so old, though I know I am.'

'Mary, do you believe in the force of evil?'

'Yes, yes, I do. Meg didn't. We almost quarrelled about it. She said you couldn't prove it and what could it be? And I couldn't explain, not properly in terms she would respect, but I knew I had felt it. She said that was just my prejudice. My mother always said I had weak nerves. I expect it comes to the same thing.'

'Leonard Wallace believes in the power of evil too. He said so. I had lunch with him today.'

Mary Dunscombe rose like a bird put up by a dog. 'Is that the time? I've stayed much longer than I should.' Tiger, rudely awakened, dropped from her lap with an indignant thud and Mary almost scurried into the hall. I fetched her mackintosh and headscarf and helped her into them. At the door she turned and looked up at me.

'I don't know how to say this, and perhaps I shouldn't even try, but ... but I can't like him. I tried, God knows, in the beginning I did try. It may be that I'm wrong, that it's my fault in some way, and you will make up your own mind, but I feel as if I don't even want to hear his name.'

'He'll be at the funeral.'

'Yes, I suppose he will and I must bear it, not make things difficult; but if there were any way to stop him, I would. Goodnight, my dear. I'm sorry. I felt I had to say something, to explain.' She almost ran down the path before I could answer as if afraid that I would let fall words that would come irrevocably between us.

I was disappointed in her. She had seemed so sane at first, someone I could lean on in my disoriented state. Now she had revealed herself as just an irrationally jealous old woman.

A little mirror hung in the hall. Aunt Meg must have had it there to give a final pat to her neat hair before leaving the house. I paused before it with a sudden impulse to check on myself although I wasn't expecting any more callers. A double image looked out at me: two identikits of what I thought of as me, but one slightly behind the right shoulder of the other. They stared back with identical expressions. She had taken on my appearance in the glass and was standing behind me.

Or was it she who stood in front? How could I tell any more which was the real me? I knew, I felt instinctively, that no one stood behind me in the hall. Even without turning round to check. I knew that was so. I raised a hand and both images did the same, following my gesture exactly.

If I could be strong now, like the Guisborough man in the shop, I could send her away forever. I only had to be firm and aggressive the book said.

'Go home,' I tried. 'Go home and leave me alone.'

Both faces smiled at me. 'This is my home,' her mouth which was my mouth said, and the two reflections slid sideways into each other, leaving only one that stared back at me in horror.

I stumbled, retching and sobbing, into the sitting room and sank into the chair that Mary Dunscombe had left. After a bit my fierce reaction wore itself out and a quiet despair took its place. I picked up the book and looked at the entry again. I had remembered a cross—reference which I wanted to follow up.

I found it at once. It was a quotation from a

seventeenth–century work called *The Secret Commonwealth of Elves, Fauns and Fairies.* 'They call this Reflex–man a Co–walker, every way like the Man, as a Twin–brother and Companion, haunting him as his shadow, as is oft seen and known among men (resembling the Originall), both before and after the Originall is dead ... This Copy, Echo or Living Picture, goes at last to his own Herd.'

Somewhere, it implied, there was a world of duplicate beings, a herd of them, waiting for time to fracture and let one of them slip through to come face to face with its original. Behind the quaint language of seventeenth century demonology might lie a truth of human psychology, I tried to reason, but my experience in the hall was too recent and too strong.

I didn't believe it signalled my death. That was too easy and something in any case that I had often yearned for since I had killed Martin. No, it was closer to that power of evil that both Leonard Wallace and Mary Dunscombe believed in. It had come to destroy me in a more potent way than my simple dying could do. I wondered if I should discuss it with Leonard Wallace. Then I wondered if he already knew about my visitant, had seen her in my eyes when she had spoken to him.

All this had come upon me since I had entered the cottage, and yet I felt no fear of it and no wish to leave. It was as if I had been brought to some inevitable confrontation, an ordeal of fire and water I must go through. The house itself had no hostility towards me, filled as it was with Aunt Meg's benign presence, but in some way it had made my confrontation possible. The cottage might almost have been asking me to release it by my trial from something that was alien to it.

I forced myself to heat some baked beans in a little saucepan and toast a couple of slices of bread to put under them. Then I poured myself some more elderflower wine and joined Tiger, who was asleep in front of the fire.

One of the few really modern things in the cottage, apart from the humming fridge, was a stereo record–player, an elegant and expensive Bang and Olufsen in matt black and natural wood. I looked through my aunt's neat catalogue of records and tapes and chose a cassette on which she had recorded several songs, including one called *Scarborough Fair*. I dropped the plastic lozenge into the tape socket and pressed down the lid. The voice was a girl's, although the words were meant for a man.

> Where are you going? To Scarborough Fair.
> Parsley, sage, rosemary and thyme.
> Remember me to a bonny lass there,
> For once she was a true lover of mine.

The girl's voice faded and it seemed to me that it was Martin I heard beneath it. The catalogue of her tasks was the sum of my failures.

> Tell her to make me a cambric shirt,
> Parsley, sage, rosemary and thyme,
> Without any needle or thread worked in it,
> And she shall be a true lover of mine.

> Tell her to wash it in yonder well,
> Parsley, sage, rosemary and thyme,
> Where water ne'er sprung nor rain never fell,
> And she shall be a true lover of mine.

Never, never again, said the words. And yet if I could have heard such bitterness in Martin's voice, I would have hoped. I knew the aridity of that well, and the harsh unseamed shirt I wore every day next to my skin.

I didn't hear the next track or two, but I was brought back to the singing by the eerie monotone of the fourth song, whose persistence cut a channel into my brain.

> I am a man upon the land,
> I am a silkie on the sea,
> And when I'm far from every strand,
> My home it is in Sule Skerry.

The words were in a dialect so foreign I found it hard to follow the tale's unwinding, but I sensed that it ended in death and mourning. How else could such a tune go?

> And ye shall marry a gunner good,
> And a very fine gunner I'm sure he'll be,
> And the very first shot that ever he shoots
> Shall slay both my young son and me.

I switched off the machine. I was as exhausted as if I had been navvying all day. Tiger was still asleep. I shut the cat door and, for the first time, locked up front and back of the cottage before I dragged myself to bed.

The next morning I spent at the dismal task of sorting through Aunt Meg's clothes and putting them in plastic sacks. I had offered Mary Dunscombe anything she might care for and she had promised to take the lot off my hands. What she didn't want herself she would put in the church jumble sale. That had led me to the question of Aunt Meg's religion and the funeral.

'She was an agnostic,' Mary Dunscombe had said. 'She said she was keeping an open mind.'

Leonard Wallace had said she was an agnostic too, but he had meant something different by the word or at least, I had understood it so.

However Aunt Meg's agnosticism in the more conventional sense meant that I could arrange a simple burial at the crematorium and there was no need to involve priests or churches. I spent a quiet day dealing with practical details, and in the evening I took myself into town to the cinema. A rather earnest film about a tug—of—love child between divorcing parents was showing. It had one of my favourite American screen actors in it, and watching the perfection of his performance, I forgot everything else and came out into the night, blinking away the tears, drained by catharsis and ready to sleep. Tiger welcomed me and we spent an untroubled night, with him curled into the small of my back.

I was halfway through my four—minute boiled egg when

the telephone rang. It was Leonard Wallace.

'I threatened to ring you if you didn't ring me first. It's a fine day, maybe one of the last we shall get this year. What about that little expedition?'

I could think of no reason against it. We arranged that I should pick him up in the town. As soon as I put the receiver down, I knew that she was back, that it was she who wanted to spend the day with Leonard Wallace and I was merely the means to their meeting.

She had been there all the time of course, keeping quietly withdrawn deep inside me, waiting for her moment. Now I felt her growing and swelling to fill out my flesh. I watched while she made me dress with extra care and add a little more lipstick and eye–shadow than I usually wore. Then I put down milk and fish for Tiger, propped up the catdoor and drove into town.

Leonard was waiting on the steps of the opulently vulgar Grand Hotel, whose Kremlin domes gleamed obscenely in the sunlight. He was right: it was a fine day for our little outing. He was wearing brown corduroy trousers and a dull green fishing jacket patched with poacher's pockets. As I drove, I was conscious of his long brown fingers resting on his knee beside the gear–lever, so that my hand was brought close to his with every change.

'The winters here are pretty mild compared with further north, or inland. We get a sort of Gulf Stream drift that keeps Scarborough from the worst extremes. Did you know it's on nearly the same latitude as Moscow? If you keep going for three hundred and fifty miles or thereabouts, across the North Sea and then straight across Denmark, you come to Copenhagen and the Baltic. That's the way the sea wolves came to burn Hilda's abbey and monastery. Scarborough is named after one of them: Skarthi, the hare–lipped.'

While he talked I could see and hear it all: the boats with their dragon snouts biting into the sand and the men leaping out of them, the sunlight catching on round shield bosses and horned helmets, the shouts and clash of iron. They had become one of the most powerful warrior images the world

42

has produced, second only perhaps to the Huns or the Mongols, and they were part of the furnishings of the collective imagination. Was there a trick of time, a chink that let their dead cries echo through or was it the untapped power of the mind that almost seemed to recreate them in my own ears?

The road followed the coast between cliff and moor, again and again revealing acres of translucent sea and a land that swam in the milk of mist shot through with the white fire of a winter sun. We turned off the A 171 after it had swung inland, to go down into Robin Hood's Bay for coffee, where the narrow streets of fishermen's cottages clung to the side of the cliff. Their roofs were blue and black slate panels set at angles against the white sky. There were few people about as we plunged down the main street that ended in a wave–dashed slipway into the harbour, and the windows of the houses had a curiously blank look.

'Most of them are holiday homes now and empty in winter,' Leonard explained.

We found coffee in a pub by the quay and then walked to the church, where Leonard pointed out a verse on a tombstone.

By storms at sea two sons I lost
Which sore distresses me,
Because I could not have their bones
To anchor here with me.

The air seemed full of the cries of the drowned and those who had lost them, the very stones of the church numb and cold with their grief. I was glad to be back in the car and on the road again.

We had to turn once more down towards the sea for Whitby, this time following the River Esk as it carved its way through the cliffs to marry the tides. We parked the car on the West Hill to look across the chasm at the ruined abbey.

'Dracula's motel,' Leonard said.

'I'd forgotten that some of it is set here.'

43

'It's quite amusing, I suppose, but it's very crude, all that vampire and werewolf stuff.'

'You don't count them in your manifestations of evil?'

'Oh, evil is a much more subtle and entrancing power, otherwise, how would men ever be seduced by it?'

'The devil has all the best tunes?'

'He must have, if he's to lure the children into the hill.'

'I thought it was always supposed to be the other way round: that evil is powerful and good is weak.'

'That's the official line, of course, but actually what most people mean by evil is merely the extra—ordinary and it's the ordinary that's so strong in human beings, the ties of the commonplace, the lack of imagination and passion, a belief in what is that crowds out what might be.'

'Aren't you rather rewriting the definitions?'

'Doesn't one have to if they're to have any meaning? Everyone has to redefine things for himself. Are you willing to brave the climb up to the Abbey? There are one hundred and ninety—nine steps.'

He took my arm and piloted me down and across the river. As we went through the narrow streets I was taken with a shop window full of uncut stones, sulphurous rock, pink quartz and snowflake obsidian.

'You see those ammonites?' Leonard's long brown index finger pointed to a large collection of perfect specimens. 'The cliffs are full of them. The legend is that Hilda turned all the local snakes to stone. And there they are. Wait here a minute. I just want to get something.'

He disappeared into the little shop. I heard the faint ping of an old—fashioned doorbell. Above me, a gull laughed and mocked as an eddy caught it, just as the gulls had shouted over my head when I first stepped out of Scarborough station. I dropped my eyes to the window again. A sudden shift of light blanked out the semi—precious rocks and fossils behind the glass making a mirror of it. A double reflection stared back.

She was anxious, I could see. I was getting on far too well with Leonard. I understood him, responded to the originality

of his mind, while she was half–frightened by it. When he had
taken her arm I had felt her flinch, whereas I had a sensation
of strength and warmth flowing through it and into me ...

He was coming out of the shop again, carrying a small
paper bag printed with the shop's name. 'Look.' He opened
the neck and took out two tissue wrapped objects.
Unwrapping the larger, he showed me an ammonite, a coil of
white stone just like a calcified serpent.

I traced it with my finger before letting him rewrap it and
put it back in the bag, together with the tissue paper from
around the smaller object. He handed me the bag.

'Give me your hand.' He took it in his own and spread the
fingers a little until he could slip a circlet of pure black over
the third finger of my right hand. I couldn't pull away.

'What is it?'

'It's jet. Queen Victoria was particularly fond of it and so it
became fashionable. There are just a couple of craftsmen left
who cut and polish it. Now up to Hilda's eyrie.' He took my
arm before I could protest and led me on to the foot of the
steps.

It was too late now for anything to be said, though I knew
she was writhing with embarrassment at the gifts, and
particularly the ring though I had felt her cringe, too, as my
finger traced the smooth stone whorl of the aeons–dead
mollusc ...

I managed to get my arm free on the climb up and as all
breath was needed for the steps it wasn't necessary to talk. I
was glad of the truce, because I felt as if I was being hurried
along and was in danger of losing control of the whole
situation. My defences were being undermined by that other
within me and I seemed unable to stop her as she whirled me
on. I must try to cool the whole thing down. We reached the
top of the steps. The seawind sighed and eddied round the
headland, but I resisted the urge to shiver in case it should
encourage a concerned reaction from Leonard Wallace that I
would be unable to repulse without rudeness. I looked up at
the remains of the Abbey.

'Why did you say Aunt Meg reminded you of Hilda?' I

tried as a piece of neutral conversation.

'She was curiously firm and incorruptible, much as I imagine Hilda must have been. She could be genuinely converted by argument, too, just like Hilda.'

'How do you know?'

'They held a synod here at Hilda's Abbey to settle the question of when Easter should be celebrated. Her side lost and she accepted the new date. This was called the Bay of the Beacon then. There's probably been a lighthouse up here of some kind since Roman times at least. The Irish came all the way down from Lindisfarne for the synod.' He waved a hand at the waste of water to the north of the headland. 'Sometimes we get seals coming down as far as Scarborough from the Farne Islands. The saints and the seal people: those were the days.'

'I don't quite see how they go together.'

'The natural and the so—called supernatural were much more closely interwoven then. Seals could shed their skins and walk about on land as men and saints gave off a perfumed aura.' He was smiling again, but whether at the idea he was proposing or at me I couldn't be sure. The repeated suggestion that he was humouring a not very bright child irritated me. At the same time I could tell that *she* was growing bored and restless at the conversation and would soon break in to refocus it on her own interests.

'I was playing one of my aunt's tapes last night. It had a song on it that I think was about the seal people. It's called *The Great Silkie*, though I'm not quite sure why. Do you know it?'

'Yes, I do. I lent her the record to tape it from. But you a Cockburn and don't know that 'silkie' is the Scots for a seal!'

'There's a great deal I don't know the Scots for,' I said, hating to sound so prissy. The wind was beginning to chill me through. I turned towards the steps and led the way down.

'Where shall we lunch?' Leonard Wallace said, when we reached the bottom.

'A sandwich in a pub will do me,' I said firmly. 'And then I must get back. I have to ring my mother.' It sounded feeble even as I said it, but at least I was in control still.

We found a pub that had once been a fisherman's haunt, but was now tarted up with nets and steering wheels for the summer visitors. Leonard Wallace insisted on paying for the drinks and sandwiches even though I protested, and as I sat sipping at a whisky for warmth, in the gloom from the brass lanterns with their low–powered candle bulbs, I felt that I was about to lose the initiative again.

He sat opposite me, and the nearest lantern lit two sharp taper sparklets in his eyes. The whisky was going straight to my head, and the bar with the other customers receded to the very far distance as if the two of us were alone on Hilda's headland. His lips were moving, but I wasn't conscious of hearing his words, although I know that I answered.

Before we left I went to the Ladies. When I looked in the glass to comb my hair I saw that she had taken over my face. My eyes and cheeks were feverish with her flowing through my blood. I must get away and back to the cottage.

I drove with intense concentration, as though on the verge of drunkenness. Leonard Wallace asked to be dropped off in the centre of Scarborough. For a moment I thought he might touch me or even kiss me before he got out of the car. The air between us sang like a plucked wire with the possibility, and I knew, although the thought made me feel sick, that I was too weak to resist both of them. I was a castle with rotten walls, and betrayed from within.

Tiger was delighted to see me, and I gathered him up for comfort. I would make us both a fire and open a tin of sardines for him. Then I would make tea for myself and sit with Tiger by the fire while I regained my sense of perspective.

I didn't mean to go out, but it seemed that I no longer had any control over my intentions. I was opening the back door and then I was in the garden going across the lawn, where worms had begun their work of dragging those unraked leaves into the mouths of their tunnels. The grass was spiked with the upright brown leaf rolls and dotted with little piles of black castings. I suddenly felt it heaving under me with the thousands of dark pink writhing coils that might shoulder the crust aside altogether to slither like entrails around my feet.

Almost running I reached the end of the lawn where there was a yew hedge to protect the house from the sea wind. A gated gap in it opened on to a path like the one that led down from the road to the cottage, indeed it might have been a single thread with the house strung on it like a bead.

Opening the gate I began to go down the path, which was screened on either side by low bushes I couldn't identify. Soon it became rocky steps that were dark with moisture, although the day had been quite dry. It was as though the rock itself wept.

The surface seemed dangerously slimy. If I slipped and broke my leg, I would lie there all night and die of exposure. Why had I come? There was still some daylight left, but if it suddenly went I would have to feel my way back up in the dark. Still I kept going down against all reason that told me to go back and investigate the path another day.

The steps turned into path again, winding round the face of the cliff, and as I followed the bush screen dwindled and I was exposed like a fly on a wall to the open sea and sky. There was a rope bannister set through a series of rings let into the rock and I clung to this against the attack of vertigo that threatened to dash me off the steps.

Yet I went on down and down. The sky was banded in opal shades of green, yellow and cream; the sea was flat, almost oily with the pearled colours from the sky, until far out it became a dull gun–metal grey. Once more the path turned a shoulder, and the last and steepest flight of steps led down onto a strip of sand walled in rock with, at one end, a small concrete jetty with two mooring stanchions and a wooden boathouse.

She was standing on the jetty. I had seen her as soon as I rounded the last face. She had come there before me, had led me down and was waiting for me. She no longer needed a glass in which to appear beside me. She had taken my body and I was the outsider now, exiled from my own flesh.

She was smiling at me. 'You are going to find out what it is like to suffer.'

'I know what it's like. I have suffered. I have suffered terribly.' I could feel the well of tears inside me, but I no longer had eyes to weep with. My heart ached with understanding for all those creatures that can't weep.

She turned to look out to sea and I followed her look. As an oily slow back of water heaved, I saw a black blob against the pallor of the sky. The wave roiled again and the dark head ducked and then surfaced. It was waiting; easily, lazily rolling with the sea, its great dark bulk gleaming as it broke into the air.

She turned back. 'You haven't even begun.' She came down the two steps from the jetty and walked slowly and purposefully towards me. 'Don't worry. I won't leave you out in the cold.'

She came on across the sand. I could feel the breath from my own body and smell my own flesh as she drew near, nearer until we met. She passed into and through me, sucking me down inside, until I lay in her like a small dead foetus, or the shrivelled leathery pouch of a shrunken womb.

Two

I lay and gazed at the spare room ceiling through half—closed eyes. An ancient leak had engraved brown islands on the white sea of it. A frozen sea powdered with snow, where great seals reared on their flippers and snorted a steamy breath that congealed and pattered down in hail. It was a landscape as locked in ice as me.

I didn't remember getting back to the cottage or into bed, nor at what point she had let herself out of my body. I knew that as I lay there, I was myself again but only like someone in a fever, unsure of consciousness and aware that at any moment they might lose their hold on it and drift away, an unmoored boat with a hand clutching at air.

If I opened my eyes fully and took them off the ceiling, let them travel the room, I might see her sitting on the stool in front of the dressing table, touching up our face in the mirror. I wasn't ready for that yet. I closed my eyes again and concentrated on feeling my way through my limbs to make sure I was their only inhabitant and that they were fully mine. They felt numb as if with cold, except for one warm patch of thigh. When I realised that this was where Tiger was lying curled up against me, I wanted to cry. I put out a hand and found his blunt forehead to rub, until he purred and stretched his neck for more.

At that moment I believed I was myself again because of

him. His sentinel presence had driven the enemy off. If Aunt Meg had been a white witch, Tiger was her benign familiar who could protect me. I hung on to that thought while I made my eyes do a gradual circuit of the room. It was empty. A window was ajar and the wind pushed against it. A strand of creeper had crept in through the gap and stirred a little in the draught, as if nodding. Perhaps she had gone out that way and was waiting for me on the strip of beach. Well, I wouldn't go. I would stay warm and safe in bed, with Tiger snoring quietly beside me.

Suppose she opened the door now and came in? I was too vulnerable lying down. I must get up and meet her upright when she came back, even though being on my feet hadn't given me much protection last night. Anyway, there were things I had to do. This was the last day before the funeral. I must get Meg's room ready for John and lay in something more conventional than elderflower wine for him to drink. Rather roughly, I threw back the bedclothes, hoping to dislodge Tiger. I needed his company downstairs.

'Breakfast Tiger,' I said ingratiatingly. 'Fishy. What about that?' He thudded to the floor with a small chirp and stalked towards the landing. I followed him quickly, unwilling as yet to be alone in a room where *she* had been so recently. My mind skated unsteadily past a series of questions. At what point had she left and let me repossess my body? Whose hands had undressed whose nakedness?

I wouldn't think about it. I would concentrate on practicalities. Tiger was demanding the promised fish. I took the remains of what I had cooked yesterday out of the fridge in its silver foil tray and broke the seaweedy steak into the scallop–shaped pure white platelets he liked before I put it down. My stomach turned queasily, but I got out the packet of muesli and the milk, filled the kettle and put it on. 'Never go to work on an empty stomach,' had been one of my father's maxims. He had had his too–often–repeated wise sayings like my mother but his had had a basis in practical common sense and weren't, like hers, merely tags to paper over a vacuum. My mother would have offered me the vague injunction to 'pull myself together', presumably derived from tugging on imaginary stay—laces, while he would have counselled a good breakfast.

Tiger demanded that the catdoor be opened, and by now I was strong enough to let him go, while I made tea and swallowed my raw porridge of cereals and dried fruit. Now I must go upstairs again to fetch my clothes, so that I could bath and dress in the little bathroom beside the kitchen. I was now convinced that *she* wouldn't come back yet and I climbed the stairs confidently. I lay in the warm bath for some time. Her invasion of my body seemed to fill it with vague pains, an aching lethargy, as though it resented her alien presence, hating the slow poison seeping through my bloodstream. I tried to will it to reject her when she came again, like the transplanted organ of a stranger, foreign tissue, but even as I did so, I knew it was my own weakness that let her in.

The truth was that I had never given my body the necessary self—love. It and I weren't one, but two. I was indeed the ghost in the machine as I had read it described somewhere. I resented my body's limitations and its imprisonment. No wonder it had been prepared to combine with another against me. Other people were at home in their own flesh. I felt that Mary Dunscombe for instance fitted into hers and filled it as she would an old cardigan that had taken on her shape. But I was always a prisoner peering out through my own barred eyes. I soaped and steeped my body in the warm perfumed water in an attempt to placate it. 'There,' I said, 'I do love you. See how kind I'm being to you?'

I towelled it gently, talcumed and deodorised it and covered it in clothes against the sea damp that morning had brought again after last night's brilliantly sulphurous sunset. I must telephone the unctuous Theale and make sure that all was ready for tomorrow. My uncle was arriving by the four o'clock train and I had promised to meet him at the station. I would make up a bed in Meg's room. Should I tell him that she had died not in it but in the hall? I didn't know how

53

squeamish he might be about such things. Perhaps it was better not to mention the subject at all.

Clean sheets and pillow cases were piled neatly in the airing cupboard in her room that housed the hot water tank. They smelled iron—fresh and faintly from the little *pot pourri* bags I found tucked among them. Again I felt the pang of never having known Meg well enough. If she had been my mother, perhaps I would have been a less disjointed person. She would certainly have been more sympathetic to my academic aspirations than my own mother, who still half—believed that too much learning ruined a girl's chances. If she had dared she would have warned me not to bother my pretty little head. My year's sabattical to finish my thesis she regarded merely as a long holiday, to be interrupted for her convenience. She had never even asked me what the subject was that the college was willing to pay me for a year to stay home and write about.

Perhaps when I had finished with servant girls in Victorian novels, I should look more closely into some of Aunt Meg's fields of interest. It might even lead to marriage with a Japanese professor. I laughed out loud as I tucked in the blankets and saw my mother's face when I announced my engagement and presented my fiancé! She would be flattered as he bowed from the waist and glittered his black oriental eyes at her, eyes like moist Greek olives ... Who else had eyes like that? Leonard Wallace of course.

I felt a sudden panic. I had forgotten to tell him that the funeral was tomorrow. I would have to ring and let him know. With a last look round at the bedroom I went downstairs to the telephone.

It crouched on the table in the sitting room like a black frog, smooth and malevolent. I couldn't stretch out my hand to pick up the receiver.

The truth was that I didn't want to ring Leonard Wallace, hear his voice, or see him at the funeral; at least, part of me didn't. It was an instinctive reluctance that I tried at once to rationalise. I told myself I didn't want him present firstly because it would create problems with Mary Dunscombe, who I felt had the earlier and probably deeper claim to be there; secondly because his confessed interest in the power of evil made him an unsuitable guest at a graveside, even the deodorised and symbolic one of the crematorium.

Yet I must. I had promised and any failure to carry out that promise would create an impossible situation. My hand reached out for the receiver. I was surprised to find I knew the number to dial without looking it up.

'I forgot to tell you in all the interesting things yesterday that Aunt Meg's funeral is tomorrow at two.' Even as I said it, I knew she was near. I fought to keep my voice steady and my will intact.

'Is there anything I can do to help? Should I go with you?'

'That's very kind, but my uncle, her brother, is coming down today, so I shan't be alone. In fact I'm just off to pick him up,' I lied. I knew I had to end the exchange quickly, if I was to keep her at bay. Fortunately Leonard Wallace didn't seem to want to prolong it. When the telephone pinged at the end of our conversation I felt a gush of relief. I had won, at least for now. I drove into the town for some mildly triumphant shopping and was punctual at the station to meet John's neat black figure as it came through the barrier.

'Did you ever stay here before?' I asked, as I drove him back to Meg's cottage.

'Never,' he said firmly, looking out at the darkening coast road, where the mist was already beginning to hover. 'I never understood why she hid herself up here unless it was to get away from us all.'

'People came to see her from all over the world.'

'What do you mean?'

'Oh, Japanese professors, American students, German folklorists, that sort of thing. They came all the way up to Scarborough.'

'Extraordinary.'

He followed me gingerly down the path, afraid, I suppose, of slipping on the wet asphalt. As we rounded the cliff and came face to face with sea and sky I heard him catch his breath. I led him on down the steps, through the garden to the front door.

'Ridiculous,' he said. 'Quite absurd.' He was breathing heavily, as if he had been running. He too lived in a seaside town but his only view was of the houses identical to his own that faced him across the road. John never went down to walk along the beach at the tide—line and bring back childish treasure of seashells and coloured pebbles.

I opened the door and called, 'Tiger, Tiger!'

He came stalking into the hall, tail up, and stood for a moment regarding John. Instinctively both Tiger and I realised in the same breath that my uncle didn't see cats. Tiger reproached me for being out so long and then bringing back such an unsatisfactory visitor.

'Just leave your bag there for now. I'll get the fire going and feed Tiger. I expect you'd like some tea.'

'I had a cup on the train. At least I bought one. It was quite disgusting, undrinkable.'

I sat him down in an armchair and fell on my knees in front of the hearth. Fortunately I had cleared it and laid the fire before leaving. I heard John's voice as I set a match to the lardy cakes of broken firelighter.

'So unsuitable these days, and unnecessary too. It's not even as if this place was old and it was a genuine inglenook.'

'I expect she found it company on a long dark evening.'

'There you are. If only she'd lived somewhere sensible she could have had central heating like the rest of us or at least gas or electric. She wouldn't have needed to compensate by lighting a messy so—called "real" fire.'

I didn't answer, but went through into the kitchen. I hoped it had been a good idea for John to come and that we should get through the evening without a row.

My uncle was inspecting Meg's books when I returned with the tray of tea—things. 'She seems to have been very single—minded. I never knew quite what she did.'

'Neither did I until I got here. I feel vaguely guilty now—and sorry. At my loss, I mean. She must have been very interesting to talk to.'

'Yes. I suppose so. If you like that sort of thing.'

I almost sighed aloud. It was going to be a long evening. There was one bonus though: I knew I was quite safe from her. John would keep her away from me by his very low–key personality. She needed energy and excitement to bring her into being. She lived on other people's nerves.

I also realised that a part of me was in collusion with her; that confronted by normality as represented by my uncle I would, after a very few hours, be in a state of rebellion that would call her up myself in spite of my fear and horror. I would become the truant, the one who would do anything for a dare, just to break the monotony, even if I frightened myself half to death in the process.

Even as this came to me I heard myself beginning to play a dangerous game. 'Do you believe in second sight? I've been told that as a Cockburn I ought to have it.'

'But then I'm a Hackstead.'

'But you don't altogether reject it?' I asked with surprise.

My uncle stirred his tea. 'When I was in Africa, I saw a lot of things my rational Western mind didn't understand or care for very much. Indeed I once wrote to Meg about them when I was feeling particularly depressed during the rains after a bout of fever.'

'What sort of things?'

'Oh, witch–doctoring, that sort of thing. It really goes on, you know.'

'But does it work?'

'Oh yes. Because people believe in it. Faith can move mountains, as we were taught at school.'

'What did Meg say?'

'She was very sensible and soothing. I was in a bit of a state, if the truth be told. I'd found the usual bits and pieces in a skin bag—a dead snake and a chicken's head and a sock of mine, laid at my door. It was the sock that did it. Someone had stolen it, of course; easy enough to do. But there was something about its very familiarity, its *me*–ness in hostile hands. I began to get pins and needles in my left leg. It was like the gipsy's curse.'

'The gipsy's curse?'

'I'm surprised your mother hasn't told you. It used to be a favourite story with them all. They thought it was very funny.'

'Mother never mentioned it to me.'

'I was still in the pram. I must have been about three. Your mother was five and Meg was nine. We were out for a walk with Ellen.'

'She was your nannie, wasn't she?'

'That's right. She was a quiet and sensible girl. We were on our way to the park when we met the gipsy. It was afternoon, rather hot. We were going away for our annual holiday at Mumbles the next week. Mother and Ellen had been packing the trunks for days. It was cooler under the trees in the avenue and we walked quite slowly. Eileen was bouncing about as usual, running ahead and back again, while Meg hung on to the pram and talked to Ellen as she pushed. I don't think they took much notice of the woman until she was up with us, thrusting out her basket with the little bundles of dry heather. There were more gipsies in London in those days. She was old, brown and leathery with her hair in two flattened snail—shaped coils over her ears. She began to badger the girls and Ellen to buy her heather and have their fortunes told. "I can see handsome husbands for you both, but there'll be none for you," she said to Ellen, "if you keep old gipsy from looking into the little misses' hands." I think Ellen would have paid her to be gone by then, but the truth was, she hadn't any money with her and neither had the rest of us. The gipsy woman didn't believe her, of course. She thought Ellen was just holding out. She leant over the pram and glared down at me. "I'll tell his fortune for nothing," she said. "You've lost one and the other won't thrive. You remember what I say, and be sorry." I started to cry. Her face was so close to mine, and all the anger and frustration in it poured down on me. I don't remember how we got away, but I was ill for a week and the others had to go down to Mumbles while Mother and I stayed in London alone until I was well enough to travel. I was haunted and terrified by the experience for years.'

58

'How awful for you.'

'Ellen was badly scolded by my mother for letting it happen, although there was really nothing she could have done to prevent it. After that she never went out without a little money, in case. When I got better it became a great joke. She was 'John's gipsy'; I suppose as a way of overcoming any left—over fear but I went on being frightened inside for years, although I never dared say so. You see, she was half right. There had been another boy between Meg and Eileen who had only lived a few hours.'

'How could she know that?'

'I don't suppose she did. It was a guess that had a fair chance of being true, and nothing lost if it wasn't. Anyway, here I am. I did thrive in a way, although sometimes I think she was right and my whole life has been rather blighted. Anyway, when I was in a village outside Nairobi, still a very red—kneed young ADC, and I found this bag of tricks at the door of my bungalow, it all came back. It was fatigue and fever, I suppose, but I began to wonder if the African magic was meant to fulfil the gipsy's prophesy. My leg swelled. I thought I had gangrene and it would have to come off. Then suddenly I had the urge to write to Meg about it all, my big sister. Do you know what she did?'

I shook my head. 'No.'

'She flew out to Africa—just like that. She calmed me, the swelling went down and I got better. That was thirty years ago. When I retired and came back to this country, I wanted her to come and live with me. She refused. So I sulked. I've been sulking ever since. That's why I've never been here before.' He put his cup down carefully.

'So you do believe?'

'I believe in the power of suggestion, certainly. It made me ill and it cured me. I believe in the power of words and events to tap our deepest fears and insecurities. I've seen Africans turn their faces to the wall and die.'

'What did Meg do to cure you?'

'In a sense she didn't have to do anything at all. Just her presence was enough. That's why I tried to get it for myself when I came back. I wasn't really thinking about her at all, only how marvellous it would be for me. She was quite right to refuse. I would have cannibalised her for my own comfort. I'm sorry if I was a bit tetchy when I arrived. I feel better now. It must be being in her house and some drinkable tea at last.'

My defences were quite shot to pieces. I had never seen this so human side of John before. I hardly knew how to answer. It would be churlish to slap him down after such a confession; such an opening up of himself but I wasn't used to such a gift and didn't know what words to receive it with. However he went on again, giving me no need to reply at once.

'I should have married, but I couldn't ever seem to manage it. That's where Meg and I were alike. Your mother was the only one of us who could cope with that side of things. Perhaps my trouble was being the youngest and the only boy. The headshrinkers would say that was it, I expect. Meg was too independent. In those days a woman like her found it hard to marry, in every sense. Chaps preferred "gals", if you see what I mean. And what man was her equal, let alone her superior? But I would have married if I could have found someone soft enough to have me. Your mother now was just like the jampot Ellen always stood on the windowsill in summer so the wasps would stay there instead of wandering about in search of sweet things and stinging people when they didn't find any. They all hung round her. Fortunately she had the sense to land your father, though I never knew how.'

'He adored her,' I said, picking up a log and throwing it into the hot seedbed of embers, so that the sparks shot high in the chimney well.

I cooked supper and then Tiger joined us to watch the news on television. My uncle expressed a strong desire for an early night, and Tiger and I soon climbed the short stairs after him.

Perhaps it was the crying itself that wakened me. Tiger was gone from the bed and surely it was his voice in the garden, mewling in distress and probably pain. I saw him at once in my mind's eye like some sickening illustration to a book on hunting, with the wire noose of a snare about his striped body as his own struggles bit it deeper into the flesh, cutting him in two, or with a paw clenched in the metal fangs of a gin that tore through to the bone.

The sound had come from the front of the house. I crept down the stairs so as not to waken John, sensing that Tiger would get little sympathy there, and opened the front door. For once the skies were clear and a frosty moon sailed high in them, lighting up the front garden with an opal luminescence.

She stood beyond the gate with the baby in her arms that for all its wailing I knew was dead. Its cries were as tenuous as its hold on life. She smiled at me, extending her hands and offering me the small, weeping bundle.

'Take it. It's yours or it might have been. Look. Hasn't it got Martin's mouth and eyes? Or are they your mother's? Whose baby is it, Paula? Shall I tell you? It's my changeling. Look.'

She drew back a fold of shawl so that I could see the baby's face. It was wizened like that of a very old person or those primitive Byzantine pictures of the Christchild, where he lies in his mother's lap older than the ancient sages who have come to his birth. Yet even as I looked, the face began to melt and run like in the story of a wax doll set too close to the fire my mother had once told me.

'I'll leave it here for you. You must come and get it and take it indoors by the fire or the cold night will kill it.'

'It's dead, dead already,' I said, feeling the tears beginning to surface behind my eyes. 'I killed it. You know I did.'

'Yes, Paula. You didn't want it, did you?'

'I did. I did want a baby. It wasn't that.' She had the power to make me weep and I wept now.

'Perhaps it isn't yours, but that other one. You'll have to take it in to find out.'

'It's dead. That baby died over seventy years ago. It only lived such a very little while.'

'Is anything ever really dead, Paula? Except Martin's love, of course. That's dead. But then you killed that. Only murdered things die. Is that the answer, Paula?' She said my name each time, as my mother did when she was angry or disappointed with me. 'I'm going now. I shall leave your baby, my baby, here.' She bent out of sight behind the low fence and when she straightened up, her arms were empty, but I could hear the thin wailing louder than before. Then she smiled at me, turned and walked away into the shadow of a yew hedge and was gone.

The invisible baby wept on. I should have to go to it. But what would I find when I bent to pick it up? The shawl would fall back and show me its little face, long corrupted, with only a pearl pale maggot in each eye socket or shrivelled like the pickled head of an elderly monkey. Yet I must see and my arms ached for it.

I moved slowly forward to the gate and peered over. The crying stopped. At first I couldn't see anything. The patch of grey wintry grass was empty, or almost. I opened the gate and went out. The moon had disappeared behind a cloud, but there was light enough to see that there was no baby, only a small shape, enough to make a little hump on the bent chill blades. I stirred it with my foot. It was a limply dead mouse.

Normally I don't scream and jump on chairs at mice. Of the creatures we have to share our lives with, they seem to me to give us in charm what they take in food. The mansion polish mice in their oversize boots, town mouse, country mouse, Mrs. Tittle Mouse were loved figures in my childhood. Therefore it wasn't because it was a mouse that I felt sick and trembling. It was the very fresh deadness of it and the fact that it was there at all. I knew that it would be warm to the touch and that she wanted me to perform the stomach–turning absurdity of picking it up, perhaps even taking it inside; but I held out against the knowledge, shut the gate and walked, though still shaking, back into the house.

I wasn't yet ready to face my bedroom again and I had crossed the hall carefully avoiding any glance at the mirror where she might be waiting for me with a smile, ready to slip into my flesh as easily as an old dressing–gown. Poking life into the fire, I went through into the kitchen to make myself some tea.

There were both teabags and loose leaves in tins in the cabinet. Automatically I stretched out my hand for the ease of a teabag; then I changed course and began to spoon leaves into the umber Woolworth's pot. The floating teabag in its moist, grey–brown softness was too much like the small furred corpse I had left outside for me to face yet.

When I had poured out my tea I went back to the sitting room fire. I was wide awake now. Should I open one of Meg's books for company? Who knew what I might stumble across? The half–played cassette was still in the machine where I had left it a couple of days ago. Turning down the volume control so as not to wake John, I switched on where I had left off. It was a new voice, a woman's, cracked with age and grief into a monotonous chant whose words I knew only too well from my own English literature studies, a classic ballad that was anthologised again and again, and now lay in wait for me on the slowly unwinding tape:

> There was a lady who lived in York
> All alone and aloney–oh.
> She proved a child by her own father's clerk,
> Down by the greenwood sidey–oh.

She had borne three babies, whom she had stabbed with a 'long penknife'. One day years later she had seen them, now boys, playing ball:

> 'Oh mother dear, when we were thine,
> You did not dress us in silk so fine,
>
> You pulled out your long penknife
> And there you took away our three lives.'

> 'Oh my fine boys, what will become of me?'
> 'You'll be seven long years a bird in a tree,
>
> You'll be seven long years a tongue in a bell
> And you'll be seven long years a porter in hell.'

63

What was the penalty for someone who killed by wilful denial, not even out of lack of love? All alone and aloney—oh! Like John. Somehow Meg's aloneness didn't seem to me a punishment but a free choice. John and I on the other hand would be punished like those sufferers in Dante's *Inferno* who had 'lived without praise or blame', stung in their half-death by wasps and hornets until the blood streamed down their faces mingled with tears, to feed the loathsome worms at their feet. Those who had never truly lived could never die. Even the murdering mother was a porter in hell, a bird or a bell, while John and I were shut out and doomed to follow the wavering flag of our own indecisiveness. Sometimes I wished I hadn't read so much. There was always an image ready-made in someone else's words to pin down my thoughts and make them inescapable as specimens under glass. Even though I no longer believed in hell as a distinct place, the power of that symbol of despair and punishment could still tear at my throat. The dead baby was the child of love that Martin and I might have had and that I had desperately wanted, even while my perverse body rejected and resented the means to it.

When I woke in the morning my eyes were swollen as if I had cried in my sleep. I knew I must get up and begin the funeral day by taking my uncle a cup of tea, but I lay there, seemingly unable to drag myself over the side of the bed. My whole being ached, especially my right arm, which felt swollen like my eyelids. Perhaps the sea-damp was eating into me or, more prosaically, I had lain awkwardly on it in the deep sleep of exhaustion. I flexed my fingers under the bedclothes, clenching and unclenching my fist to get the blood flowing.

In the end I made myself throw back the warm cocoon of blanket and duvet, like ripping off sticking plaster, and swing my legs down to the cold floor. Aunt Meg had belonged to the generation that believed in linoleum with an oasis of an occasional rug here and there for bedrooms. No doubt it was meant to be bracing, but in my view it simply led to lying in sloth longer while you worked up the necessary courage to go over the top. The lino, I knew, would feel not just cold but moist, as if some sea beast had breathed frozenly on it.

After I had pulled on my dressing—gown and poked my feet into clammy shoes, I sat for a moment on the edge of the bed and looked at my throbbing arm and splayed out hand. The black circlet of the jet ring was a dark weal about the third finger. Perhaps it was restricting my circulation and that was making my arm ache. I pulled at it, but the knuckle seemed swollen too and I couldn't get the black band over it.

Still half asleep, I went down to the kitchen and filled the electric kettle from the cold tap. I pressed down the little red tongue to switch it on and turned back to the sink. I let the hot tap run until the water was warm and then soaped my bound finger and tried to slide the ring off, but it only seemed to bite deeper into the puffy flesh. Taking a teaspoon from the cutlery drawer, I levered the handle between ring and finger and jerked. Jet was brittle; it should snap, but my own skin cushioned it.

For a moment I felt terror rise in my throat. Perhaps the ring was poisoned. I had read of such things. It had been a favourite device of the Borgias, Lucrezia and her unholy brother. But was that true or only historical fantasy about victims who were really suffering already from one of the short fatal diseases that carried off people in earlier unscientific times with all the appearance of witchcraft or murder? One of today's tragic viral cot—deaths would have had some mumbling old woman burnt at the stake, I thought, desperately trying to control my panic.

'Slowly the poison the whole bloodstream fills,' my brain chanted from an almost forgotten poem. I imagined it flowing up from the black band of the ring, darkening the veins as it climbed slowly through my body. And yet I knew that my attempts to break it were half—hearted. Suddenly I knew too that she had lain down in me in the night, twisting the shiny circle against the bone until it swelled so that I was unable to slip it off, and that now it was she who held my hand from breaking it. I would have to force my will against hers. I saw myself taking Aunt Meg's sharpest kitchen knife, laying its edge against my flesh and then slamming it down like a cleaver

65

through skin and bone to free myself. Where had I read of the mutilation of dead hands for their wedding rings?

She was daring me to take down the knife from where it dangled with other harmless utensils, spoons, fish—slice, potato—masher, on a rack above the cooker, and to turn it against myself.

'That's the way to get it off, if you really want to. But you don't do you? You're a little fish that loves the hook and only struggles to make it sink deeper and deeper.'

It wasn't true. It was she who wanted to keep it, to wear Leonard Wallace's black ring. I squirted a green slime of washing—up liquid against it and began to turn it round and press it against the joint. My skin was red and bruised now, and my whole arm ached. Then, as I looked at my two hands, the one tearing against the other, I saw that the right one, the ringed one, was becoming transparent, as if I was seeing it in an X—ray. At the same time the pain receded. It was numb, chilled with a creeping cold that grew like a lengthening icicle towards my shoulder. The flesh was quite translucent so that I could see through to the bone. It was no longer my hand but hers.

The kettle began to belch steam and shut itself off with a loud metallic click that brought me back to the demands of everyday. I turned automatically towards it and saw that the hand that picked it up and tilted it over the teapot was solid again, though slippery with detergent and water. I held on tightly to the handle, afraid that it would slither from my hand and pour scalding water over me. At that moment I was convinced that she wanted to injure me, either to punish me for resisting her, or for some other reason I couldn't divine.

I leant against the cooker while I waited for the tea to draw and concentrated on remembering whether John took milk and sugar. He was already awake when I went into his room, sitting half up with the pillows stuffed vertically behind him. The grey morning light showed up his own pallor, the lines and faded hair with vulnerable clarity.

'Listen to the sea. That's what woke me. I suppose Meg was used to it, but I know I never would be.' He was thinking of the comfort of his bachelor flat, warm and with everything to hand.

'Can't you hear it where you are?' I put the cup carefully on the bedside table.

'Only if you go down onto the beach. Then you get that long, lazy noise of waves uncurling along a shore—not this boom, boom against the cliffs.'

'You must wrap up warm. It'll be cold.'

'Funerals are, always, even in summer.'

There was no sign of Tiger when we were ready to leave. Indeed, for once he hadn't slept on my bed. It was as if he disapproved of, was perhaps jealous of, my uncle's presence that didn't leave me all to himself. I called his name in the damp garden but he didn't come, and in the end I had to prop open the catdoor and leave what I hoped was a tantalising display of breakfast just inside.

We drove to the cemetery in my car. The unctuous Theale and his partners were meeting us there and it seemed pointless to hire a black saloon just for the two of us. Somehow I was convinced that Aunt Meg wouldn't have wanted it and would have thought it merely wasteful. To reach the cemetery we had to go through the southern part of the town and I tried as we passed along the winter forlorn streets to imagine it in summer, when its million visitors were streaming through, there was singing and laughter, children played on the sands and their parents dozed in deckchairs. Had Meg liked the summer bustle, or had she grumbled at it as residents so often do, and shut herself away in the cottage on the cliff? Perhaps Mary could tell me.

At first I had intended to have Aunt Meg's body cremated and the ashes scattered in some memorial park as the tidiest solution. Then I had thought again. It was clear from going through her correspondence that she had been a respected figure in her field. It seemed to me that I had a duty to leave some more tangible record of her for posterity almost as if she were one of her own folklore relics.

Quite frankly too I suddenly felt rather unsure of my ability to cope with the ghoulish vulgarity of a crematorium, the sepulchral musak and the soundless rollers that glided the coffin through the curtains to the flames, while everyone tried not to watch or rather was unsure whether it was right to look or not. In the end I decided that the verbal dignity of the truncated official C of E burying was best and probably no more superstitious than crossing one's fingers or touching wood, or even the automatic, 'Thank God!' of everyday speech, that now had no more religious overtones than 'goodbye'.

Winter damps had made the cemetery chapel turnover rather rapid. I was aware that we were part of a chain: the mourners before were just getting back into their cars as we drew up. Theale and partners hadn't yet arrived. I hoped there wasn't going to be some hideous and inevitable fiasco. It was my first funeral from the standpoint of producer and I found that grief was firmly displaced by first–night nerves. Since the chief mourners are usually the chief movers on these occasions, I reflected that that might be part of the funereal function.

I was aware too that it was the kind of raw day that ate into what my mother always described as 'the marrow of your bones.' It would be all my fault if John caught literally his death of cold through some incompetence of mine. What then should have given me a pang, the arrival of the hearse, brought only a sense of relief.

'Should we go in and wait?' I asked John.

'I think they'll tell us when but perhaps we ought to get out of the car.'

We got out, into deeper cold. Ridiculously, my mind threw up a picture of John's lean and sinewy shanks in an old–fashioned bathing costume, going shivering down into the sea. I was relieved again by the sight of Mary Dunscombe's small figure coming along the leafless avenue although I at once realised with remorse that I should have offered her a lift. I introduced her to John and found I was soon deep in a matchmaking fantasy, which ended with them joining elderly hands and running off to Seaford. Then I reflected that anyone who had needed to love Aunt Meg's commonsense and strength was unlikely to find comfort in her brother.

For the elderly, funerals must be bitter with foretaste. I was young and strong, physically anyway; yet the atmosphere wound itself into the imagination. A few more people were arriving, none of whom I knew, until I saw the tall, dark shape of Leonard Wallace approaching down the avenue with a small white–haired man remarkably like one of Snow White's dwarfs. He was undoubtedly an organiser, the secretary of some local group which would collapse without him they all agreed and was 'marvellous for his age'. Even so I was glad Leonard Wallace wasn't alone. At once my black banded finger began to throb inside my glove. Mary had seen him too, for I felt her start and bristle much as Tiger might do at the sight of a stranger.

A lugubrious member of Theale's team stepped towards us and made ushering motions of his hands. We were to go in. They had been busy while I gaped around me, and the coffin was on a trestle heaped with flowers. I was amazed by their quantity. John and I filed into the front row. Mary had dropped decently behind; I for one would have been pleased to have her with us, but hierarchy had to be observed even in death, and here we were the chiefest. John went down into the Protestant crouch, with his head resting in his rope–veined hands. I sat upright and stared at the Pre–Raphaelite decoration of that part of the Victorian memorial chapel that was dead ahead. Aunt Meg and I were possibly the only non–believers present.

My father's death had seen away the last shreds of any residual belief I had had in traditional Christianity. I had wanted, longed to believe that I would see him again, that a spirit so brave and funny couldn't be just snuffed out; but confronted by the reality of his closed eyes and waxy skin I couldn't, my little stock of faith ran out at every pore and left me with dry reason.

A young clergyman had swished in, his surplice looking faintly grubby in the grey light. We stood up, and he began: 'We brought nothing into this world and it is certain we can carry nothing out. The Lord gave, and the Lord hath taken away; blessed be the name of the Lord.'

Job's comfort, I thought. His manner seemed to me perfunctory, but then, who were Meg and I to complain? Somehow the dead had to be seen off, grief assuaged. No doubt the clergy on chapel duty realised that they were burying unbelievers, otherwise their own pastors would have come to perform the last ministrations. He announced a hymn.

It was one I have always found most stirring: '*For All the Saints.*' Meg hadn't been a saint in the young clergyman's sense, but in my reinterpretation perhaps she might be. At least I could be grateful for her life. *Alleluia*! I could hear John and Mary both singing out surprisingly strongly. No doubt the weekly practice kept their voices in better condition than my unexercised instrument would be at their age.

Now it was time for the psalm. Perhaps sensing that some of his audience were with him in spirit as well as in the flesh, the young clergyman gave the words their full weight: 'Every man living is altogether vanity; For man walketh in a vain shadow and disquieteth himself in vain.' And then suddenly, as is the way with words, there was a sentence that struck me through: 'Thou makest his beauty to consume away, like as it were a moth fretting a garment ...'

'*Gather ye rosebuds,*' sang my school choir in my head, and, '*The grave's a fine and private place But none I think do there embrace*' said Martin when we had spent a sweet hour kissing and touching, before the old, cold panic had gripped me and I had flinched away when I had felt his mounting eagerness.

Was it wrong to be thinking about lust and my lack of it at such a time and place? I didn't believe Meg would have thought so. Surely, implicit in the strange customs and lore she had gathered and studied was a cycle of 'birth, copulation, death,' as Eliot had degradingly put it, the nitrogen cycle of other poets, the seed falling into the earth and dying only to spring up as John Barleycorn to amaze us all, and be cut down in his prime, to go into the earth, and begin again. 'Behold I shew you a mystery,' as the young clergyman was now telling us. It was time to get up and go into the even chiller outdoors. Theale's men hoisted up the coffin and we fell into procession behind, walking the bare avenues till we came to a place of freshly—dug graves. Aunt Meg was lowered into one of them. The flowers brought from the chapel were added to those already miraculously there.

The clergyman gathered himself for the real business. 'Man that is born of a woman hath but a short time to live, and is full of misery. He cometh up and is cut down like a flower ...'

I raised my eyes, which had been trying not to look into the oblong clayey hole whose sides were faintly shiny with a slime of moisture from the dank air as if the earth sweated. I looked across it to those standing on the other side, Leonard Wallace among them, and then a movement further back caught my eye.

She was coming out of the stark trees towards me, and she was smiling. She was dressed in black for the occasion, but it was an unseemly long black gown more suitable for a dance floor than a graveside. She moved between the few mourners until she reached the front rank opposite me, where Leonard Wallace stood. As I stared across at him, he too smiled faintly. She slipped her arm through his and, for a moment, a second's break in the overcast let a ray of light ring the finger resting on his arm in black fire. I seemed to be transfixed by their smiling stares, to be drowning in their eyes ...

'Earth to earth, ashes to ashes ...' the clergyman intoned and she bent, as I dared not do, picked up a little soil and threw it down into the hole, still smiling.

I have never been a fainter but it was touch and go then. Lady My—Death had come to the funeral and, contrary to what the book had said, the sign of the cross from the young clergyman, even that traditionally most potent of prayers, which the little congregation had now embarked on, 'Our Father which art in heaven ...' had no power to dismiss her. How could it, when it had no power either to make me believe or able to accept the comfortable words the priest was saying for those who believed? Meg and I were both shut out by them and such, as I say, is the power of words that even in my unbelief they hurt me like knives in their exclusiveness. I bent my head for the blessing in order not to offend my uncle and Mary Dunscombe, and when I looked up again she had gone. Leonard Wallace was turning away alone.

I offered Mary a lift, making up for my previous omission and asked her to join John and me for lunch. She accepted, I could see, with relief. Obviously she had dreaded going back home by herself. I lingered to inspect the labels on the flowers to give Leonard Wallace a good start on us. There were tributes from all over the world, both from individuals and organisations. Mary introduced the spry old man I had seen with Leonard Wallace as the secretary of the town's field club, and he shook my hand with vigour, shouting, 'A great loss, a great loss.'

None of us felt like making small talk as I drove back, but at the door I tried to pull myself together by speculating about Tiger's possible return.

'I'd love to see him,' Mary said.

'I'm afraid he doesn't care for me,' John pouted.

'It's men,' said Mary. 'He prefers the ladies. It's nothing personal.' In her relief at not being left alone to grieve, she was almost coy. Perhaps my matchmaking fantasy wasn't too far out after all. I left them to revive the fire, which showed every sign of having died on us in sympathy, and went into the kitchen. I longed to be alone to think and come to terms with the morning's events, yet I dreaded that when the time came, I wouldn't be left alone for long.

My prospective couple got on splendidly over lunch, and soon John was saying Mary must visit him in Seaford and she was crying that that would be lovely but that she hoped I was going to keep Meg's bungalow, and that he would come and stay when the weather was warmer.

'What are you going to do?' John asked me.

'I haven't decided yet. There's been too much else to think about.' I was avoiding a decision, and I knew it.

After lunch I drove John to the station, dropping Mary at

her gate on the way.

'I do hope you haven't caught cold,' I said anxiously at the barrier.

'Oh, I'm tougher than I look. But I must confess I shall be glad to get back to my central heating. I know we grew up in that Spartan way, but I seem to have lost both the knack and the taste for it.'

I kissed his thin cold cheek and hoped I hadn't killed him. Then I drove back, stopping at the fishmonger's for a treat to entice Tiger home.

Back in the car I found scraps of our lunchtime conversation going through my head. My uncle had wanted to know who the other people had been who had come to Meg's funeral. Most of them I hadn't been able to speak about any more than he could and it had given Mary a chance to be sprightly and informative. I had wondered what she would say about Leonard Wallace, but she had chosen to ignore his presence completely.

John, however, had noticed him. 'And who was the tall dark chap with the secretary of the field club?'

It was as if the air began to sing and glitter with an electric charge. I felt my lips start to move and knew that she was about to speak with them; that when I had bowed my head after she had flung the earth into the grave, *she* had entered into me. When I had looked up and she had gone, it was because she was curled tight inside me and now she was unfurling through my body.

'That's our local warlock, Leonard Wallace. Mary doesn't approve of him. She didn't think he should be there.'

'Just the sort of person Meg would have found "interesting". There must be a great temptation to dabble in all kinds of dubious fringe activities under the blanket, so to speak, of folklore.' Mary and John's mouths were both pursed with disapproval.

'He wormed his way in. I watched him do it. I warned Meg that he was ... unreliable, but she wouldn't listen. It was the only thing we ever disagreed about, really disagreed. He can be very insinuating.'

'She could be very self—willed; even as a child she was the most determined of the three of us, though your mother could always get her way by being charming.'

'He's rather charming, I think,' I heard my mouth say. 'Quite the gallant, when he chooses. I can well imagine Meg being taken by him.'

'Taken *in*,' Mary clucked, stretching up like an indignant hen.

Frantically I fought to get control of my speech before the whole occasion fell into chaos. John rescued us.

'All those flowers from people abroad were an unexpected tribute. Perhaps someone will do a collection of essays as a memorial. I believe that sometimes happens, doesn't it, Paula? You'd know more about it than I would.'

I felt *her* retreat inside me. The dangerous moment had passed. But I had been badly shaken by my loss of control, even in the usually safe company of my uncle and Mary Dunscombe. I pondered the word 'warlock' as I drove back. I hadn't known that I even knew it as a word to use. It had sounded quite foreign on my lips. Was that what I really thought about Leonard Wallace, or was it merely what she had made me say out of mischief?

Back at the bungalow I was drawn irresistibly to the faery dictionary, but the word wasn't there. I turned to 'wizard' and found that there were black and white among them, that they had the power of shape—shifting and separate souls. Shape—shifting was easy; we've all been brought up on Snow White and the disguises of the wicked witch queen but the idea of a soul that could be taken out of its body and hidden in an egg was entirely new to me. The thought of the creature that was left going about its business like an empty and quite indestructible casing I found very chilling even though I wasn't quite sure what I meant by 'a soul'.

Was she my true soul? If so, what was I? Or does the body house more than one soul? *The Secret Commonwealth* said she was my 'copy, echo or living picture' and that suggested that she wasn't a soul and hadn't one. But if she was only an appearance, a wraith, she often seemed to have more substance than me and certainly more strength of will.

It was dangerous even to sit beside the fire thinking of her, and I felt her begin to stir in me. Sometimes I seemed to be no more than the water in which she swam freely. When the phone rang I knew who it would be and that she had been waiting for it. I felt her stretch and rise.

'I didn't come and speak to you today because I didn't want to intrude. Was that your uncle?' Leonard Wallace's smooth voice asked.

'John, yes. He's gone back. I put him on the train this afternoon.' Those words were mine, but they were my last though my voice went on. 'It's as well you didn't come up because we had Mary Dunscombe with us.'

'So I saw. You mean I'm not popular with her?'

'She hates you bitterly. She told John you were "insinuating and unreliable". I gather she and Aunt Meg used to quarrel about you.'

'Did she tell your uncle that?'

'At lunch, yes.'

'She was very jealous of my relationship with your aunt, it's true. What I mean is, I always suspected it, but I wasn't sure. Meg was very loyal and the soul of discretion. I know Mary Dunscombe resented my coming into her cosy arrangement. But she wasn't really up to Meg, not her equal in any way. She gave Meg no stimulus, nothing for her mind to bite on. She's very foolish to try to turn other people against me, very foolish. I really can't have her going about saying that kind of thing. However, I didn't ring you up to talk about the hysterical outbursts of a senile old woman. I wanted to explain why I didn't speak and to hope you weren't leaving us at once, but would come and see my house before you go.'

'No, I haven't made any plans to go yet. I'd love to see your house sometime.' The part of me that was still me had noted his use of 'senile' and 'old' as if he didn't know they were essentially the same, and this slip the pedant in the real me had seized on to try to regain control. 'If you don't mind I'd rather not fix a precise date now. I feel so tired I can't really concentrate. I think I'd better go to bed early and ring you in the next few days when I'm more organised.'

At once he made soothing noises and soon put the phone down.

I was trembling with exhaustion. My tiredness had been no on—the—spot invention, the social white lie to avoid committing myself. It was real in every fibre of my body as though I had personally dug Meg's grave and carried her to it. Even to get myself to bed was a haul up a sheer cliff face I could hardly contemplate, although it was only six o'clock, but I set myself to it. She would leave me alone now. I sank into a drowned sleep almost at once, even though I was uneasy about Tiger's continued absence.

I woke in the grey winter morning with tears on my cheeks and a hand between my thighs. My nightdress was rucked up to my waist and I lay flat on my back with her hand on my flesh. Horror and revulsion flowed through me as I felt her fingers begin to move. It wasn't that I condemned self-satisfaction in principle for those who wanted or needed it. It was just that I never had and her hand on me was a violation of my deepest nature. I tried to close my thighs against her, but she insinuated herself deeper and slid inside me. I felt myself becoming detached as I had with Martin, but with the difference that her possession of my body flooded out from her hands, for the other was now on my breast, and made it all hers.

As I looked down I could hear her beginning to grunt with pleasure. 'Come back,' she said. 'You don't get away so easily, my Paul. You're in on this too.'

She was drawing me back into my body, which had begun to respond to her touch. I was open as a sea anemone and helpless in the warm salt waves that poured through my lips. Spasm after spasm of anguished pleasure tore at my flesh that was her flesh and my mouth opened in cries that were almost shrieks. I had never cried with Martin, or felt the exquisite charges that now jerked my limbs, that were no longer mine. When it was still again, I sank back into sleep.

My mouth when I woke was full of ash and my own smell

76

of sweat and shame reeked up at me from under the bedclothes, in spite of the deodorising cold of the bedroom. Adding extra cologne–scented foam to my bath I lowered myself into it and began to soak and scrub the skin I was almost ashamed to look at. I knew that she had left it like an emptied husk for me to cleanse and make sweet for her use when she should need it again. My poor flesh ached as if it had been whipped or had run all night. Only the arrival of Tiger when I went downstairs brought me any comfort; and Mary Dunscombe's telephoned invitation to have tea and see her house that afternoon merely increased my guilt. I rang my mother.

'They say I can come out in a few days, probably for the weekend. How did it all go, darling? I'm sure John was a tower of strength.'

I held the phone slightly away from my ear and let her voice drop into emptiness; the little tinny syllables fell like sparks onto a damp hearth and hissed out. 'When are you coming home?'

She paused there. It was the only question she wanted an answer to, and she used the word 'home' for a place that was her home not mine in order to exert the maximum leverage.

'I haven't decided yet. There's still a lot to clear up here.'

'Surely there can't be that much? Just a little house and her books, I suppose. You could give them to the local hospital: they're always glad of books.'

'I don't think they'd want these.'

'Why not?' Her tone was sharpening.

'Try asking your burser or whatever he's called if a seventeenth–century first edition of a treatise on demonology would be suitable light reading for women's surgical.'

'Really Paul, you're impossible. You make difficulties. How can I come home if there's no one there to look after me?'

'There's Bob.'

'You can't expect a man to do that sort of thing.'

'I think you're unfair to him. I think he'd be perfectly willing and entirely capable of looking after you for a bit.'

And he was of course. I had no worries about that. Though I found him dull and personally irritating, I had no doubt that he loved her and would be perfectly content to bring her a bedpan, wash her and fetch her light meals on a tray. It was she who wanted me there to dance attendance, so that Bob, a man, her man, shouldn't see her at a disadvantage, subject to a real rather than an assumed helplessness.

'You could put Meg's things into store until you have time to sort them out. Get Carter Pattersons or Pickfords to crate them up for you, if there are so many.'

'There are letters from all over the world that have to be answered and thanks that should be sent. Perhaps if I send you a bundle you could write some while you're in bed. You must be getting awfully bored.'

'Who are they all from?'

'Oh, professors and associations, folklorists and so on.'

'They sound more like your kind of thing than mine.'

I knew this. My mother's epistolary style, full of dashes and exclamation marks, would hardly do for the learned enquirer from Wiesbaden into 'the British rustic mythology in the poems of John Clare'. 'There are some you could manage: more personal ones. I'll pick some out. I must go. I've got to pay Theales.'

'Whose?'

'The undertakers.'

I hadn't; I could perfectly well have sent them a cheque but it was such a good parting shot I couldn't resist it. 'I'm up here harassed with all these unpleasant details, while you lie in bed being looked after,' it said. I put the receiver down with a brisk ' 'Bye!'

Even so she had rattled me. I knew I had to decide what to do with the house and its contents, and indeed, Tiger himself. I would discuss it with Mary Dunscombe over tea. She would want me to stay. My mother would say any such idea was 'quite ludicrous'. Perhaps it was. I stood still for a moment and listened to the house.

All houses have their own sounds, a small voice almost. I

heard Aunt Meg's house speaking to me now. It wanted me to stay; it said I wasn't finished there, that I still had things to do or to undergo. I felt it tug at me and heard the slight creakings as the wind pushed at it or rubbed a bare branch against the verandah, and far off, as in a shell held to the ear, I could almost catch the sigh of the sea.

Mary's cottage was so close I decided to walk. The mist had cleared off by afternoon and there was even a pale sun and a view from South Cliff almost it seemed 'to Norroway o'er the foam', with the water for once not an Atlantic grey but a steely blue.

A white–painted gate led up a path to a whitewashed cottage with a red–tiled roof, set under the brow of the hill. Before I rang the bell, I turned to look back the way I had come, and found that the land had fallen away completely and the world become simply sea and sky of such a vastness that I didn't know whether my spirit would be uplifted or dwindled by the complete loss of human scale between them. Mary's small figure when she opened the door reminded me of a knitting bag of my grandmother's, stuffed with balls of wool and unfinished pieces. Mankind's, and especially womankind's, doings seemed laughable against that backdrop. She drew me in to a blazing fire and a tea display of so many species of cakes, scones, cheese straws and little sandwiches that I knew I could never eat enough to try everything.

'I thought you should have at least one good Yorkshire tea before you go. When will that be? Have you decided yet?'

'I wanted to talk to you about it. I can't make up my mind what to do. My mother would say I'm quite mad and she wants me to go home straight away, but something seems to be holding me back.'

'I feel I shouldn't try to influence you. I should like you to stay very much, but I mustn't. You have your own life to lead, and perhaps there's someone you want to get back to.'

'Not now; not at the moment.' Martin seemed almost a ghost, glancing back with a sigh and slipping away into the netherworld of memory. 'There's Tiger too. I've grown very

79

fond of him.'

'I'd be glad to give him a home, of course, if he was a problem. I think he'd stay with me though he's obviously taken to you.'

'I'm afraid I've been rather relying on you for that. It's the house itself, too. I feel I haven't finished with it. Does that sound quite mad? Or perhaps you can understand.'

'Oh, I do, I do.' She paused, with the brown teapot in its maize wool cosy, the colour of a harvest festival loaf and sprinkled with bright woolly flowers, held against her cardigan in hands whose joints showed the faint telltale of arthritis. 'I haven't told anyone this, but I've never been altogether happy about Meg's death. I think I can speak of it now without crying. Perhaps the house is unhappy too. Meg would laugh at that, but I think we may leave ripples, a kind of psychic disturbance that other people can pick up. It was so sudden. She wasn't ready to die and it isn't as if she was peacefully asleep in bed. She was in the hall. It must have been a great wrench, a tremendous struggle.'

I knew she saw it as a soul tearing from the body, but I didn't want to argue with her. It was her, and thousands of others', symbolic view of something that I, and Meg too I imagined, saw in what we thought were more scientific ways, that were our metaphors for the inescapable yet unacceptable fact of death.

Suddenly I longed to tell her about my own unhappy spirit. I knew she had no power to disturb me in Mary's serene house, and I knew too that Mary would believe me. But shame from the morning was still on me. There were things I couldn't tell her, and that made it somehow impossible to tell her anything.

It was dark when she said goodbye to me. 'I'll just come down to the gate. Are you sure you can find your way back? Thank you so much for coming. I've enjoyed it. You'll let me know what you decide? Give my love to Tiger.'

When I reached the rim of darkness where the light above her gate no longer stretched, I turned to wave. She was still standing there with her slightly swollen knuckles resting on the top of the gate and the lamplight showering down on her.

The fire was almost out and needed a lot of blowing on ritual hands and knees to coax it back. Perhaps my uncle was right and it was an anachronistic nuisance. I felt lost for what to do next and no nearer any decisions. It was a relief when the telephone bell broke the silence. As I picked it up I wondered fleetingly what people in the country had done before it, but life was different then; fewer people lived alone.

'You were out when I rang before.'

'I was having tea with Mary Dunscombe.' My voice was deliberately cool. Where and when I went out was no business of Leonard Wallace.

'Did she say anything more about me?'

'No. She was mainly talking about Aunt Meg. She seems unhappy about the suddenness of her death.'

'The coroner wasn't.'

'No, but then he must see that sort of thing all the time.'

'What sort of thing?'

'Heart attacks, sudden strokes.'

'Yes, yes, he must. And what else have you been doing? I hope you're coming to see my house soon. I don't know whether I've told you: it's rather special. It's called the House of the Five Ways.'

'Why's that?'

'I'll tell you more when I see you. Just now there's something else I want to talk about ...'

His voice was trailing away. 'You're very faint. I can hardly hear you.'

'You must listen very carefully. It's a bad line. Don't try to answer. Just listen, listen to my words ...'

The line was very bad indeed. He seemed to be almost whispering, but although I concentrated hard, I couldn't make out the sense of what he was saying. Dutifully I didn't interrupt, but went on listening. Then the line seemed to clear. 'Did you get that, Paula?'

'Yes, yes I did.'

'Good. I'll see you soon then. Goodbye.'

I had taken the call sitting on the rug by the fire, with the now leaping flames warming my face and making me drowsy after the cold walk home. I put the receiver back, pulled down a cushion from the nearest armchair and rested my head on it. It wouldn't matter if I slept for a bit; I had nothing urgent to do.

I don't know what the time was or how long I had slept, when she woke me. My eyes opened to her voice. She was bending over me where I lay on the rug.

'Come on, Paula, wake up. We're going for a little walk.'

'Please let me sleep. I'm so tired. It's too cold and dark. I ought to go to bed.' Even to myself I sounded like a fretful child.

'A walk will do you good; blow away the cobwebs, as mother would say,' she laughed. 'Come along. I'm in charge now. You must do as you're told. You know you can't help it, so why try to resist?'

She put out a hand to mine to pull me to my feet. Looking up, I saw the two hands with the black band on identical fingers, stretching out towards each other, for mine had moved irresistibly to take hers, like metal to a magnet as she reached out. As they touched, it was as if a charge arced between the two rings in a spasm of black lightning. Lifted by that charge, I seemed to rise to my feet like a dancer or as if in a dream. Her hand in mine drew me across the sitting room and into the hall, but by now I could no longer tell who led and who followed, which of us was her and which me. We seemed to flow into one another through our joined hands. The front door was opened. We went out into a night, where, for the first time since I had come to Scarborough, a pale moon had eaten holes in the mist which lay in ragged banks of torn candy floss across the polished dark steel plate of the sea. I felt neither cold nor fear as we climbed the path effortlessly, the path that usually had me puffing by the time I reached the little gate onto the road. No wind bit into our faces as we rounded the bluff, and no sound came from the still sea.

The cliff road under the moon was a grey, silent wash on which our feet made no sound.

'Where are you taking me?'

'You'll see. Come on.'

We were retracing my steps of the afternoon, but how long before I had come this way I couldn't tell. Would we go on towards the town? Perhaps she meant to lead me to a cliff top and then over but if that had been her intention, she would have held my hand tight as we climbed round the bluff and torn me from the rope banister to shatter on the flat, hard surface of the sea ...

Whatever she intended, I didn't care. I no longer felt or had any true apprehension that I was Paula. The outside world I saw as if through a glass cage, and my fingers were numb against the smooth walls that shut out sound and feeling. We had come to Mary's gate, where I had last seen her small figure stand and wave. It hung a little open as if something had shouldered through. She stood aside for me to go first up the path.

No lights came from the little house under the brow of the hill. I walked on between Mary's two small strips of lawn neatly bedded round. Then I saw that the front door was open. I moved forward and pushed it further back.

'Go in, Paula,' the whisper came from behind.

I went in, my hand seeking automatically for a light switch inside the hall. A familiar little knob met my fingers. I pressed it down and the light sprang on, dazzling after the dark.

The hall was a shambles. A coat stand inside the door had fallen or been flung into the middle, throwing old coats and hats onto the floor. A wall barometer was splintered face—down on the rug.

'Mary?' I called. 'Mary?' I pushed open the sitting room door and switched on the light. The confusion of the hall was everywhere here too. Ornaments were smashed, little tables and chairs overturned, pictures crazily awry. I backed out of the room and turned towards the little kitchen. Again I pushed at a half—open door and felt for the comfort of a light switch. As the gleaming surfaces sprang up under the snapped—on whiteness, it was as if something broke in my head, letting me see and hear for the first time.

Blood had fountained over the white enamel tops of the drainer and fridge, and slashed across the walls. It screamed at me from every side, and underfoot among the shattered china and glassware. And now I heard them, even though I knew they were gone: shrieks and cries, smashing and shattering, and the roaring of a bloody beast of prey. They pounded and screamed at me from the spattered walls.

I leant against the table, afraid I should faint or be sick. I must go upstairs. I looked down at my hand on the formica top and saw it was sticky with a bloody ketchup that seemed to start from every surface to smear itself against me. In the winter cold it was still fresh and thick. Horrified, I rubbed my hands against my clothes but I only managed to stain them, while the rich juice still oozed between my fingers.

Stumbling to the door I made for the stairs. And now I saw what I had missed before as I stood in the hall: the deep puddles of blood in the carpet, the living drops that had splashed the banisters and wall, as if a lunatic painter had daubed them in his frenzy. The trail led to an open bedroom door. I knew it must end soon. I switched on the last light.

She had fled up the stairs, her lifeblood pumping out with every heartbeat but I couldn't tell from which gash or which among the gaping mouthed wounds had been the first. She lay on the floor, her body still in its blue wool cardigan, slashed and bloody. One hand hung by a flap of skin, a hand that I had seen resting quietly on the top of the gate, its elderly blue veins flattened now and empty. But it was the head, severed from the pathetic huddle of the body and split open lengthwise like a peapod that caused me to retch, and stumble away to the door from the butcher's shop window of halved brain and muzzle, and the absurd scatter of broken false teeth.

I tottered down the stairs, not caring that my hand on the banister was bloodied again and again. I knew I was alone in the house, that the foul beast had done its work and gone. I knew I should ring the police or someone, but I held back. There was nothing to be done for Mary Dunscombe, and I felt too ill to answer questions. I must get away, out into the air, away from the terrible reek of blood that filled my nostrils. I staggered out of the house and down the path I had come up a century ago.

Then I was on the road and running. At Aunt Meg's gate I paused. My hands were still bloody. Instinct told me not to smear the gate with tell—tale stains. I wrenched the front tail of my shirt out from my waistband and wrapped my hand in it. Then I opened the gate and began my way down the steps and path without holding on to the guiding rope. Once my foot caught and I almost fell. My ears were full of my own breathing and thudding heart, and I was quite alone. *She* had led me to Mary's and left me there.

I reached the still—open front door and went in, leaning my back against it to close it. I went upstairs to the bathroom, took off my clothes and bundled them up with trembling hands. Then I ran a bath and climbed in to wash away the contagion of blood. Looking down, I saw my own body showing white through water that had turned a thin pink. I hauled myself up, and shuddering and almost vomiting with disgust, I pulled out the plug and let the contaminated liquid ooze away. Sluicing out the bath vigorously first, I ran fresh water and began again. Mary's death had taught me all about Lady Macbeth's frenzied washing of her hands.

'Who would have thought the old man had so much blood in him,' went round and round in my head.

Towelled dry and in clean clothes, I went down to the sitting room, raked up the embers and burnt my bloodied cast—offs. I was acting in a daze of horror or perhaps it would be truer to say, *re*acting, for nothing I did was thought out. The instinct to rid myself of any trace of Mary's blood was part of my recoil from the shock of what I had seen. As the flames licked over the smouldering cloth, I tried to think what to do. I still couldn't face the police, but I knew I ought to do something.

I imagined myself picking up the phone and dialling 999. What would I say? As I followed the conversation through in my mind I suddenly saw that I too could be suspect. I hadn't touched Mary, indeed, my stomach heaved even now at the very thought, but I knew she hadn't been dead long and by the morning that gap between her murder and my visit would be insignificant when they came to fix a provisional time for her death.

Surely no one would seriously think I could do anything so bestial. Would I even have had the physical strength? No, the murder would almost certainly resemble the previous attacks by the man Leonard Wallace had called 'a redcap'. There had been blood enough to dye a wardrobe of caps. I cursed myself for not having asked more about him and what he had done, but after my initial fright when Mary Dunscombe had come looking for Tiger, he had faded from my mind, driven out by more immediate terrors.

Should I be afraid for myself alone in this isolated place? Not tonight anyway. He had had his fill of blood. A sentence of Mary Dunscombe's floated into my consciousness. 'He likes them young.'

She had thought she was safe, just as I did ... But somehow I couldn't be afraid. Death, even one so horrific, seemed almost welcome. I wouldn't resist as Mary had done. Then it would be over quickly. There would be no more need to think or make decisions. My life held nothing that I wanted to struggle on for, and this latest manifestation of brutality and meaninglessness had sickened me of the whole business.

She had taken me there so that I should see it. But why? If it was to drive me to despair and self—murder, surely that would kill us both. Or would I be bound in her forever and she in me? I no longer knew what I believed, and I had no one to ask. Martin's voice whispered at me out of the shadows, but I couldn't catch the words. We had discussed everything together, walking in the park or on the sitting room carpet with a drink between us and a growing island chain of books as we read this or that to each other.

'All alone and aloney—oh.'

I switched on Aunt Meg's expensive record player, rewound the tape that was still on it and pressed the button for play. I had to have the sound of a human voice, even if it sang of my desolation.

> Where are you going? To Scarborough Fair.
> Parsley, sage, rosemary and thyme.
> Remember me to a bonny lass there
> For once she was a true lover of mine.

As the reproach unwound into the air, I heard the soft thud of Tiger coming through the catdoor into the kitchen. In a moment his furry head, with the ginger ears pricked was pushed round the door and at the sight of me he came forward and began to purr, one of the most flattering sounds in the world. I hugged him to me and then carried him into the kitchen, where I thanked him with milk and fish. Then he was ready to lead me up to bed. I hadn't thought that I would ever sleep again, but I did.

In the morning I switched on the radio and found the local station. There was nothing. Mary was still lying there undiscovered, at least by the media. But it couldn't be long: a postman or a milkman would notice the door I had left open and the lights still on.

The murderer had carefully switched them off, or, I paused in washing dried fibres of fish from Tiger's supper bowl, he had gone about his work in the dark with a night vision as good as a cat's under that sickly moon.

It broke at eleven o'clock. Police called by milkman ... Brutal murder, following pattern of two previous attacks on women ... Not since the Yorkshire Ripper ... York murder squad intensifying hunt—and so on. The clichés dribbled out of the plastic box. Mary was a kind old lady who lived alone in an old world cottage on the edge of a popular resort. The milkman was brought on to tell how he had been disturbed to find no note in a bottle beside the open gate and had gone up to investigate. He stumbled into the pun as people will, suddenly finding themselves at the centre of happenings and with the questions and the little viperous head of the microphone thrust under their noses.

The murder seemed a copybook of its forerunners, with a single difference that the other women had been much younger: a mother in her early thirties living alone with her child; a waitress at one of the town's hotels, living in for the summer season. I found myself waiting for the police to call on me. I doubted if Mary had gone out for a walk after I had left her at the gate. She had no dog and no reason to go into the town. The chances were that I had been the last person to see her alive, except one. I might myself have been seen by a passing motorist though I didn't remember any cars going by on my way there or back, or while we stood at the gate.

My own ambiguity puzzled me. Why was I so unwilling to go to the police? I've never been a great fan of the law, since experiencing the contempt policemen generally have for students, unless they happen to be the more gilded youth at one of our older universities, but I had always assumed that I was a more or less law-abiding and co—operative citizen. Now I was skulking like a criminal myself.

Then, as I began to run through my conversation with an anonymous detective inspector in my head, I realised why. I couldn't explain my second visit and I would have to pretend that I had first learnt of the murder from the news, like everybody else, apart of course from the murderer, the milkman and the police themselves. If they came I should have to lie, or at least be evasive, and I wasn't at all sure I could. Once again there was no one I could ask.

Only Leonard Wallace.

I knew immediately that she had slid that thought into my mind. It had the dangerous, dubious tone of all her actions. She wanted me to ring him so that she could talk to him. The ring began to bite into my throbbing flesh. There was a bond between them and I was just the necessary go—between, the pimp that brought them together.

I reached for the telephone.

'I've just heard something quite shocking on the radio.'

'Oh?'

'It's Mary Dunscombe. I know you two didn't get on ... but even so.'

'What is it?'

'She's been found dead, murdered. I've been expecting the police and wondering if I ought to ring them.'

'Why should you?'

'Well, I expect I was the last person to see her alive.'

'I can't see that that would help them much.'

'It might establish the time or something.'

'Oh, I think they can do that quite easily these days.'

'He must have been covered in blood.'

'He?'

'The murderer. The man you once called a "redcap". I looked it up.'

'Perhaps it wasn't a "he". Men don't have a monopoly of evil.'

'But to *do* that, to mutilate her in that way …'

'You speak as if you'd been there.'

'It must have needed great physical strength, that's all I mean.'

'Women can find such strength, especially in a fit of madness, what was known in classical times as a divine frenzy.'

'You mean like the bacchantes tearing Orpheus to pieces?'

'She was small and elderly. A strong younger woman could have killed her quite easily with some sort of weapon, a meat cleaver, or an axe for chopping firewood. You must be her nearest neighbour, so I expect the police will visit you soon enough. I'll ring you in a day or two to arrange about your coming to see me.'

I put the phone down in horror. He was suggesting that *I* might have killed Mary Dunscombe and warning me not to go to the police, almost as if he knew … I remembered our conversation of yesterday, or at least listening to his distant voice and then falling asleep. Suppose I hadn't really been asleep but in some kind of trance and had gone out and come back? Suppose my memory of my second visit was only what I wanted to remember and that the reality had been quite different? Wouldn't I want to blot out something like that, to pretend she hadn't done it, for it couldn't be me, not the real me?

She had hated Mary. She might well have killed her, using me as instrument, either while I thought I was asleep on the rug or when she took me there the second time. Why else had I burned my clothes? It was the first thing a guilty person would do.

But how could I have done it? I had no weapon. And then I knew I had. I saw it quite clearly in my mind's eye, in the wooden box beneath the verandah steps, under a pile of sacking, beside the slice of tree trunk that served as a chopping block, sharp and clean, as you would expect of the axe that Aunt Meg had used to split her kindling.

I went out through the kitchen door onto the wooden platform. It was greasily dark with moisture. Spiders had spun overnight webs between the verandah rails, and these were seeded with leaden droplets, evil necklaces that would trap and cling. I went slowly down the steps, which were patched with a livid green moss, a leprous slime that might make me skid and fall. At the bottom I pulled out the box and turned up a corner of the sacking. The axe wasn't there.

Ever since I had seen it in my mind's eye I had known it was the weapon, 'the murder weapon' as crime novelists, and perhaps the police themselves for all I know, call it. That it was gone was in some ways a relief: it might have been nestling in there, hideously stained, waiting for me to pull back the sacking like moving the washing up bowl in the morning and the spider darting or opening the cupboard door on the sharp face of a rat.

Where was it? Was it lying somewhere in Mary's garden where the police would find it, or at the bottom of the sea hurled from the cliff? When they examined it, they would have a mess of Aunt Meg's fingerprints and possibly the murderer's. Aunt Meg's would be unidentifiable, I thought. I doubt if she had ever been 'mugged and printed' in her life. They would only know that they weren't Mary's; that the murder weapon had been brought deliberately to the house. There must be dozens of identical wood choppers in the town and countryside about, and probably more than one shop that sold them. I didn't really believe it could be traced back to me even if it was found. Then I caught my breath: *I was thinking like a criminal.* I looked down at my hand, which all this time had been gripping one of the uprights to the verandah steps, and saw that I had been clenching it so hard that some of the slimy moss mixed with the broken pustules of an orange fungus had crushed up between the fingers.

The mush began to redden as I looked at it, until Mary's blood oozed again on to the back of my hand which stuck to the post as if nailed there. Hadn't people once believed that at the approach of the murderer, the victim's wounds would bleed afresh and hadn't Lady Macbeth been unable to wash away the blood from her hand? If I could wrench mine away and take it down the steps to the little cove and plunge it into the sea, would the waves run red through North and South Bay and cast up my guilt on the shore?

Her guilt, not mine. I was only her tool, her accomplice at most. I hadn't wanted Mary's death. What I felt wasn't guilt, but horror. I tore my hand away and went up the steps into the house, where I scrubbed my fingers with a nailbrush. I felt no compulsion to telephone the police now. If they were coming, let them come. If my body was guilty, then I too was a victim.

They came as it was growing dusk. I had been sitting with Tiger by the fire, trying to compose a letter in my head that would break the news most gently to John though I was probably already too late and the national press would have it in the morning. He would learn all the hideous details from them.

The detective inspector introduced himself and his two constables. I offered them tea, which they accepted. One of the constables took notes.

'We shall be pursuing a house–to–house enquiry, but as you're her nearest neighbour we'd like to check with you first.'

The interview had begun ludicrously on the doorstep when he had addressed me as 'Miss Hackstead,' while the wind whipped his trousers tight to show the outline of his calves.

When I told him my name was Cockburn and that Miss Hackstead was dead, I almost expected the old B—movie response, 'Then who might you be, Miss?'

'Won't you come in? It's turning very cold. I'm Miss Hackstead's niece. She died a couple of weeks ago.'

'We've no record of anyone else living here.'

'I don't, not really. I came up to arrange the funeral and things.'

'I see. And your name again, just to keep the records straight?'

'Paula Cockburn.' I spelt it out for him.

He was warming his backside at the fire, the privilege of rank, when I brought in the tea, while his constables sat and stared about or seemed to doze. No doubt it had been a long day since the milkman's call.

'It's a bit of a long shot, but we have to ask whether you saw or heard anything that might help.'

'No, nothing, I'm afraid; that's why I didn't ring you before—that and the shock. You see, I went to tea with Miss Dunscombe yesterday afternoon.'

'What time would that be?'

'I got there at three and I suppose I left about five or half past.'

'A motorcyclist reported seeing a woman walking along the road at five—twenty. That fits.'

I didn't remember him, but then I'd have been busy with my thoughts and my head was down against the cold. Anyway, motor bikes go by in a flash and make much less impression on the eye than cars. It was as well, however, that I had decided on this much of the truth.

'Did Miss Dunscombe say anything to you about expecting another visitor?'

'No, she didn't.'

'You say you've only been here a couple of weeks. How well did you know her? What were her movements likely to be?'

'She was a friend of my aunt's, a great friend, but I hadn't met her until two weeks ago.'

'Would she make enemies, do you think? Some elderly people can be very sharp—tongued.'

'Mary wasn't a bit like that. She was rather kind and gentle. I think she went to church. The vicar and people there will probably be able to tell you more. Anyway, I thought this was only one of several crimes, presumably by the same person according to the news.'

'We don't believe all we hear from the media even when we've given it to them. There are certainly similarities, but there are one or two differences as well. Miss Dunscombe was a lot older, and there was no evidence of sexual activity. She hadn't died easily, or swiftly either. She fought for her life.'

'There was an old lady once who was going to be executed on the scaffold and she fought with the headsman because she wouldn't be party to her own murder. Mary might have felt like that.'

I longed to ask what time she had died, but even if they had told me it wouldn't have been much help since I didn't know how long I had been asleep on the rug, if indeed I had slept, or what the time of my second visit had been.

'It's funny you should say that.' The inspector put his teacup down carefully on the stone hearth. 'Because her head was cut off.'

I gasped and put my hand to my mouth. It needed no dissimulation to make me gag and gasp: the memory of the split pod was enough.

'How awful! Does he usually do that sort of thing?'

'He mutilates them, but usually in a rather different way.'

They asked me one or two more questions, but it was clear that although they had expressed caution they were only too glad to put this one down to the local favourite. I told them that I might be going back to London soon, but that I would leave them my address. He went through the motions of thanking me, but it was clear that I wasn't on their list, at least not anywhere near the top. Whatever Leonard Wallace said, to them it wasn't 'a woman's crime'.

I felt quite pleased when they had gone. I hadn't let her say something silly and destroy us both. I let her make a fresh cup of tea, while I slid deep down inside to wait for my next opportunity to take charge.

Tiger had been waiting for the policemen to go before he made his appearance. Now he came to sit beside me, as had become our custom. The death of Mary had made his future more certain in one respect: he would have to stay with me. It was unthinkable that I should hand him over to a stranger. But that didn't solve the problem of the house. I felt it too didn't want to be given to strangers, that it clung to me in some way.

Pushing the problem from me with Scarlet O'Hara's immortal words: 'I'll think about that tomorrow,' I switched on the television, but it was still showing children's programmes. Tiger was growing tired of my restlessness. He opened his pink mouth wide in a yawn of protest, showing off his pointed white teeth.

'Alright, I'll find a book to read. There must be something among all this lot.' A guilty memory of my neglected thesis came to me. Something on my period, whatever Victorian servant girls might read if they could or at least tell each other in bed at night or repeat for the little masters and misses in their charge, would satisfy my Puritan conscience.

I began to look among the fairy stories; Jacob's *English Fairy Tales*: that might do. I picked it off the shelf and looked at the date: 1890. It was just right.

There was a slim leather–bound book next to it with no title on the spine. What was that? It might suit me better, since I already knew several of the Jacob's stories as the stuff of pantomime: *Dick Whittington, Jack and the Beanstalk* and the *Three Little Pigs*. I pulled it out and opened it.

Although it was bound, it wasn't a printed book at all. It was handwritten in Meg's own clear script. It seemed to be some form of diary. But what was it doing among the printed books? That wasn't at all like my methodical aunt. It must be there for a reason. I replaced it, and Jacob beside it, and stood back. It blended in perfectly. You wouldn't have known it was there or anything special; it was the perfect hiding–place. I took the slim book out and went back to the rug. Wood charred and fell in the grate as I read. From time to time I remembered and threw a fresh log on when Tiger shuffled in protest or I felt myself beginning to chill. When I had finished the last page I went back and read the whole thing through again.

Three

I do not know quite why I have decided to put down these notes or for whom. I do it, I think, out of a feeling of unease, out of a sense that at some point it may be important to know exactly what happened or was said in chronological order. I have therefore decided to go back to the beginning and with the help of the dates in my engagement book to record what has happened up to this moment, while it is still all clear in my memory. In putting it into this particular book I have to admit to myself that I am using a form of disguise, because I am no longer sure whether the house is safe or whether anything I write can be kept private. Yet it still seems absurd to think so and I should feel both ridiculous and somehow disturbed if I had to resort to hiding things under the floorboards. This seems a dignified and, I hope, effective form of concealment. Even so, I resent being forced to it. It is against my nature to be secretive, against everything I have tried to do in my work by way of making a science out of something that has too often been in the hands of cranks, not to put it too kindly, or those whose imaginations are too easily stimulated. I do not mean the ordinary people whose stories and customs are our source material, but the self—deluded hangers—on, shading into the dubious fringe cults of the present day. There is material for a much—needed lecture on the subject, and perhaps I should try it on some conference when I am next asked to speak on a theme of my choice.

I had been worrying in a rather subdued way about the problem, when I suddenly remembered this handsomely bound notebook presented to me by a visiting student, an Italian, if I recall correctly, and until now sitting quite blank on the bookcase. I shall try to tell it all exactly as it happened as they say in American detective fiction. I have retold enough odd tales by now to be able to manage that, I think, even against my own instinct to reduce everything to notes, except when it is a matter for publication.

I have always kept an open mind about what I was recording. As Briggs put it: 'We must make allowance ... for the likelihood that people see what they expect to see.' I shall try to keep to that lifelong practice although I now realise much more clearly how easy it is for what she called 'The constructive power of the imagination' to creep in when one is at the centre of an event rather than merely an historian of it. I shall begin with our first meeting.

March 16th

Today being the second Monday in the month was the meeting of the Field Club. The County Archivist, surprisingly young and pretty, came to lecture on Thoresby and the early days of the society. More and more girls seem to be taking to archives; a good sign of the times, I think. In the coffee interval Harry Chalmers introduced me to her. I was foolishly flattered when she knew my name. Silly, but there it is. So much interest comes from abroad that one does get the feeling of 'a prophet is not without honour except in his own country' rather too often in dear old England. It is absurd to be Honorary Something–or–Other of Wichita University and not, say, Bristol, and absurder still, I suppose, to mind. However, the ego was to be further soothed when Harry introduced me to a new member, especially as we don't get them all that often.

First impressions—I wonder if I can reconstruct them: tall, dark and intense. Not what our mother would have called a gentleman; a faint flavour of what used to be dubbed a cad or a bounder. Early forties, I should guess. He bent over my hand in a rather foreign way that I took to be assumed because of the lack of proper social courtesies in English, but also because of a certain theatricality in his own make–up. Indeed, he almost looked made–up in another sense, because of the darkness of his hair and the intensity of his eyes against the tanned skin, itself unusual for an Englishman in Winter. When I heard his name I realised he might not be English, but Celtic fringe. I thought he looked like a magician or a conjurer. At any moment he would produce the top hat from behind his back and pull out silk scarves, paper flowers or rabbits. Not at all the sort of thing the Field Club was accustomed to! I could just imagine the consternation and I almost laughed aloud.

'I didn't quite catch the name …'

'Leonard Wallace.'

'Mine's Margaret Hackstead. I always think we should adopt the Continental custom of shaking hands firmly and stating one's name. That way there would be less embarrassment all round. All that asking about afterwards.'

'I'm sure people don't have that problem with yours, Dr Hackstead. You're much too famous.'

If time and circumstance had been other, I would have been expected to strike him lightly with my fan and cry: 'Flatterer!'

'Mr Wallace has only recently moved to Scarborough,' Harry Chalmers shouted at me—he gets increasingly deaf. 'He's taken a rather splendid house. I don't know if you know it, Dr Hackstead: one of Paxton's few domestic flights of fancy. What's it called, Wallace?'

'The House of the Five Ways.'

'What an interesting name.'

'It's a pentagon, basically; a tower built to get a view in five directions. It was in such a tumbledown state that no one else wanted it. You must come and see it now I've got it a little more under control.'

'I'd love to. I didn't even know it existed.'

'Few people do. Actually, there are some matters I've wanted to discuss with you for some time. I've been working on a series of pamphlets, privately printed, on Gaelic folklore and related themes, and I'd like your advice on type and motif classification.'

Flattery again, of course, and a line I couldn't resist. 'I'd be delighted. Why don't you bring them round to me and we can use Stith Thompson's index on them.'

'That would be so kind. May I telephone you to fix a date?'

'Yes, do. I'll wait to hear from you. I'm going to Norway for a few days next week.'

'Ah, yes, the Scandinavian Conference. You're giving a paper, I assume?'

'The Shetland Trows and their Scandinavian cousins. It's long been my theory that the Nordic delegates are really all trolls themselves. They certainly behave like it.'

'I won't ask you to be more precise now. I'll wait till you come back with it all fresh in your memory. Then I'll ring you and ask to be invited over for the full accounting. I've heard a great deal about your brilliant storytelling.'

I would like to think that I didn't lap all this up at the time like Tiger with a sardine tin to lick out; but in the interests of truth I have to record that I went home refreshed and invigorated with the encounter, and that I flew off to Stockholm eager to absorb every detail and find an amusing way to retail it because I knew I had an audience waiting.

March 26th

Jet lag is receding and the ground stays firm underfoot. Tiger delighted to see me. L.W. rang to hold me to my promise. I found myself less taken by him on the telephone after a week of a rather high–powered international gathering and rather disinclined to be sociable. It suddenly seemed a chore to have to produce a string of anecdotes and character sketches for someone I scarcely knew. Nevertheless I was committed to the invitation and there was no option but to follow it through. I invited him to tea on the day after next.

March 28th

I found myself very apprehensive before he arrived, bundling up papers and shelving books with a nervousness usually attached to being in love, that almost forgotten state. At one point I caught myself actually plumping a cushion, and stood quite still with it in my hands to consider. I didn't really want Leonard Wallace to come, and yet here I was, almost girlishly on my best behaviour and tenterhooks too. Firmly I stopped that foolishness of tidying. I combed my hair and freshened my face and neck with a little cologne, but refused to do any more. He must 'love me for myself alone and not my yellow hair.' It was still very cold, with no hint of spring yet, apart from a sprinkling of snowdrops under the hedge. Sometimes I think that the lateness of spring up here might be the one thing that could drive me South at last. The very flower bells seemed carved from ice, as if some Fabergé had been making exquisites that would melt if brought indoors like faery gold turning to leaves. In protest at the bitter outside, Tiger was curled right round in front of the fire, a furry ginger ammonite with his head at the centre of the whorl. The knock startled me. It seemed only a second since I had been looking out into the frozen garden and had seen no one.

He was hooded up in a kind of green parka with dark fur round the face, which gave him the appearance of human and animal dissolving into each other. I suddenly saw how people could have believed in werewolves and was as disconcerted as if he had begun to howl. Then he smiled and threw back the hood, holding out his hand to shake mine almost as though he knew the impression he had made and was trying to correct it. It was strange to find a conventional sports jacket and corduroy trousers under the parka when he took it off, but reassuring.

I made tea and brought in cake and biscuits and a pyrex dish of buttered crumpets to stand on the hearth to keep warm. Tiger opened an eye and then uncurled, stretching both forelegs out rigidly to accompany a yawn. Then he stood and finished his stretch by arching his back. Leonard

Wallace put down a hand and rubbed his index finger and thumb together in what was meant to be a cat–fetching way. Tiger lowered his back, stood quite still for a moment considering and then turned and stalked from the room, his buttocks stiff with rebuff.

'Your familiar isn't very sociable.'

There is no way of apologising decently for a cat's rudeness. I didn't try. 'Like all of us, he sometimes gets out of bed the wrong side.'

'I hope it isn't an omen.'

'An omen?'

'Or perhaps a forerunner of his mistress's feelings.'

The remark annoyed me with its heavy gallantry. Did he think I was just a silly old woman to be flattered? I offered him the dish from the hearth.

'Will you have a crumpet while they're hot——or at least warm?' I rather hoped the butter would run down his chin.

'How was Scandinavia? Very cold, I expect.'

'Somehow it's a dryer cold and anyway they're better organised to cope with it. Our cold is always damp. I find theirs invigorating. I could walk about in it and feel warm and brisk even in the snow, whereas here I would have been chilled through and just wanting to get back to the fire and be sluggish.'

'I can't imagine you ever being sluggish.'

'Oh, I am often. I'm quite lazy.'

'I'm afraid your list of publications gives you the lie. Those of us who have the same interests but without your energy, can only admire and recognise that we're really just dilettantes.' He bit into a crumpet but efficiently and anyway by now I wasn't sure I wanted to see the greasy rivulets shining on his skin.

'You said you've been publishing some things of your own. I hope you've brought them for me to look at.'

'Of course. How could I resist?'

'Perhaps when we've had the crumpets. Literature doesn't go well with buttered fingers.'

'I'd hardly designate them literature, but then they're not

meant to be, just jottings.'

'Oh, we can all say that in this field: pickers up of unconsidered trifles. We're the last of the line, for Britain anyway.'

'Do you think so?'

'Surely. I often think of myself as a kind of archaeologist of folklore, called in at the last minute before the bulldozers and the concrete foundations destroy the evidence forever, sterilising our particular piece of earth.'

'I don't quite follow.'

'I'm sorry; I'm rerunning what I said in Oslo. I haven't quite got back yet if you know what I mean.'

'No, please go on. It isn't often, I've discovered since I've been here, that one gets a chance for sustained conversation. How does the parallel with archaeology work out, I mean the sterilising part? I can see that you dig up snatches of custom and story as an archaeologist digs up pots and things.'

'Well, once he's done that, the earth is sterilised of the past, cleaned out and then the modern bits are put in. Until now, we humans have largely built on top of what was there already, adding to the layer cake, to be crushed down in our turn by the next layer and become part of the whole history that the earth held and that the next generation had its roots in. There is a sense in which archaeology, by exploring destroys that. I feel it's the same in a way with folklorists. We record bits of belief before the television and radio blot them out forever, sink their foundations into the unconscious, replace the old beliefs in children's minds with science and technology which is our equivalent of reinforced concrete. We record what's left and put it into books, where it gets remade into television just like putting pots in a museum really.'

'There's your difference, though. It isn't destroyed, merely, how shall I say, transmuted. Because it's spiritual not physical like pots and sword blades, it's indestructible. It goes on in another form.'

'Spiritual shape—changing?'

'Yes, that's it!' His eyes were almost giving off heat with

103

the intensity of his excitement and his skin was flushed under that strange Winter tan to a kind of dull brick. 'Exactly the right phrase. The intangible *can't* be physically destroyed. It will break out, even though no one believes in the old forms of goblin and faery.'

'But doesn't that make the recording and codifying of all the old scraps absolutely pointless?'

'Not at all. Because it needs channels to work through, and the mere act of dealing with this material in its old shapes provides a channel, and it also reminds people of those old shapes from which they, as it were, get the designs for new.'

'What is *it* then?'

'A force, a power.'

'The power of the supernatural?'

'I don't think the label is important, really. One knows it, one feels its presence. You've felt it.'

'I think you may regard what I'm going to say as heretical.'

'Do go on.'

'I have felt something, yes, when people have told me stories, or taken me to places where something has happened. Stonehenge, for example: it's impossible not to be moved by it in some way. But I've never been able to separate it from the influence of the mind that is telling me. I am moved because they are.'

'But in the case of Stonehenge, no one is telling you.'

'Not now. But I have been told; we all have in the past, in dozens of books, from Geoffrey onwards. You would say this is a tribute to the power making itself felt down the ages. I think I would say it's a tribute to the powers of the human mind, which I do believe we hardly understand as yet, and to the need or will of the human psyche to believe in the seemingly inexplicable. Perhaps it's an image of the fourth dimension the scientists are telling us is there.'

'Brilliant, quite brilliant. I am enjoying this. Did you give them all that in Oslo?'

'Good heavens, no. No, I stuck much more to my trows and trolls. Not a fair example, because they simply came over

104

to the Orkneys in the settler's boats or rather, their heads. If your own work is in things Scottish, you've probably come across them.'

He laughed. 'One of them was an uncle of mine. At least, I thought so as a child. I don't think our views are that far apart. Not if you're prepared to believe in a fourth dimension.'

He had laughed the discussion and our differences off as though he didn't want to say any more and reveal his own ideas any further but I had seen a glimpse of something in his intensity when he was talking about supernatural power to make me uneasy.

After we had finished eating, he produced his series of booklets, rehashes of Scottish material from nine-teenth—century collections in the main. I was a little surprised after what had been said to find them so conventional.

'These are from just one of my series, the ones I thought you might help me classify,' he explained. 'If I do a new edition of them I should like to add the codes as a footnote.'

I didn't say it aloud, but I thought that he could quite easily have got the information he needed without coming to me. However, we went through them systematically, typing and coding. All the time I had the feeling that we were playing some kind of game and that the whole exercise had to do with something else. I suddenly had a picture of us, heads bent together over our work, in front of the fire, and felt I was taking part in a charade I didn't know the key—word to. Soon after this he left, but not before he had made me promise to visit him. I managed to delay it for a week, but that was all.

Tiger came in so jump upon his cue when Wallace had gone that I decided he had been waiting and listening for his going. I sat for a little, wondering why I wasn't delighted at the thought of visiting Leonard Wallace. After all, I have been known to complain to Mary that there's little enough intellectual social life here, apart from the theatre and I don't move in the same circles as our distinguished local playwright.

There were too many things that I didn't care for about Wallace or rather that in some cases I found puzzling. How, for example, did he make a living? He seemed without visible occupation or means of support. Yet I couldn't see him living on inherited income. With the snob's antennae of a Hackstead, I had already divined this at our first meeting.

Another thing that had disturbed me was his calling Tiger my 'familiar'. It hadn't been quite a joke. I didn't want to be made to see myself as the traditional old witch in her cottage with a cat, dabbling in curses and herb teas. It's true I make my own wine, but I regard that as a mild form of alcoholism not a healthy country craft or 'double, double, toil and trouble' over the magic potion.

Nor did I like Tiger being reduced to my creature. I regard him as his own person, not a projection of me. One of the things he hadn't cared for about Wallace, I was sure, was that he had treated Tiger as an animal, a lower order, whereas he is used to being a companion, different but, in his own way, equal. After all Tiger knows that I am an animal too. Wallace's attitude trembled on the edge of treating him as an automaton, a thing. He was expected to come running to an invitation as if he had no choice. It showed a distinct lack of knowledge of cats and made me wonder if the whole little episode had been for my benefit, so that I should think well of its perpetrator.

Yet I really had no grounds for any of this and if I had come across a judgement so speculative and ill–founded in a book I would have been down on it like a ton of bricks, as Eileen would say. It was such a relief to me to find when I met her that Paula hadn't acquired my sister's weakness for the cliché. It comes, I'm sure, from a deliberate decision not to use her mind and indeed, I can remember it growing on her as I became what she thought more eccentric and less marriageable. However, all that's beside the point of my reactions then to Leonard Wallace though it does show how, having embarked on this exercise, I am almost enjoying it. I suppose it's the chance to write something freer and fuller than I allow myself as a rule.

What did he want of me? Why was he pursuing me in this way with invitations to his home? Clearly it wasn't an entrée to the delights of the Field Club, since it was there I had met him. Perhaps he was just a bit lonely up here and feeling the intellectual isolation that I sometimes complained of. Without Mary I should be quite desolate, and yet I don't want to live in the South. John and I have nothing in common. Paula I could see a lot of without any strain, but she has her own life to lead and I mustn't cannibalise it as the aging sometimes do to the young. Eileen fortunately has got herself a pleasantly boring man who dotes on her, so I need feel no guilt there.

I love it here in so many ways, and that's the truth. I have Tiger and Mary, the sea and the sweep of the two bays, with my own private cove that appeals to the child in me. I have peace to work at something which is the nearest I have come to a passion since Larne was killed. And from time to time I have the excitement of being invited to a conference, setting off from home to see the world at someone else's expense, with the knowledge that it will all be waiting safely here for me to come back to.

There, I've digressed again from the point of L.W. Perhaps it's the first sign of senility, a tendency to ramble. It was at about that point in my thoughts, when I was speculating on his motives, that Tiger got bored with me and began to play with something under the chair where L.W. had been sitting, an old–fashioned armchair with a kind of frilled skirt of heavy chintz round its legs that I kept because it was comfortable and because I liked to watch Tiger batting a ping–pong ball in and out of the ruffles and pouncing as if a live thing was hiding there. Cats are very like us in their ability to set up exciting games that need imagination to make them fun. Dogs are realists: they chase the ball or stick, knowing exactly what they're doing, like footballers. Cats like to pretend.

I thought it must be one of his ping–pong balls that he was playing with now, but it was the white corner of a piece of paper that his paw was pushing at. I bent down to pull it out. It must be a note or letter that had been knocked from the desk and that, if Tiger hadn't found it, I would have spent hours looking for. But it wasn't. It wasn't anything I had seen before.

It was a change of address card. 'Dear subscriber,' it said. 'The Pentacle Press, formerly of Leatherhead, Surrey, has moved to Scarborough, Yorks. I hope that you will continue to subscribe to our mailing list. Remember: only the Pentacle Press offers you truly alternative publications and opens up a new dimension of thought and experience.' The address was The House of the Five Ways and the logo of the press was the five–pointed star of conjuration. The card must have fallen out of one of L.W.'s pamphlets.

Here was a small source of income; but a living could hardly be made out of the sale of the kind of thing he had shown me. The card gave substance and colour to my half suspicions. Wallace probably dabbled in just the kind of thing that gives the whole field a bad name. If I was ever to give the lecture I had been thinking of a few days before, I probably had a fund of material right to hand. I still didn't see how I fitted in to his requirements, but I could see how he might fit mine. I mentally straightened my back to observe and record for future use.

April 7th
In the event it was ten days before the proposed visit came off: man proposes and streptococci dispose. They disposed of me with a fluey cold indoors for a couple of days, and then a few more had to pass before I felt strong enough to cycle into town and out on the other side to the bottom of the hill which led up one of Scarborough's several natural ravines. I got off and began to push, still feeling a little weak and easily puffed after my dose of flu. As I leant against the handlebars and looked up, I could see what I took to be Wallace's house rising above a brush of still leafless trees. The late afternoon sun caught one of the windowed facets obliquely before me and flamed there for a moment, so that my eyes dazzled and black shapes flared across my vision when I looked away. It was several seconds before they cleared and I could see the handlebars, the basket between them and the ground below

108

again.

When I lifted my eyes once more to see how much further I had to go, the flame had died and the two flattened planes of windows nearest to me were dead eyes with a long nose between under a conical leaded cap with a ball on top like a tassel. Had Leonard Wallace come here because of the name of the house and its unusual architecture, or had that been a coincidence? Obviously it was the ideal home for the Pentacle Press. It must have an amazing view from the top windows.

The road was cut into by a kind of peninsula on which the house stood, inside what must be a walled garden. There was an arched black door in the weathered brick, with a brass bell pull beside it. I was aware of the house behind the high wall, bulking above me. It must be quite big. Did he live there alone? I thought of John's neat bachelor flat the last time I had seen it. I pulled on the brass bell knob that was clammy with the sea air, but bright and obviously kept cleaned, not easy in Scarborough, where the salt tarnishes metal in a day. I imagined it clanging somewhere away in the old servants' quarters on a mahogany board still marked 'Footman,' but I could hear nothing.

The door itself opened with a click and a whirr, and seemingly without human agency. I paused for a moment, looking up a flagged path through a shrubbed garden. Then I jolted my front wheel up the step and through the archway. When the bike and I were safely inside, the door closed itself again. I propped my bike against the wall and set off up the path towards a handsome columned portico. The wall must have been a later addition. Originally there must have been some form of carriage drive, perhaps before the roads were built that had isolated the house on its own neck of land like a lighthouse whose waters were the shrubs and flowing rivers of tarmac.

I hardly had time to pause under the canopy of the porch before the inner door opened. There was a lobby where wet umbrellas and galoshes were meant to be left before an inner glass door. My hair had blown about on my ride and I put up a hand to pat it into place. As I stepped forward, the glass door opened and I could see Leonard Wallace descending the last treads of a balustered staircase. He wore a black velvet jacket that might have been part of Highland evening dress over a polo—necked black fine—knit sweater. His trousers were black too. It was a spectacular entrance. I was almost as impressed as I was meant to be and I was on the point of regretting my own dingy tweeds, until I remembered the ride back. I pulled off my gloves, unwound my woolly scarf and presented them to him, realising that I probably bore at that moment a distinct resemblance to Margaret Rutherford playing Madame Arcate in *Blithe Spirit*.

'Your mechanical footmen are rather unnerving.'

'But useful. If I'm working upstairs, they give me time to descend without keeping a visitor waiting in the cold. Come in to the fire you must be as we say 'starved'. Should you have cycled this far so soon after your flu?'

'Well, since I don't drive and I don't like spending money on a taxi, it's that or walking. I'm too impatient to wait for the bus, or to organise my life to suit their timetable.' I felt a little put out by this concern, since after all it was he who had set up the whole visit. Now I was being made to feel that I was eagerly irresponsible in coming out, when truly I would have much rather been home by my own fire although I had to admit that, when he opened the door into the drawing room, his was larger and brighter. Again, looking discreetly around, I had to wonder about his income and in a sense to feel a little ashamed of myself. It was, I hoped, uncharacteristic of me to concern myself with other people's status or financing. I had always prided myself on not caring about such things or even giving them a moment's thought, but now I discovered inside me a deep snobbery that must have been implanted when we were children and had lain there ever since. I didn't like it, partly because I felt I was being unfair to Leonard Wallace and that it coloured my judgement.

The room was lined with leatherbound books in glazed bookcases. Some of them, I suspected, would turn out to be identical to ones I had at home. There were heavy curtains at the windows which were still drawn back to let in the cold Northern April light. In spite of the warm bright fire I was glad we were already in official summertime and that it wouldn't be dark for several hours. I didn't know why this thought went through my mind, but even the studied attractiveness of the drawing room, where a round black table, topped by what I thought was a Benares brass tray, was laid rather fetchingly with the paraphernalia for tea, couldn't quite dispel my sense of unease.

'What a splendid room!'

'I'm glad you like it.'

'Indeed, what a splendid house altogether. How did you find it?'

'Quite by accident. I was looking through *Exchange and Mart* and my eye just fell on it. At the time I was wanting to move and it seemed—heaven sent.'

Was I imagining things or had there been a slight pause, the merest microsecond of hesitation before that last expression, almost a crossing of the mental fingers?

'How do you manage it all by yourself?'

'I don't. I've a sort of companion/handyman, a friendly trow, who does most of it. Now, as it's a cold day, I suggest we follow the ancient Scottish custom of a dram to our tea. I expect you're ready for yours now?'

I was indeed ready for a cup, but I would have preferred it unlaced. However, there was no way of saying so without appearing old–maidish. I was trapped by my vanity into drinking something I didn't want as so often happens under the tyrannies, usually called the niceties, of social convention.

Leonard Wallace produced a decanter of dark liquor that must have been a heavy malt whisky and added a large splash to the two cups of tea he had been pouring.

'I found my friendly trow in Germany when I was stationed there, and he's been with me ever since.'

'You were in the Forces?' This didn't fit my image at all.

'The last gasp of National Service caught me. Not that I minded, in a way. It gave me a chance to travel. In fact, I

111

decided to bow to the inevitable and get the most out of it, so I took a three–year commission.'

Curiouser and curiouser, I thought. Then I saw that it explained some of the things that had been puzzling me. A clever boy from Scotland who became a short–term officer might well, twenty or so years later, have much of Wallace's manner and accent. It still didn't explain the invisible means of support however. And young officers living on their pay don't usually pick up handy native batmen they can afford to keep once they're demobbed.

The heavy dram of whisky had totally obscured the taste of the tea and rose in an alcoholic haze as I lifted the cup Leonard Wallace had placed in front of me with his remarkably beautiful brown hands, which made mine look coarse and peasantish from gardening and scouring Tiger's innumerable dishes.

'You said he was a trow and the other day you said you had an uncle who was a trow. Do you always give people such labels?' I laughed as I said it, to show I was joking but he answered quite seriously.

'I think they often fit remarkably well. After all there are only so many variations on the human personality, and most of them, probably all of them if we knew, have or had their shadow counterpart.'

This was an intriguing idea: a mixture of Plato and folklore I hadn't heard expounded before. ·

'But how can you tell which is the shadow and which the real?'

'I don't think you have to. Perhaps neither is real and they are interchangeable, like twins.'

'Twin souls or entities coming and going between this world and another?'

'I think that's a possible explanation of changelings, for example, and those who were said to have gone to fairyland while a fairy took their place in daily life.'

'Does everyone have a double? It's certainly been a widely–held belief. Do I in your scheme? And you?

'Perhaps some people, a very few, are able to be wholly

one. I'm sure you are, if anyone can. It takes a strong will and personality to hold the various manifestations together, but if you can, then it gives you great strength and singleness of purpose because other people are fragmenting themselves all the time.'

As he spoke, I saw a series of images, transparent flat prints floating in dark water that I knew I had to bundle together, one on top of the other, to make one clear picture. It was Paula. She looked up at me from the water, as if she were drowning. Behind my thoughts I could hear Leonard Wallace's voice going on. The heat of the fire and the dazzle of its high flames, the fumes of hot whisky were making me drowsy after my cold ride. It must be a hangover from the flu. I gave myself a strong mental shake. There was a pretty china clock on the mantelpiece. I had noticed when I sat down that its hands said five past four. Now it was showing just twenty minutes past. I was very relieved that I hadn't fallen asleep. However, I must be careful. There was a difference between human and other time. I must pay closer attention to what Leonard Wallace was saying in his rather flat, soporific voice.

'You're feeling drowsy, very relaxed by the warm fire. Why don't you just go to sleep, relax completely, put your head back on the cushion and close your eyes?' It wasn't so much a question as a suggestion.

'I wouldn't dream of it. I think I had better have some more tea without any additive except milk and one of those tempting scones.'

'I'm so sorry. I should have offered them to you or told you to please help yourself. Kasper's learned to make them just like a native.'

I took a scone and a liberal helping of butter and jam. With a great effort of will my dreadful drowsiness was passing. It would have been too humiliating to fall asleep like a tired old woman on his sofa. Briefly I wondered what obscure worry about Paula had surfaced in the image of her drowning reflections, but I put the worry away to look at later. I decided on a piece of Dundee cake, reminiscent both of nursery tea and railways, and very steadying.

'I must show you some of the rest of the house when you've finished your tea. We won't bother Kasper in the kitchen. I want you to see the view from the tower.'

The house was rather like a ship with the tower as the bridge rising above the deck. The inside of it was plain and almost disappointing, bare of both furniture and ornament except for a telescope on a brass swivel; but the light that cascaded in through the five windows was a dazzling shower and the view in every direction was as I had expected, always interesting and twice magnificent.

'If you look right to the furthest corner of that pane, you can see a rock edge like a wall. Do you see?'

'Yes, a sort of curtain of rock.'

'That's the face that cuts off your own little cove. You don't know how I envy you that, your own private beach.'

'And I envy you your tower. How strange that you should find something so aptly named just when you needed it.'

'What do you mean? I'm afraid I don't quite understand.'

'For the Pentacle Press. It's perfect, surely.'

'Oh yes, yes, of course. But I don't believe in coincidence; I believe in fate.' He laughed, but again I thought it was to hide his seriousness.

The pouring light was beginning to make me feel almost dizzy, the light and staring at the black line of rock against the pale sea and white sky. I knew that when we left the tower I should be blind in the dark like a mole come up into the day from his earthly night. I didn't want to have to grope or to stumble. Somehow it seemed very important not to show weakness in front of Leonard Wallace, not to appear doddery. I felt him behind me as we turned towards the glass wall that was part door.

'Where does the other door go?' I had barely noticed it before: a narrow slot that we had passed on the other side of the spiral iron staircase that led to the tower.

'It opens onto a little glass corridor between the leads.'

I felt for the iron banister. 'What do you think the tower was built for? Was it just the views?'

'I think the first owner, the commissioner, used it fc astronomical views as well as more conventional ones.'

'Yes, of course. It's ideal for making observations of the stars. You must take it up.'

'I dabble a little sometimes but I haven't really the patience. You need to be able to sit all night watching for the slightest movement. The five windows cut up the sky into equal portions, so that you can plot any change, a sort of fixed grid. Divide each one in half and you have a convenient ten points. I suspect he had some kind of attachment to his instruments that divided each sighting horizontally into ten as well.'

'Then you could plot it all on a graph?'

'That's right. I'm not a true astronomer because I'm inclined to go for the spectaculars, comets and interesting conjunctions, rather than the infinitesimal shifts of obscure stars, or simply studying a little pane of space night after night to see whether anything happens in it.'

'I'm afraid I would find that rather absorbing. That makes me dull, I fear.' With relief I felt my feet reach ground level. Wallace leaned forward to open the door politely, but I was aware only of a sudden moment of claustrophobic panic as I stood at the bottom of the black stairwell, with the blind steepness of the stairs behind me, a closed door in front and his breathing warmth there in the darkness almost touching. I knew for a second or two what it must have been like to be in the labyrinth with the minotaur, and hear the snuffle of its breath and the clattering of hooves on the rock floor. With relief I heard the handle turn and the lock click and saw a strip of light widen in front.

'But then you're a true scholar, whereas I ... I'm what some people, many people, would call an intellectual charlatan.'

His calm statement almost threw me into confusion. Was I meant to cry 'No, no'? If so, my tongue wouldn't frame it. It was like asking an early Christian to put the obligatory pinch of incense on the altar of Jupiter. The will paralysed all motion. Hadn't I in my own mind used just such language of

115

him? It was almost as if he had heard my thought and was asking me, or rather attempting to force me by subtle social blackmail, to retract.

'I'm thinking of starting a new series of booklets,' he went on, as we crossed the hall back to the drawing room. 'I hope I can persuade you to contribute to it.'

'What would you want me to do?'

'Oh, anything you like. Use it as a platform to put across some view you couldn't perhaps find an outlet for otherwise. My intention is to make them a fairly controversial run, theoretical, rather than just recording new folklore material.'

'Suppose you didn't agree with what I wanted to say?'

He laughed. 'Let's worry about that when it happens.'

'I'll think about it. I may not have time for a bit. The summer is always a busy period for me. I do most of my writing in the winter.'

'It only needs to be two or three thousand words.'

'It's the thinking first that takes the time.'

When I got home I tried to analyse what I really thought and felt about Leonard Wallace. I had to admit to myself that I was attracted and repelled at the same time which seemed to me an emotional mixture so clichéd that surely my sister Eileen would have some saw to cover it. There was a kind of combat going on between us, which part of me enjoyed. For some reason, and in some way I didn't quite understand, he was attempting to subdue me, to bring me under his influence, if not control.

The showiness of his mind and personality both amused me and yet seemed cheap. It was good to have someone to talk to, to sharpen one's wit against, but there was an undoubted tinge of vulgarity about his thinking. I felt, too, a kind of threat sometimes beneath his laughter, a feeling that if he was thwarted, he might lash out like a spoilt child. It was his desire to be master, I thought, that had made me feel claustrophobic in the dark of the stairwell, yet I couldn't truthfully say that I feared he might attack me in some way. The menace wasn't quite definable, although I had felt it there unmistakably.

April 13th

Saw L.W. briefly at Field Club. He bowed across the room and came up in the coffee interval. He asked if I'd thought any more about his pamphlet. I said I'd been too busy preparing for an Easter conference at Liverpool but would try to think of a title when I came back, although I didn't promise to write it for months. He said he didn't expect it, but that a title would help him in planning the series, all of which seemed perfectly reasonable. Why did I feel my arm was being twisted? Yet I was glad to talk to him, if only to stop dear old Harry from booming in my ear for five minutes. I found my mind beginning almost against my will to turn over possible titles or rather subjects.

April 29th

L.W. rang almost as soon as I got in even before I had had time to go into the garden and call Tiger, who was sulking because I had been gone for a whole fortnight.

'Welcome back,' he said. 'It's been very dull without you. I've had no one to argue with.'

'Why don't you come to tea tomorrow?' I said on an impulse. 'I shall be feeling rather flat and post—conference.' He said at once that he'd 'love to'.

April 30th

I often think I suffer worse jet lag coming Intercity rail from some remote corner of our English fields that are forever foreign than when I really have touched down at the airport only a few hours before. Perhaps it is because every railway journey brings with it a train of old memories, whereas flying is uncluttered with nostalgia as yet, at least for me. It belongs to the freedom of late adulthood. Whatever the explanation, I realised I had made a mistake in inviting L.W. today. Mary would be expecting to come to tea as she always did when I'd been away, so that we could exchange news. And of course she must come; there was no question of her not. They must come together. It was time they met.

'Mary,' I said when she telephoned, 'you're coming to tea,

117

aren't you?'

'Yes, yes. If that's alright.'

'Of course. There's just one thing: we shan't be able to have our proper gossip, because I got bounced and we shan't be alone. Leonard Wallace, you know, the man from the Field Club, rang as soon as I got back when I was still not quite compos after the journey and I was somehow manoeuvred into inviting him; mainly I think I did it to forestall his inviting me.'

'Well, if it's awkward ...'

'No, I'd rather you came. I'd like you to meet him anyway, so you know who I'm talking about. I'll be interested to hear what you make of him. You come a bit before. He's due at four.'

I spent the rest of the morning making a start on the stack of correspondence that always greets my return. Then I cycled to the garage on Filey Road that is half a general store and bought bread, cake, milk and some frozen fillets for Tiger and came back to the letters and bills.

Mary arrived at three–thirty and we sneaked in a quick cup and sat by the fire sorting out Scarborough, until my rusty old doorbell burbled a bit and I went down to let Leonard Wallace in. I took the green parka and hung it in the hall wondering why the black fur of the hood never struck me as faintly sinister on other wearers. After all, it's a common enough country garment, sold by hundreds of shops up and down the land. I led him into the sitting room.

'I don't believe you've met. Mary Dunscombe, this is Leonard Wallace.'

'How do you do? I won't get up because of disturbing Tiger. He seems to have taken root here.' He was indeed as oblivious as a cat can be deep in a warm lap. I turned to L.W. and saw that he had flushed a dark red. He was very put out, I could see, and finding it hard to speak.

'How do you do.'

'It's as well to let sleeping cats lie, I think. Tiger hasn't quite forgiven me yet for going away. That's why he's sitting on Mary to punish me. I'll make some fresh tea.' I hurried off

118

into the kitchen, glad that that sticky moment was over. I had expected him to be slightly miffed, but not to the point of stalking out, as I realised had almost happened. I could hear Mary's voice as I went, making conversation and sounding, as one does, a little foolish.

'Cat's are so subtle, Mr Wallace, don't you think?'

'I've had little opportunity to consider the question. I understand they are traditionally thought so.'

'I believe you're a member of the Field Club?'

'I don't think I've seen you there.'

'No, I don't belong. I hardly need to go. I hear so much about it from Meg. You seem to have some very interesting speakers. And of course, I know Harry Chalmers, because he's a sidesman at St Martin's.'

I carried in the tea. 'I don't know if you've seen inside St Martin's, Mr Wallace? It's the Pre–Raphaelite repository for Scarborough. Really a remarkable collection, even if you don't care for Rossetti and Burne–Jones in profusion. I tell Mary she only goes for the stained glass.'

'And where does St Martin's stand on the ordination of women?'

'Personally, I'm all for it. I'm sure Meg for instance is quite as competent to preach and take services as any man.'

'There is the small matter of faith,' I murmured.

L.W. laughed. I was glad he was relaxing his first anger. 'I sometimes think St Hilda must have borne a great resemblance to Margaret.'

I was startled by the use of my name, and in a form he couldn't have heard from anyone else. As he said it, he sounded more Scottish than his careful rather flat voice usually allowed. I was also a little angry. It implied an intimacy that was quite untrue.

'Tell me, Miss Dunscombe,' he went on, 'what you would think of a little theory of mine that some of those outstanding women of the early Christian church were really wise women?'

'Wise women? I don't quite understand.'

'The great ladies of Anglo–Saxon times often dabbled in

what later ages called magic: cures involving charms and herbs gathered in a special way, spells against elfshot and supernatural happenings generally. By the Middle Ages, they would have been thought witches, but of course their power in every sense had been lost by then. I have a theory that when Christianity came they became abbesses and suchlike and carried their knowledge and power into the church with them. The Norman Conquest finally destroyed them by introducing the masculine magic that was at its strongest and purest in the Knights Templar.'

'You're suggesting that they were witches?'

'White ones, of course.'

'I don't think I like the idea. It seems to call everything in doubt. I suppose that, like Meg, you're not a believer, Mr Wallace?'

'On the contrary: unlike her, I believe in everything.'

'Everything?'

'I believe the whole universe is the battleground of warring powers.'

'I'm not very strong theologically, but isn't that close to Manicheanism?'

'I would agree that that was one of the manifestations of the belief. But it's very ancient and crops up continually in different mythologies all over the world.'

I laughed. 'I don't think you'll get Mr Wallace to St Martin's, Mary; at least, not for any purpose you'd approve of.'

The dark flush came back into his face. I had said the wrong thing. He leant towards Mary and put out a hand to the sleeping Tiger. Startled, the cat leapt awake, thrashing out a paw that caught the back of Wallace's hand to leave a fine stitching of blood, and digging his claws into Mary for a purchase as he thudded to the floor.

I jumped up too. 'I am sorry. You must have woken him suddenly. I'll get some TCP and cotton wool. Come up to the bathroom and I'll bathe it.'

He took a clean handkerchief from his pocket and dabbed at the bubbles of blood. Sharp red stains flowered on the white ground. 'Don't worry. It'll soon stop. I'd forgotten how sharp a cat's claws are.'

'Are you sure you don't want to wash it or put something on?'

'No really. Look, it's stopping already.'

I was very relieved. I had realised even as I was offering that I didn't want to take his hand and bathe it or touch the smooth brown skin even with an antiseptic cotton wool swab. Fleetingly, I wondered why my remark had angered him. I had expected him to laugh and agree.

'Let me give you some fresh tea. I'd put something stronger in it to steady your nerves, but I'm afraid I've only got homemade wine and I don't think that would mix with tea.'

'My father used to put rum in his coffee,' Mary said, 'We put it down to his having been at sea, but I think my mother always found it faintly shocking.'

'What kind of wines do you make?'

'Any fruits and flowers in season. I don't always get the time, of course. I find I miss the crucial week when something's at its best. Dandelions for wine are supposed to be gathered on St George's day, for instance. I usually seem to miss that, but I don't mind much as they're pretty fiddly to do. You have to pluck off all the little green calyxes.'

'And mandrake: when do you gather that?'

'St John's Eve,' I said without thinking. Then I added, 'Not that I do, but it's the correct time.'

'So you say.' Wallace was laughing now, but it was a laughter that somehow drew me into complicity with him and excluded Mary. I hoped she wouldn't be forced by it into leaving before he did. I was beginning to feel like the rope in a tug-of-war. I knew it wasn't Mary's doing, but L.W.'s. He had been angry to find her there and now he was trying to shut her out. I wondered if she knew or whether only I was sensitive to it.

'I'd like to try the brew you make from that,' he went on.

'I'm afraid you'll have to be content with ordinary tea.' I went out into the kitchen. When I came back, L.W. was on

121

his feet by the bookcase, taking out volumes at random. Mary had leant forward to stretch her hands to the fire. 'Throw on another log or two, would you?' I asked her, as I went across to hand him his cup.

'I'll borrow this if I may?' He held out my copy of the *Saducismus Triumphatus* of Joseph Glanville, the first edition of 1681.

'By all means. Mary, would you like another cup?'

'No, thank you. I think I should be going.'

'Must you? Can't you wait a bit for Tiger to come back? There's something I want to ask you about a little bald patch he has.'

'Oh well, in that case I could stretch it a bit longer.'

'I'm afraid I must be off soon. Have you had any thoughts about your subject yet?' Wallace closed the book and drank some of his tea.

'Not really. Liverpool wasn't conducive to new ideas. I'll try to let you know soon.'

'Be as unconventional as you like; I almost said "as you can". You can't go too far for me.' He put the cup down empty.

Did he intend the double meaning or was I merely starting at shadows? I fetched the green parka and handed it to him. Mary stood up to shake hands. She looked very frail, almost shrunken, beside him. I suddenly realised that he was young enough to be the son of either of us.

'Thank you for the loan of this.' He held up the *Saducismus* at the front door. 'I'll ring you when I've finished to let you have it back. It must be worth quite a bit. I'll take great care of it.'

'I don't suppose it's worth more than a hundred, but it might be difficult to replace.'

'You won't have to; I promise.'

'Well, what did you make of him?' I asked Mary.

'It's hard to tell on such a brief acquaintance. I didn't warm to him at once, I have to say. But that sounds uncharitable.'

'I don't quite know why he seems to be cultivating me.'

'Oh really, Meg. You never think well enough of yourself. In your field, which he seems so interested in, you're an acknowledged expert. He's probably after a little reflected glory, to be able to say he knows you, is a friend of yours.'

'Well, it's certainly not my youth and beauty.'

That evening after Mary had gone, I took out one of the little notebooks in which I collect songs and tales and comments. L.W. didn't perhaps belong with my usual type of subject. It's true, a few of my little books are devoted to one person, but that's been when I've found some old singer with a fund of material. In L.W.'s case I thought it might be his ideas I wanted to note down and comment on, but when I had sat with it on my knee for some time, half–listening for Tiger, who still hadn't come back, I could write only one sentence:

Is L.W. a Ganconer?

May 3rd

Tiger has been missing for two nights and Mary and I are quite distraught. He came back the evening of L.W.'s visit, was here for two nights, went out the next morning after his breakfast and hasn't been home since. I haven't rung the police yet. I know they'll say they get dozens of ginger and white cats, and that I should try the R.S.P.C.A. I'll ring them tomorrow if he doesn't come back tonight.

May 4th

Tiger is back. I heard him come in through the catdoor. I must have been sleeping with half an ear open. I got up at once and went downstairs into the kitchen. I switched the light on. He was crouching under the table and ready to turn and run out again when he heard me. His eyes were staring and slightly glazed at the same time and he didn't seem to recognise me. I moved very gently and got between him and the door, talking to him quietly, saying what a good boy he was to come home and how we'd missed him until I got close enough to drop the catdoor and I could relax a bit.

His coat was filthy and matted, smeared in places with

what might be mud or blood. The first thing was to calm him down and bring him back to himself, so that he would let me inspect the damage. I got some milk and fish out of the fridge, being very careful to close the door gently, ran the fish under the hot tap in a sieve to thaw it out as he likes it and bring out the smell. Then I put it on his saucer and gently pushed it towards him under the table and stood back.

As I approached him he shrank away from me. I decided it was best not to leave him alone in the hope that he would eat, but to go on talking quietly, to try and get him to accept my presence as soon as possible. He hesitated for a few seconds. Then he stretched out his neck and started to chew on the fish. He was obviously ravenous. The fish gone, he turned to the milk and began to lap, throwing up little splashes of milk in his thirst over the rim of the saucer. I hoped as I watched him eat that he wasn't too badly hurt, not the internal damage I dreaded from his being hit by a car.

It was hard waiting for him to come to me, but I *had* to do it. I leant patiently against the cooker while he inspected both empty dishes, rasping his tongue round the fish one for every taste of juice and fibre of meat. He was obviously still hungry, but I didn't want to make him sick with overeating.

'Tiger,' I tried, 'how are you feeling now? Would you let me have a look at you? Come on. Who's my boy?' I moved a little nearer and bent down to his level. He flattened himself to the floor, but didn't run. I put out a cautious hand and began to scratch between his ears and smooth down his neck.

This close I could see that the mattings in his fur were mud and blood mixed, as I had feared. Presumably, he had been hit by a car, or even set on by a dog and lain too injured to move under a hedge or in a ditch until he had recovered sufficiently to make his way home. I would have to get him calm enough to put in the cat basket and take to Miss Hedges in the morning.

'Would you like me to make up the fire and we'll go and sit by it? Come along, let's go into the sitting room.'

I stood up quietly and led the way, calling to him from the door. He slunk towards me, favouring one paw but he was becoming himself again and beginning to recognise me. In the sitting room I put more wood on the fire and piled up all the cushions beside it. Then I lay down myself. After a few moments I felt him approach stealthily and curl round beside me. It was a minute or so before I dared put out my hand to touch him. I could feel the lumps in his fur and one particularly large one under his left jowl, but he stirred complainingly when I touched it and I decided to wait until morning before investigating further. I think we both fell asleep at the same moment.

At nine, I rang Mary to tell her he was back and that we were off to Miss Hedges for a check–up. I'd decided this was a better course than trying to bathe him and inspect his wounds myself. I managed to get him in to the cat basket and battened down surprisingly easily. Then I lugged him to my bicycle and strapped him onto the carrier. For once there were no howls of complaint as we rode into town.

Miss Hedges has the knack of making all owners feel incompetent and neglectful. Not that she croons sentimentally over her patients; she is firmly kind and efficient. In her hands Tiger, who would protest if *I* tried to minister to him, is respectful, almost docile. Yet I knew that when I opened the basket I should be made to feel that his tattered appearance was really *my* fault, and indeed there was a disapproving silence, followed by a, 'Well, well, what have you been up to?' as Miss Hedges lifted him out that I knew meant that I had wilfully let him get into this state.

First she put him to the indignity of having his temperature taken. 'It's up a bit, but not too much. Now let's have a look at you.' She began to feel him for tender places.

'Do you think it was a car?' I asked.

'Hard to say. Nothing seems to be broken. Has he eaten?'

'Ravenously.'

'I don't think there's any internal damage. Let's have a look at the feet.'

'He seems to be favouring that right front one.'

Tiger winced and complained as she gently examined it. 'It's badly cut and he's lost a claw. It almost looks as if it's

125

been in a snare. Perhaps that's where some of the blood has come from.' She continued her examination. 'No, these seem to be all little gashes. They do look more like a car.'

'I thought when I stroked him in the night I felt a particularly nasty one under his chin.'

Miss Hedges turned his head sideways and tilted it up. Tiger swore. 'That's very nasty indeed. Look. I'll have to stitch it. You'll have to leave him for a couple of hours. I'll give him a light anaesthetic. Take him downstairs, will you, Sarah?'

Her assistant picked him up and carried him out of the room. I saw his blunt face accusing me over her green—overalled shoulder as he was taken away. It was a nuisance, but I would have to go home and come back for Tiger later.

The wind was blowing against me down the Filey Road, but I was so relieved that Tiger didn't seem to have suffered any fatal damage that I hardly noticed it, and indeed even enjoyed pedalling vigorously into it, until my cheeks were numb and my eyes watering. Once home I made myself a cup of instant coffee and went to tidy the drawing room.

The cushions were still as Tiger and I had slept on them beside the dead and dismal hearth. I began to pick them up and bang them before restoring them to their rightful places. As I seized a sprigged blue—and—green—covered one that belonged to the sofa, a small object rolled to the floor. I bent to pick it up.

At first it meant nothing to me. It seemed to be a minute purse or little bag of thin leather, not more than about three—quarters of an inch wide or long, with gilt markings on both sides and some ravellings of thread like a broken drawstring at the top. It was soft, almost spongy to the touch, and seemed to be empty.

I stared at it lying in the palm of my hand, completely bewildered. It was nothing of mine, nothing that I had ever seen before, and I was almost certain it wasn't Mary's either. I put it down on my desk and picked up the telephone.

'Mary?'

126

'How's Tiger?'

'He's going to be alright. Just a little temperature and a few cuts. One of them big enough to need stitching, so I've left him with Miss Hedges and I have to pick him up in a couple of hours.'

'Did she think it was a car?'

'She didn't say what exactly. I think she was rather puzzled. He's hurt one foot; lost a claw.'

'I expect she'll fill him full of antibiotics just in case.'

'Bound to. As usual, she made me feel it was all my fault somehow. Mary, there's something I want to show you. Could I drop over on my way back to Miss Hedges?'

'Why don't you come and have a sandwich lunch and then go on?'

'That would be such a help. I'll be over as soon as I've straightened up here, in about half an hour.' I found an envelope and put the strange object in it.

'Have you ever seen this before?' I asked, as I handed it to her later.

'What is it?' She opened the flap and peered. Then she tipped the little leather pouch into her hand.

'I've no idea. It looks like a doll's purse, or a bag for keeping some small piece of jewellery in, a ring, for instance.'

'I don't understand. Where did it come from?'

'I found it on the sitting room floor this morning.'

'But how did it get there? What is it?'

I sipped at my coffee. 'It's the sort of thing that used to make people believe in fairies. You could easily say it's some elf or brownie's purse.'

Mary turned it over. 'What are these markings? They look faintly familiar.'

'They're Gnostic symbols.'

'Gnostic?'

'I think so. I'll have to look them up. I haven't had time yet. I think I'll find I'm right, though.'

'But I wouldn't recognise a Gnostic symbol. I've never seen one in my life.'

'You probably have, though you didn't know it. They're

127

used for magic. Even a children's conjuror might have one on his cloak. "Abracadabra" is a Gnostic charm.'

'Good heavens! What's inside?'

'Nothing. It feels quite flat and empty.'

Mary felt it between her fingers, as I had done. Then, unlike me, she pulled open the neck of the little bag. It's one of the differences between us: I believe in what reason and observation tell me; she doesn't. Because the bag felt empty, I hadn't opened it. Reason told me there couldn't be anything in there. I was wrong.

She poked a forefinger into the neck. 'It's sticky.' She drew it out and held it up. Her finger was covered in a thick red glue. Gingerly she sniffed at it and wrinkled her nose. 'I think it's blood. But it can't be!'

'Are you sure?'

'Almost. I'm going to wash my hands. I feel a little sick.'

While she was gone, I studied the object from a distance, but without getting any further in deciding where it had come from.

'Perhaps it was used as a fingerstall,' Mary suggested hopefully, as she came back.

I tried to focus on a memory niggling at the back of my mind. I made myself pick the purse up and open it as she had done. I put the whole thing back in the envelope, not knowing quite what to do with it. I didn't really want to put it in my bag or pocket and yet I didn't want to leave it for Mary to get rid of. I felt I ought to keep it.

'I must go and rescue Tiger. He'll be livid with me. He's another one who believes it's all my fault.'

Miss Hedges sent an assistant down to fetch him. 'Keep him quiet and no going out. Let him eat anything he fancies, but don't worry if he doesn't want to eat for a bit. He's had a shock and then a general anaesthetic. He'll feel a bit off–colour. I've bound that foot up too, but I expect he'll soon have that off.'

'What was it? A car?'

'I can't say. The cut under the chin was very nasty. A little more and it would have severed the jugular, and that would have been that. He wouldn't have made it home. Even so, he must have lost quite a lot of blood. Give him one of these three times a day if you can without opening the wound up.' She handed me a little white envelope with the hard nodules of pills inside. Tiger was carried in, looking like the proverbial wounded soldier and very sorry for himself. I knew he would give me that special kind of hell only pets can when they are ill, but not ill enough.

'The little gashes all over him have been done with barbed wire or glass, or sharp metal. I've cleaned them up. Perhaps now you'll stay home,' she said to Tiger. 'You're not supposed to be interested in nights on the tiles. Bring him back on Monday or before, if you're worried,' she instructed me as I held the basket lid while she thrust him expertly inside with no fuss. He was too glad to be out of there to howl on the way home.

May 14th
Tiger completely recovered. Miss Hedges doesn't want to see him any more. Took his picture with Mary in garden to celebrate. Nothing from L.W. for some time. Perhaps he's away. He wasn't at Field Club.

June 8th
L.W. back. Came up to me tonight and said he must talk to me. Would I come to tea? I said he should come to me. He made it clear, though I'm not sure how, that he wanted a *tête à tête*, no one else. Why don't I want to go to Five Ways again? Is it only the distance and the hill? Or is it that I feel at a disadvantage off my home ground?

June 15th
L.W. to tea. Tiger bolted. He has become an anti–male chauvinist since his accident and watches for them from some hideout until he sees them leave. L.W. all charm, asked if we could proceed to first names. So I am to call him Leonard and he will call me Margaret, after the Scottish queen, since he doesn't like Meg. He was, of course, pursuing

129

me for my contribution to his booklets. I am finding it hard to fix on a theme. The subjects that really interest him are all so theoretical, almost on the edge of Margaret Murray's witch cult writings and similar efforts. He wants me to take him down to the cove. There was no time today, but he is coming again in a fortnight if the weather's fine.

June 28th

L. came over and I took him down to the cove. He seemed quite fascinated by it, and it was certainly looking its most attractive. He brought a camera with him and took a lot of pictures. He insisted on taking one of me, so I had to reply with some of him. I found Tiger scowling under the hedge watching us, and just managed to get him into the edge of a snap with L. before he was off again. In the process I got rather scratched. There's no reconciling him, I'm afraid. I'm worried about what I shall do with him while I'm away. I think he will have to go to a cattery. I should be too anxious if he was roaming loose, with Mary just dropping in, as we've always done in the past.

I've offered L. one or two possible titles. He said something today about my will being too strong. He was off on his me–as–Hilda theme. When I said again that I was an agnostic about most things he stared very hard at me and said he hoped to effect my conversion. For a moment I felt quite chilled or, no better, transfixed like a rabbit in a car headlight. And I still don't know how he makes a living and manages to afford to go to some hot country where he keeps that tan topped up. Yet if one were to be suspicious of everybody living on private means, paranoia would soon set in. What about me on the last of Dad's shares and the bits and pieces I earn here and there? Does that make me suspect? And anyway, what do I suspect? Nothing I could be precise about. He is just a man who likes to exploit his charm and slightly wolfish good looks to get some kind of rapport going. Perhaps he does it to a lot of people, but likes to keep them all apart. He never speaks of anyone else except Kasper when he's with me so that I could believe I was the only one in his world, but I don't. Nor does he say where he goes on his 'holidays,' as I suppose I must call them. On the other hand, he knows all about my trips away. Is there any basis for a relationship, a friendship, in something so one-sided?

July 5th
Went to Mary's to talk about Tiger going to the cattery and had the most awful quiet row. She thinks I'm making a fool of myself with L.W. and that he is insinuating himself into my life. She asked if he'd enquired about my will, whom I was leaving the house to. I refused to discuss it. She has hit a disturbing note, however, since somehow the other day I found myself telling him about Paula and that she was my heir. I realise that Mary is jealous. My life pattern *is* changed, I have to admit. L. comes here once a week now, or we meet for coffee in the town. I still shy at going up to Five Ways: some residual spinsterly qualms, I suppose. And yet there is nothing in it except his persistence, the fact that he is there. My heart certainly wouldn't be broken if I never saw him again, but as long as he pursues, telephones, invites himself, arranges meetings, I respond. It's shown me a new aspect of my own character; a weakness, a susceptibility to being manipulated, I didn't know I had. Partly I'm intrigued, but if I'm honest, I'm also flattered. That far Mary is right. Where she is wrong is in supposing that I am not aware of it.

L. has been able to find something like a geological fault in me that makes me vulnerable, a feeling of neglect perhaps, an ego that needs more bolstering than the outside world sees.

Aug. 1st
Came back last night. It was very strange and empty without Tiger, whom I must fetch from the cattery today. Always before he's seemed to sense when I was coming home and would be here to greet me. Perhaps it was just that he hung about in hopes while I was away or some clock of habit told him I'd been gone my usual length of time. Knowing he wouldn't be here made all the difference to coming down the path with a suitcase getting progressively heavier after the

taxi (I got the nice local driver who always makes me feel welcome back) had dropped me at the gate. The house looked forlorn and abandoned too, which it doesn't as a rule. I must get the sign repainted. The lettering is badly weathered.

I let myself in and humped the case into the hall. I shut the front door and stood a moment to get my breath and as I stood there with the house very quiet around me, I suddenly had the extraordinary conviction that I wasn't alone. There was a feeling of presence there. I can't describe it any other way, of alien presence. And yet I wasn't sure whether it was present at that moment or had been and left a kind of footprint in the air, rather as the scientists tell us light may still be reaching us from a star dead light years ago. It was a kind of pyschic shadow after the body has gone. The house felt violated and reproachful. I tried to shrug the feeling off and put it down to fatigue and went round switching things on and making tea. I could have gone up the path to Mary's and stayed the night but that seemed like an admission of weakness. I felt I had to stay here and dispel the sensation with commonsense and will.

Suddenly I had an impulse to open the back door, lift the flowerpot and check on the back door key I kept under it in a little plastic bag. The little packet was safely there. I picked it up with a feeling of relief. Then I hesitated. I always put an elastic band round it twice. The band was there but only once, making a looser, softer parcel. I can't prove anything but I don't think that was how I left it. At first I thought, or rather hoped it must be Mary popping in to make sure the house was alright. I knew she'd been in, because the letters were all stacked on the hall table as usual. But she has her own set of keys. There's no need for her to use that one unless she's lost her own. That might be it. I doubled up the elastic band and put the key under the flower pot again and went back into the house to telephone her.

'I'm back.'

'How was Toronto?'

'Very crowded. The Americans dominated as they always do when it's on their side of the Atlantic. Thank you for keeping an eye on things; picking up the post so that I could get through the front door. Was everything alright?' I waited for her answer. She would tell me now if she had lost her keys and had to take the one from the garden.

'It was fine except that I missed Tiger terribly. The house seemed very bleak whenever I dropped in without him. He usually does the round of the rooms with me, when I check for leaks or windows blown open.'

'I know; it feels like that now.'

'You wouldn't rather come here for the night?'

'In many ways, yes. But I feel I ought to stick it out. After all, I'm old enough not to mind a night on my own surely. I must be firm with myself. I'll come in for a cup of coffee on my way to collect Tiger.'

When I had put the receiver down and broken the connection, I lifted it off the hook again and laid it on its side. Anyone telephoning me would think first that it was engaged and then that it had gone out of order in my absence. I didn't *want* to be rung; I wanted to think.

On an impulse, I went over to my desk and opened the lid. I knew at once that someone had been through it. I'm inclined to be tidy and systematic in a rather boring way that's necessary to my work; I could see the slight disarrangement, as if fingers had rifled through, searching. My little notebooks had been taken out and put back, not quite precisely enough. My will and my paying—in book were out of line. All my papers, Tiger's vaccination certificates, the TV licence and so on, had been ruffled. I opened each of the drawers in turn and felt them make the same impression on me.

In the bottom right—hand one I had put the envelope containing the little bag. Now the envelope was empty, except for an iodine brown stain of dried blood, as I was sure it was. Was that the object of the search or had it been taken as a curiosity in the course of it? A burglar might be intrigued. They were, after all, only human. I didn't believe anyone other than Mary had known it was there, and she certainly had no hankering after it. I wasn't in the least upset that it

133

was gone from the point of view of wanting to keep it; only because its loss confirmed my other observations.

The house had been entered, my desk inspected and not just by Mary. But I couldn't prove it. My hand began to reach out for the telephone and then drew back. I saw myself getting on my bicycle and going down to the police station where some young constable, a girl like Paula perhaps, would ask me what I wanted. I saw the look of pity come into her eyes as she listened to what I was saying, the carefully blanked expression that covered: *Poor old thing.* And then aloud: 'Has anything been taken, Miss Hackstead? Is there any damage to property? Then I'm afraid we've nothing to go on.' I saw myself turning away, humiliated by her pity.

It's my Achilles' heel, my 'mole in nature' that L.W. has found, this pride that wouldn't let me lift the telephone receiver, or get on my bicycle, and with that self–knowledge I felt a kind of despair. My home, my personal things had been violated and yet, like a rape victim, I was afraid to complain, afraid of their eyes, of pity, and almost with a certain shame, as if I had somehow connived at my own dishonour. 'You say you keep a key under a flower–pot, Miss Hackstead? You know, we warn people against that. It's just asking for trouble.'

No, I couldn't go to the police. I would just have to try to protect myself somehow, at least until I had more positive evidence, some proof to offer. Tomorrow I would deposit my will at the bank. Suddenly exhaustion began to drag at me. I had to go to bed and think about it all in the morning.

I woke suddenly. It was a hot still night. Toronto had been blazing, but there was the hotel air-conditioning to offset it. This was an English summer heat that made me feel sticky and stifled. I had forgotten to put my usual glass of water by my bed on the table. I wanted a drink, but I felt reluctant to get out of bed and go to the bathroom.

The feeling of presence was as strong as before. It hung in the air like the smell of fried fish or cigars the morning after a party. I had never been afraid alone in my cottage. It had always fitted comfortably around me. Now I sensed someone downstairs. I wished I hadn't put the key back, but had brought it inside. Whoever had searched my desk and taken the little bag knew it was there under the flower pot.

I was in danger of panicking completely. My heart thudded, my head sang and there seemed to be a lump in my throat, making it hard to breathe. I must get up and move about to calm myself. I threw back the sheet and swung my legs over the side of the bed, scrabbling for my slippers. Reaching for my dressing–gown, I pulled it on and tied the belt tightly. Somehow more clothes made me feel less vulnerable. I moved to the window to get some fresh air and look out at the sky. Light from the full summer moon fell in panes on the bedroom floor.

A man was standing in the shadow behind the hedge. The shock of seeing the blackly anonymous human figure passed through me like an electric charge. It was *his* presence that was filling the house. I looked away and back again, hoping that I had been merely 'seeing things' in my overtired condition, mistaking a shadow or a tree for a human form. But there was no mistake: the figure was cut out from its background quite precisely, like a Victorian silhouette in a picture frame. I was terrified that it would step forward and begin an inexorable movement towards the house. At the moment it was as faceless as figures in dreams. I didn't want the moonlight to fall on it and show up the features. Whatever they were I didn't want to see them.

I could call the police and tell them there was a burglar in the garden, except that somehow I knew he wouldn't be there when they came and I should look like a silly old woman, imagining men on her doorstep. I hurried towards the landing. Even as I took my eyes off him he might begin to move towards the house. I must be quick. I put a hand round the spare room door, pulled the light cord and shut the door. Then I hurried back to the darkness beside my bedroom window. The figure turned sideways and became indistinguishable from the shadows behind. It had worked. He was going away.

For a long time I stood there, watching, until I was sure he wouldn't return. Even then it seemed impossible to lie down. I propped up on my pillows against the bed head and leant against them until I fell into a doze. At some point I must have slipped down under the sheet, for when I woke it was full daylight and I was lying beneath it, still tightly wrapped in my dressing—gown, with the two pillows forming an arch above my head and my neck painfully cricked. I felt as squalid and aching as from a night sitting in a train.

After a bath and breakfast I felt better. I retrieved the key from the flower pot and put it in my desk. I still intended to deposit my will with my bank and took it with me on my journey to fetch Tiger. I said nothing to Mary about any of it. There was no point in alarming her. She said I looked tired. I said the journey had been hell.

Now I am back, with Tiger dispelling all fears, although he still hasn't quite forgiven me, and the will safely deposited. I no longer have any confidence, however, that the house is private if I go away. It's not that as a rule I have any great secrets, but I might have; and in any case, it's the sense of violation I object to, as I would to the intrusion of a burglar, even if nothing was taken. I suppose it's the remains of some primitive territorial instinct about one's own nest or burrow.

What really disturbs me, though, is that none of it makes any sense. I have moved out of the real world into one of my own folk tales. I understand emotionally perhaps for the first time what it was like to have, or believe you had, contact with that other world where our laws of reason and physics don't apply, even though nothing that has happened so far couldn't have some rational explanation.

I found today, going through the last copy of the local paper that had come while I was abroad, that we have had a murder up on Oliver's Mount. Somehow this seems to fit in with my feelings at the moment. It may of course be just the usual domestic homicide, as Perry Mason would no doubt put it, and the husband or lover will be arrested and charged but I feel the intrusion of a darkness, like a mist coming into the cove from the sea and creeping up the path to envelop the cottage, a darkness that I have never believed in, and still don't. I feel ridiculously like a kind of spiritual Canute, ordering the waves back and all because I have had that most common of phenomena a peeping Tom looking over my hedge. No, that isn't quite all. There is the searching of my desk. I must remember that. I am not irrationally disturbed, then. Something which I can't explain is happening to me.

Aug. 4th
Didn't go to Field Club last night. I still feel tired from Toronto and my disturbed sleep when I got back, although I have slept better since, with Tiger curled up beside me. I have an article to write for *The Folklorist*, but I can't get up the energy to begin. And then there is L.W.'s wretched pamphlet. I know he will ring today and badger me about it because I wasn't there last night.

Aug. 18th
L.W. to tea. Had to tell him I haven't even settled on the title yet. Said I was feeling very off–colour and that progress on my *Folklorist* article is consequently slow. He put on a little boy's sulky face for a moment, and then became all concern about my health. He took my hand and stared hard into my eyes in the way that he does, and said that something was clearly troubling me and that I should rest more. If I would relax, it would all be smoothed away. I almost believed him for a second or two.

Aug. 24th
When I got back from a trip to York today, I knew the house had been entered again. There was no sign of Tiger, but mercifully he came in an hour after me, and before I'd had time to get really worried to the point where I had to ring Mary and tell her all my fears and feelings. I *knew*, that's the thing, as soon as I opened the front door and stepped into the hall. Everything's been so quiet that I had been lulled into a calmness, the beginnings of a disbelief as to what I had seen the night I came back from Toronto. Yet as I stood there and listened, I expected the searcher, would–be burglar, whatever

137

he is, to be there in the house. I went cautiously to the sitting room door and could almost see an anonymous figure standing at my desk and going through it. There wasn't anyone, but when I opened the lid, I saw that I was right in a sense. There had been someone. My photograph album was misplaced and one or two other things. I imagined hands picking up the album and turning the pages, going through my notebooks, and I wanted to be sick; with fear, I suppose.

How is it getting in, this anonymous figure? There's no longer a key under the flower pot and the windows are all shut. And if it can get in when the key isn't there, I might just as well put it back for my own convenience. I begin to feel a little angry which is probably better for me than being afraid.

Another murder in the paper today, this time up on the North Cliff golf links. No details, but a young woman again, so perhaps the last wasn't a domestic affair. I don't read the kind of newspaper that gives all the background which might tell me. What would a girl be doing up on the golf course at night, except inviting trouble? But then ... At such times I think about Paula and worry about her life. I find myself wishing sometimes that she were my daughter instead of Eileen's and I had the right to ask if she's happy. I wonder if she would consider it an interference.

The Field Club is having a day trip to Harkness for its annual outing and in a weak moment I said I would go.

Sept. 5th
L.W. of course insisted on sitting next to me on the coach. I was trapped between him and the glass of the window like some wretched insect—I carefully don't say butterfly—under a jam—jar while we see—sawed up and down the Dales and he poured a stream of insinuating words into my left ear until I felt like Hamlet's father in the orchard, with the poison trickling through his auricle. It is in some ways so absurd and childish all this talk of powers and the combat between good and evil presented in these terms, that when I'm alone I want to laugh. Yet when I'm with him, I find myself discussing the subject with total seriousness. He probably believes that he is

winning: that I am coming to accept his propositions about the nature of things and abandon my agnosticism; but in fact it's only that when I am with him I can't hurt his feelings, or anyone's by simply laughing at their beliefs, and I therefore begin to argue against them rationally. His very conviction and persistence has a kind of hypnotic force to draw me on.

What I hadn't quite realised before is where L.W. stands in 'the combat'. Most of us, when asked in these terms, say we are on the side of the angels of light, but he is on the side of the fallen. He talked today about a pamphlet he is writing for his series on how misunderstood Satan—Lucifer has been; that he is in fact a kind of Prometheus figure, indeed L.W. says that was merely the Greek mythological version of the same story; the same truth, he would say. Prometheus plucking fire flowers from the fields of the gods to give to man to warm himself is the same as Satan giving the first man knowledge of good and evil. In a way, of course, I have to agree with him that they are versions of the same truth, which, as I see it, is a psychological one. But he sees it as much more literal, more as a Christian fundamentalist would, oddly enough, although he wouldn't be pleased at the comparison.

Harkness was as beautiful as ever, but by the time we got back, my head was aching and I was as exhausted as if I had been in an obstacle race. The worst of it is I can't discuss any of it with Mary. She disapproves of him so much that she is quite unapproachable on the subject.

Sept. 10th
The figure was there again last night. I woke out of a deep sleep in which I'd been dreaming about Larne for the first time for months, and knew that the house was under threat. I got out of bed and went to the window. This time there was no moon, but I could see the shape standing beyond the hedge looking, it seemed, straight at me. Though I was sick with fright at first and my heart seemed to be running wild with horror, I made myself stand there and watch. Gradually I steadied a little. I reasoned that he couldn't see me, whereas

I could see him and this gave me an advantage. My night vision began to adjust, too, until I could make out that, whoever it was there, was wearing a hood like an old—fashioned balaclava, but covering more of the face: the sort of thing terrorists wear. And he *is* a kind of terrorist. For some reason, whoever he is, he wants to terrorise me or at least the occupant of this cottage; I mustn't assume that it's personal. It may simply be some kind of lunatic who gets satisfaction from this kind of thing; it may even be our murderer.

I have to face that thought, too, unpleasant as it is. From bits I've picked up in shops, I gather the police think that both killings were done by the same person and that they certainly aren't family affairs. My voyeur and the murderer may or may not be the same person. I am so afraid of being laughed at, even behind my back; of being thought a hysterical woman. And yet two women have died. In a way that makes it more difficult. The police must be inundated with false alarms, sightings and confessions. What can I prove? Nothing, and so my report will merely seem another of those. And yet again, if they are one and the same, isn't it my duty to report it, even at the risk of appearing foolish? I resolve it by doing nothing, which is a kind of decision.

I was determined to outwatch the watcher this time. I began to feel a cold curiosity about what it would do. In the morning I shall ring the telephone people and ask the cost of an extension in my bedroom. Meanwhile, I decided to creep down to the sitting room and if it made any move towards the house, I would ring the police. I had to be quick and silent, because I knew that if he had gone by the time I got to the sitting room window, I would be terrified, not knowing where he was. Losing sight of him, even for that minute of going downstairs, was a risk I had to take if I was to get to the telephone.

I took it, very afraid that I might fall on the stairs, a thought that normally never crosses my mind. And he was still there when I got to the sitting room window and peered round the edge of the curtain. I could see the two eye—slits in the hood. It was then I realised that what he really reminded me of was the headsman, the executioner. But I felt safe with the telephone to hand and, as if he sensed that, he turned slowly and went away. I sat up for a while, but I knew somehow that he wouldn't come back.

In the morning I poked about behind the hedge like an amateur detective for signs that someone had been there, but without any success. There were no footprints, cigarette ends or cloth fragments on the bushes or steps that I could see.

L.W. is off on his mysterious travels again, which gives me a sense of relief. I must try to get down to some work.

Sept. 20th
I have seen the figure three more times. I am exhausted with so many sleepless nights. I can't think or work. Mary says I look dreadful, and I still can't bring myself to tell anyone about it. All I seem fit for is to rake up the leaves in the garden, even they are falling early this year, and make it tidy for Winter.

Sept. 28th
L.W. dropped in to see me without warning, something he has never done before, all fresh and tanned from his holiday while I felt tired, old and defeated. He exuded an almost electric animal energy that was overpowering. I felt more and more my little remaining strength drain away. He asked if I had ever thought of selling off the cove. Did I ever use it and, if not, why not sell it? I said something feeble about its going with the cottage, and why should anyone want to buy it anyway. The only access is through my back garden after coming down my path from the road. He said there could be access by boat, if someone was really keen. I felt him trying to force his will on me, even though he didn't actually say that he wanted to buy it. When he had gone, I sat for a long time by the fire as if I was very old. These last few months I feel as if I have aged ten years.

Sept. 30th
Woke this morning after a good night's sleep, determined to

try to get back to my old self. Thinking things over as I lay there with the comfort of Tiger's faint snoring beside me, I decided that my present low state dates from my first meeting with L.W. Ever since, I've been in a sort of decline, as though I had contracted some slow illness, a bit like a consumption. It came into my mind that tuberculosis used to be thought a fairy sickness, because of its symptoms; the wasting away, changes of mood, not wanting to eat human food, and so on. In a sense I have been bewitched, I think, even though I can't put my finger on it. Yet I don't know why and the whole idea seems preposterous. I decided as I lay there that this evening I shall begin to write an account of these last few months, in the hope of pulling myself together and trying to get certain things clear in my mind. When I'd settled that, I got up, feeling more cheerful at the prospect of a day than I have for weeks.

Oct. 5th
I have written and written over the last few days and am now up to date. It has been like, I imagine, a course of psychotherapy, draining the system of some kind of psychic poison. I feel stronger than for months and I have gone to bed after my writing and slept without waking all night. If there has been anyone there, I quite simply haven't looked to see.

   Field Club this evening. L.W. came up and asked me how I was. I said I was feeling much better and hoped to get down to some work soon. A shadow crossed his face for a second. I don't think he is altogether pleased with my recovery. I saw him quite calmly this evening. His power to disturb and drain me, like being in love, but somehow a back–to–front version of it, had gone but I didn't invite him to tea this coming week as I should have done before; I'm not sure if I'm strong enough for that yet.

Oct. 6th
The figure was there last night. I suppose because I was a little disturbed by seeing L.W. I didn't sleep as well as I have

142

done this last week and at two o'clock when I looked at my watch on waking, I became convinced that it was there and got up to look. I wasn't surprised or even greatly frightened, since I know now that all it does is stand and watch. When it had gone I went back to bed and slept soundly and therefore didn't feel too tired when I woke again this morning.

I decided to go down to the cove this afternoon. I felt I wanted to smell great quantities of sea, to gulp it down, that it would do me good in the same way in which it used to be prescribed for convalescents, and it might be my last chance before the Spring. The path gets very slippery in Winter and I feel less like the climb back.

The view was as magnificent as ever, and I felt quite uplifted, almost exultant with the wind in my face and a great open wash of sea and sky, clear of any human element, in front of me as I hung onto the rope banister and climbed round the bluff. It was as if I could step off into space and fly away. Then I turned the corner and saw the jetty and the boathouse below me. I love to walk along the tideline, picking up bits of flotsam and jetsam, rubbish really, but a treasure trove that goes on appealing to the child in all of us: little pink–lined slipper limpet shells, long flat razors, sea–polished black stones that might be Whitby jet, the hope of finding one of Hilda's snaky ammonites, old bottles that must have messages in them and wave carved wood bleached with salt. I love the stretch of pure sand between them and the sea when the tide is low, with only the little arrow marks of birds' feet drawn neatly across it.

I saw at once that today it was quite different. The tide had turned; the waves were slapping higher across the beach every time, to rub out the markings. A little later, and they would have been gone. But I was in time to see them. The sand was scuffed and disordered by human feet, some shod, some naked. Here and there, a shape was imprinted with Man–Friday–like clarity. I walked slowly over the sand examining every mark but I was no real detective to be able to interpret them, even to say whether they were male or female, although I thought there were both.

143

In the Orkneys they used to believe that the seal people came ashore to dance on the beach, casting off their sealskins and taking their human form. The story came back to me now as I crouched down with the waves running up behind me, darkening the sand and sucking out the prints. Perhaps a group of children had rowed round, not knowing it was a private beach. I stood up and walked on towards the jetty. Even from the sand below I could see that one part of it seemed to be blackened. I climbed the concrete steps.

A fire had been lit there. There were the remains of driftwood burned to charcoal fragments, wood ash and soot stains. I took a clean spar and poked among the dead embers. In the middle were the fire—whitened bones of a small animal. I cast around, looking for an explanation. I walked along to the wooden boathouse. The padlock was in place and I hadn't brought the key. Then I looked again. It was a different, newer padlock. My key wouldn't have fitted. I was locked out. I went round to peer through the window in the side.

There had been an old rowing boat in there when I had bought the cottage, but it had gone long since. Idly I had considered replacing it from time to time and then had decided that just for myself it wasn't worth it. I didn't really use it very often. Now I could just make out some dark shapes through the window, but not enough light came in to identify them properly. However, it was clear that someone was using the boathouse and it certainly wasn't me. Ineffectually I rattled the doorknob. The answer was to bring down a hacksaw and cut through the arm of the padlock. I was determined to see what was inside.

As I turned away, a small object near my foot caught my eye. I bent to pick it up, but I knew already what it was. It was the little pouch from the envelope in my desk drawer. I squeezed at the top to make it open as one does with a snapdragon, but there was hardly any need. The outer rim was caked with a brownish crust and the inside viscid with a thick mucus of blood, as I had known it would be …

Four

The diary stopped there, less than a week before her death. Reading it had brought me a kind of comfort, the tone of voice was so clearly Aunt Meg's, but my heart had ached to see her brought down, exhausted as the weeks passed, by the strange combat with Leonard Wallace. For that was what it had been: a struggle, like the great fight in *Paradise Lost* when the angels tore up the hills of heaven to hurl against each other. Aunt Meg's voice from the pages had restored my power to reason a little, or at least to see through the fog which seemed to have drifted into my head. But the return of reason brought an endless succession of questions and no one to answer them.

Except, of course, Leonard Wallace. Unless the whole thing was a fantasy dreamt up between two old women or a product of my aunt's illness, for she must have been ill, even if she hadn't known it, then he was the other person, the *only* other person who would know the truth, and the one person it was impossible to ask.

I felt elated, almost light—headed, as if I were on the verge of grasping some very difficult problem. At any moment I would understand everything. But I knew from past experience that this was a false effect born of exhaustion and some change in the body's chemistry and that the sensible thing to do was to go to bed and sleep on it.

As soon as I woke in the morning I knew I had slept better than for days and I lay there trying to regain, but more rationally than the night before, the conviction that understanding was within my grasp. The answer was to try to find out for myself without asking Wallace. That was it: quite simple, really. I had only to telephone and he would invite me to his house, that strange house where Aunt Meg had been before me. Perhaps there I would be able to pick up some clues.

With a night's sleep there had come too, the conviction that I had had no hand, even as some other's instrument, in Mary's death. My whole being cried out that this was so. However different in detail from the earlier murders of women, hers must have been by the same agency. After all, killers often began in one pattern and deviated a little as they repeated their crime. What I still had to explain to myself was the missing axe. And then I felt myself go quite rigid with fear as I lay there. I hadn't sufficiently taken in Aunt Meg's nocturnal visitor. Had his visits ended with her death? If not, he could easily have gone to the back of the house and taken the axe from under the verandah. The gap between her death and my arrival would have given him plenty of time to search all round outside, if he was curious. He could easily have found out where it was kept.

And what about the inside? Meg had felt, had been sure, that the house had been entered and her desk searched. Had those visits ended too? Had the searcher found whatever he or she was looking for? I couldn't be sure, except that I felt that Leonard Wallace was the key to it all. My fear receded, driven out by the excitement of what I intended to do. My hand reached out for the telephone and then drew back. I wasn't quite done with my thoughts yet.

Should I go down to the cove first, before I rang Leonard Wallace? I had seen nothing unusual when *she* had drawn me down there before, but then I hadn't known there was anything to look for; and besides, all my attention was on her. It was logical that she should have drawn me to the cove if there was some mystery or danger attached to the place.

She would be strong there, might even be waiting for me now, putting the thought into my head that would bring me to her. Then it would be she, not I who went to Five Ways. As it was, I knew I was already inviting her appearance by going there. Yet I had to find out and there was no other way. I had to risk it.

I looked at Tiger, curled up beside me. Not for the first time, I longed for him to be able to speak and answer my questions, as Aunt Meg must have longed for him to be able to tell her where he had been and what had happened to him. I turned his head to one side and ran my finger under his chin as I knew he liked but this time I was searching for something. My finger found it: a seam in his ginger—and—white coat. Gently I turned his head a little further and parted the fur. There it was. A long, thin line of white skin was sliced through the fine hairs where they would never grow again in the scar tissue.

This confirmation of part of the diary convinced me that the rest was true. Not that I had really doubted it. Aunt Meg and Mary weren't really the sort to alarm themselves unnecessarily. I believed there had been a night walker, and that someone had been using the cove. I got out of bed determined to find some answers. My excuse for ringing Leonard Wallace was the visit of the police.

'I've had my gentlemen callers. They didn't seem interested in locking me up.'

'Perhaps they were just being clever, giving you enough rope to hang yourself with.' He laughed as he said it, but there was an edge behind the laughter.

It was my fault for starting the conversation off in this dangerous way, and all at once I realised that I had already lost control. They were her words, not mine. I heard with a kind of horror my mouth opening on her phrases, that revealed the conspiracy between them.

'I don't think they'll be back. They're only going through the motions. They really believe it's the same one.'

'So there's no need for you to stay home any more. You can pay us a visit. Come to tea this afternoon.'

There it was. I had done it. Or had I merely been the ventriloquist's dummy? Whatever the answer, I was committed to going. The telephone cut into my thoughts. It was John, shocked by the news of Mary's death.

'I knew it was an unsuitable place. Why Meg ever chose it I don't know. When are you coming home? I don't think you should stay a moment longer than necessary.'

'Please don't set Eileen off,' I said. 'I've a lot to do still and she'd only waste my time. I promise I'll leave as soon as I can.'

He went on a bit longer about police inefficiency and locking up carefully at night. I didn't give him any more detail than he had got from the newspapers. 'Such a gentle person. I keep thinking how frightened she must have been. At least it was probably quick. They say she was stabbed.'

I held my tongue. There was no point in distressing him any further. Slashed, I thought, slashed to bits. I hoped my mother wouldn't have seen a report of it.

But I was unlucky. The receiver was soon shrill with her cries and somehow it was all made to seem my fault, part of my wickedness in not coming home to look after her although Bob had, of course, been 'an angel' at what wasn't really 'a man's job'. At least the familiarity of her lamentations helped restore me to myself.

It was strange and somehow comforting to be driving out of town in the wheeltracks of Aunt Meg's old roadster. There was the hill just as she had described it, with the tower of the house silhouetted against the afternoon sky, except that I sailed up it in my hired car while she had been forced to get off and push. Almost as if she was there inside ahead of me, I could see her pat her windblown hair into place and her hand on the bell I reached for. The automatic opening of the door brought me no surprise. I would have to watch myself and not betray that I knew as much about the house as I did.

But the knowledge made me tongue—tied. As I waited at the inner glass door and saw Leonard Wallace's legs descending the stairs, I tried to compose my face and a suitable sentence for the amazement I didn't feel. He was

148

wearing the all—black clothes that Aunt Meg had described instead of the country slacks and windcheater I was used to. They at once gave him a more formal appearance and emphasised the dark eyes and hair and the tan that was fading a little now. If my aunt was right he would soon be going on his travels to deepen it. I tried to cultivate her almost satirical way of looking at him, but inside I knew I was hollow, even as the last door opened and he smiled down at me.

'It's almost as good as the entrance to Heathrow,' I tried.

'When I'm working upstairs it gives me time to get down without keeping my guests out in the cold.' The almost exact repetition of what he had said to her made me shiver inwardly. I felt his closeness as he took my coat, holding the collar while I struggled out of the sleeves and fought back the sensation of being bound. Suddenly I knew how wrong I had been to come here and to think that I was strong enough to find out anything he didn't want me to know or to do battle with him. I was in a trap, if they cared to close it and, like all silly creatures, I had walked into it of my own free will, betrayed by my own curiosity. I followed him through into the drawing room, where the fire was still blazing as it had for Meg. If he tried to put whisky in my tea I would refuse it. The very thought made me feel sick.

He must have known he had no need of such extremes with me. 'I hope you like china. I was sure you would. I prefer bowls for china. It makes the whole ceremony more elegant.' He poured a scented stream from a painted porcelain teapot in a little wicker cradle. Then he picked up another matching bowl full of pink—and—white petals and dropped some onto each steaming surface, where they spun like fragile coracles.

'There.' He held out a bowl to me. 'That makes the whole experience pleasing to the eye, as well as to the palate. Look at them whirling around.'

I looked into the bowl offered in his long fingers, and began to drown. As the petals slowed, he delicately touched them into motion again. I have always been susceptible to the eddies in a cup, but surely he wasn't to know. Or *was* he?

'You take it and look at them. Smell the fragrance.' He placed the bowl in my hands and I stared into it through a haze of warm orange blossom. The bowl swelled, carrying my hands out of sight. I could no longer see the bottom properly, only the steep white sides, and far off the moon gleaming up through the clear, dark waters, where two water lilies turned and turned, bearing my eyes with them round and round and down ...

'Drink.'

I lifted the great well towards me and bent my head over the spinning waters to drink. The hot steam filled my eyes and nostrils. My lips touched the rim numbly and the fragrant river flowed into me and along my veins. I put the bowl down.

'Look at the fire. How the flames leap and flicker. Follow them, Paula. Follow them up and up. Now look at me. Can you see them still in my eyes? Look. Can you see them?'

Twin flames flared at the centre of the brown pupils, and as I looked I could no longer see his face, but only the dancing points of fire. A part of me deep inside still held back, but my will was gone and I could feel *her* stirring lazily in my blood, turning in the warm, perfumed streams that had filled my veins.

Leonard Wallace took my hand. 'I'm glad to see you're still wearing my ring.'

'It wouldn't come off. It's stuck.'

'But of course it will. Look.' He placed his other hand round my finger with the tips of his touching the ring, so that his hand was a hollow phial of warm flesh, and drew the jet circlet effortlessly up and down several times until shivers of pleasure ran through me. 'Can you still see the flames?'

'Yes.'

'Keep looking at them for a moment.'

My ears roared and the whole room fell away. There were only two hot points of light in the universe and the 'I' that beheld them was nothing but a reflecting glass in which they could shine. 'If you look hard you will find your own sight

150

becoming clearer with a new vision. You will see into things behind the façade to the true reality, the true nature of existence, including your own.'

I looked down at my hands resting in my lap. Each had a double outline, as if two perfect copies had been placed one on top of the other, but slightly overlapping. I didn't know which was mine and which was hers, except that she had somehow split my body between us. She was like a snake about to slide from the old identical skin. At any moment *she* could step sideways and stand twinned beside me.

'What do you see, Paula?'

'She sees me.'

'Who are you?'

'Paul, Paula—whatever you like to call me. But I'm the real one. She's tried to keep us from each other, you and me. She knows we speak the same language, you see, that we know what we want, that we're strong and we don't care what the rest of the world thinks. Come on, let's do something. I'm restless. Show me something. Amuse me. We'll leave her here if she doesn't want to come.'

'Perhaps I like her better than you. Suppose I find her more ... pliable?'

'Alright, I'll be good. I'll stay quietly deep down inside her, so that you hardly know I'm there.'

'Come, Paula. I want to show you the rest of the house.'

Obediently I stood up. Their little pretence didn't deceive me. They might appear not to know each other and he might suggest that he preferred me to her, but I knew how strong the affinity was between them. I followed him out of the drawing room, carrying her like a monstrous child inside me.

I had expected to be taken up to the tower, but instead he led me along corridors and up another flight of stairs at what must be the other end of the house. Even in my confused state, part of my mind continued to function almost normally, the scholar's part that noted and assessed facts. The house must run up the little peninsula it stood on. The tower was at one end, linked by the glass passage between the leads my aunt had noticed, and we were now coming to

151

whatever that ended in.

'You are going to see my study, where very few people are allowed. But first the print shop.'

I had gradually become aware of the noise of machinery at work, a noise that was louder with every step we took. Steps led down from the corridor, iron steps with black filigree rails. Leonard Wallace turned down them, and I followed. At the bottom the noise was at its height. In front was a black door with a figure drawn on it that was almost a Christmas tree star.

'This is where the Pentacle Press lives.' He opened the door and the sound of metal on metal engulfed us.

Inside a long, windowless basement a printing press was automatically churning out pages. The walls were lined with shelves of what I took to be his publications, and other equipment stood about whose function I couldn't guess.

'Modern technology is magic now. How the contemporaries of Caxton would have cried witchcraft if they'd seen this printroom, making its own books under the green eyes of the devil computer. The Pentacle Press sends its message all over the world. I have another main branch in California where I shall be going in a week or two to get some sun before the winter closes in here.'

As he talked he led me round. 'We must give you some of our works to take home. Now you must see my study.' We climbed the stairs again and went along the corridor. Another black door with its star sign blocked off the end. It slid open onto complete darkness as we drew near.

Leonard Wallace was behind me now. 'Go in, Paula.' I felt his warmth at my back and the soft brush of his breath against my hair, pushing me gently forward when I wanted to turn and run back. I took two steps and stood still. The door slid shut. I was in a darkness so thick it lay on me like the black fur of an animal. My only comfort was that I knew no one had come in behind me.

I sensed that I was in an anteroom or lobby, very small, a coffin of a room. Although I could breathe quite well, there was a sensation of airlessness. I knew there were no windows.

152

I began to feel stifled. Panic was rising in me, making my breathing shallow and quick. My own fear threatened to suffocate me. No one knew I was here. I could die and no one would be any the wiser, except Wallace and presumably the invisible Kasper.

'Paula, Paula, can you hear me?' It was as if the voice was inside my head.

'Yes.'

'In a moment you will see a sign. Go towards it, and a way will open for you.'

I waited, trembling, in the stagnant blackness. Then I made out a little green blur on the air, growing brighter, until it took the shape of the same five—sided figure which, as my eyes stared at it, swam in an inky sea, a luminous starfish beckoning me towards it.

I don't know quite what I feared, or even expected. That scholar's part of me wanted to say even then that these silly, childish games must stop. We were all grown up and not to be frightened by phosphorus and hidden doors. But the other part of me was frightened and at the same time a little excited. The conjuror had come to the children's tea party, and I still couldn't see how the tricks were done.

As I moved towards the glowing light, a bar of colour sprang open below it and widened as if two hands were rolling back the ends of a scroll. After the total darkness that had muffled my eyes I was dazzled by a sudden burst of light that leapt at me and drowned my sight again with first a beam of pure white, and then the purple, red and orange of an infernal discotheque whirling around my head so that I wanted to duck or shrink away. The air was full of moving shadows, and then suddenly the noise of laughter and high voices.

The lights shifted again, and the walls became visible for the first time, but they were oblong glasses set at angles, each one showing a still figure dressed in black, with the hood or mask over its face that Aunt Meg had seen beyond the hedge.

Suddenly I realised that the figures were coming down to meet me. No, that wasn't it. It was I who was rising towards them! The square of floor on which I stood had detached itself from the rest and was raising me up towards them on a lengthening column. I looked down and it was already too late to jump. The floor seemed far, far away. I heard myself begin to whimper a little. I felt myself swaying, wanting to jump or fall.

'Look up, Paula. You won't fall if you do as I tell you and look up. Now look at us.'

I was on a level with the figures now, but in the strange lighting it was impossible to tell which of them were real and which reflections and yet that was what the voice was now asking me to do.

'This is a test, Paula. Most people think they understand the nature of reality, that they know the real from its shadow. But you know it isn't so simple. I want you to try. Turn round slowly and point to the one which is real.'

'But what if I can't? What if I get it wrong?'

'You must wait and find out. Begin now. Turn round slowly.'

Again, I did as I was told, although my muscles ached with vertigo. I looked at each one in turn, and then I heard my voice cry out: '*You are all a lie. None of you is real!*'

There was a loud crash and a jangle of harsh laughter as the lights went out and on again in a brilliant flash. The mirrors were empty. I felt the column slowly sinking towards the ground or the floor rising to meet it. I couldn't be sure just as you can't tell from the train window whether it's your compartment beginning to draw away from the station, or the one on the next platform while you stay still.

'It's time for you to continue your journey,' the voice said. 'Watch, and you will find another way out than the one you came in by.'

The light had changed to a deep green now, as though I was at the bottom of the sea. Again, shadows drifted through, shapes that turned slowly, fish that might nose at me, or weed to cling and wrap itself about my limbs and hold me down. I seemed to push forward through a weight of water towards where the starfish glowed blue above an oblong that grew at my approach. At the last moment, dark thongs of weed caught at me, so that I cried out and tore at them, struggling through the door like a netted fish and was out with an iron stair before me. When I turned, there was only the blank wall behind.

I began to climb. At the top there was a glass door with a handle. I grasped it and turned. The door opened and I stepped through. I was in the narrow glass passage between the leads, which fell away on either side. The wind plucked at the glass and moaned in my ears. I wanted to run, but I put my hands against the windows on either side and made myself walk calmly. The glass was very cold, numbing the palms of my hands. It seemed as if I were walking a tightrope towards the tower ahead. I was an insect in a test tube, or Alice grown so small she had fallen into her own bottle of 'Drink Me'.

Below I could see the tops of trees, and behind spread a livid orange radiance from the invisible sun. The sky on either side was grey, with skeins of darker grey dropped here and there like dirty unspun fleece. Somewhere there must be toy houses and people in them, watching television and eating bread and jam, but I was no part of their life.

On that short journey I learnt that all fears contain an element of attraction. That gives them their power. On the high pinnacle, part of us longs to dash ourselves down. I wanted to smash the glass and fall over and over with the air rushing past, until I, too, smashed to pieces at the bottom. And the noise of the wind although I couldn't feel its pull, tore at me with the illusion that it might bear me up if I jumped, and carry me away across the town and out to sea. Now I understood why old women had thought they could fly, or be carried through the air to their sabbats ...

The far door was like the one I had come through. I turned the handle, and for the first time I had a choice. I could go down, or into the tower where Aunt Meg had been. I like to think it was the desire to follow her and be close to her sheer saneness that turned the balance, but I'm not sure that even that decision didn't have some element of perversity. In my own defence I say that I had no reason to be suspicious of the tower. Meg, like an explorer, had been there, seen and described it. It, too, had a door with a simple handle. I went in.

The loud click of the lock behind made me turn back. I tried the handle. It didn't move. Once more I was locked in and this was no longer the tower as Aunt Meg had seen it.

Now the windows looked on nothing but an illusory night sky full of stars. Leonard Wallace had turned the tower into his own planetarium. The simple domestic techniques of double–glazing could do it, I thought, before the illusion began to take hold of me. The floor, too, was different. I stood on a black shiny disc, with the symbols of the zodiac etched on it in white. There was no sign of the telescope Aunt Meg had looked through.

It was then that the black circle of the heavens under my feet began to revolve. The whole floor had become a spinning record on a high turntable. I fell on my knees and then lay down. The starry windows whirled faster and faster. I was a speck of dust in space. My head swam and my ears roared. Then I lost consciousness and the false stars were doused. At one point I thought I woke. The turning circle was still and a figure stood over me, its feet planted between my spreadeagled legs, flung open like some limp rag doll's by the centrifugal force. It held a little axe and was hooded. I sank away again into unconsciousness.

When I woke it was to Leonard Wallace's eyes looking at me over the rim of his teacup. Evening was darkening the windows of the drawing room. The fire was hot and bright.

'How did you enjoy your imaginary tour?'

'Imaginary?'

'That's right.'

'I don't understand.'

'You nearly fell asleep. It must have been the heat of the fire. So I tried a little experiment. I suggested a tour of the house and left your imagination to do the rest. You must tell me what you saw.'

My whole body felt bruised and shaken as it had before. I

156

couldn't believe I had sat there quietly dozing. 'Do you mean you hypnotised me?'

'What is hypnosis? No one knows. It's a power of the mind; that's all they can say. Do you remember me hypnotising you?'

'No, not really.' Some instinct made me fudge the truth, a truth I didn't anyway fully grasp.

'What in any case does the so—called hypnotist do? Nothing. At most he makes a few suggestions that the mind is free to accept or reject. It is the subject who acts; it is his imagination which supplies the power. The other merely suggests that there is a channel it might flow through. What did you see?'

'I can't quite remember. There are just some confused images of lights and rooms.'

Leonard Wallace smiled. I had made the right answer. Soon I could decently get up and say I must go. I knew somehow that this time no attempt would be made to keep me. What I had been through, however it had been done, had been a kind of initiation, a softening up. My limbs were suffused by a heaviness, a lethargy, as if I had been ill in bed or run a long race. I must go now before I fell asleep again. I stood up.

I don't remember any part of the drive back, only the relief of being 'home' again as I now thought of the cottage. I fell asleep in front of Aunt Meg's fire at once, even though I had been determined to stay awake and think through the afternoon to try to come to some conclusions. By the time I woke, there was nothing of the evening left, and anyway, I was still too tired to think except that, as I dragged myself up the short stairs, it came to me that Meg too, had felt this terrible lassitude, this draining of all energy, and that it was close to the torture technique of not letting the prisoner sleep in order to break the will and confuse the mind.

My body still felt bruised when I went down the stairs again in the morning. I took my tea and toast into the sitting room and tried to think as I ate. There was no longer anything to hold me there. I could put the house up for sale.

The friendly bank manager would see to that for me, even though he would be disappointed that I was leaving. I could take Tiger back to London with me; it wouldn't be as free and easy for him as having the gardens and the cliffs to wander, but I thought he would prefer it to the possible alternatives. Or could there be only *one* alternative my pedant's mind asked, as I bit into a browned crust.

It was then that I first wondered if *she* would go away, would be left behind when I got into the train to go south. All at once I had a clear picture of her smiling at me from the corner seat opposite, and knew she wouldn't. If I was ever to be free of her, I had to do it here. Once let loose in my London life, she would be with me for ever.

Vaguely I wondered if there was anything I could or should do about Mary, but I supposed there would be relatives whose responsibility it was and who might resent my interference. My thoughts had shied away from yesterday, but I was determined to bring them back.

What exactly had happened to me? Had anything happened at all, or had it, as Leonard Wallace had said, all taken place in my mind while I dozed by his fire? I went to the bookcase, took out Aunt Meg's diary and read the account of her visit again. Her tour of the house had been real. It was clear that he had tried to influence her in the same way that he had me, but had failed. I had read somewhere that one or two people in every ten aren't susceptible to hypnosis if that was what he had tried. It would be quite feasible that she wasn't and I was. That still, however, left open the question of whether what I had experienced was real, in the usually accepted sense or not. And why was any of this happening? If he had tried to subdue first my aunt and then me, what was his motive?

Here I was up against a brick wall. Unless he wanted the cove so badly that he hoped to persuade us to sell it to him I could think of no reason. I should go and look for signs of use, perhaps taking some instrument to deal with the padlock which Aunt Meg had mentioned on the boathouse—if it was still there. But even if I found them, what would they prove?

There was hardly likely to be an explanatory leaflet pinned to the door.

So I threshed about in my search for an answer, and as I struggled I felt I was watched, that just outside the edge of my range of vision, she was leaning and laughing at me, while Leonard Wallace smiled over the rim of his cup ...

The thought of Mary pushed itself back into my consciousness. Even though I no longer believed I had killed her, I felt uneasily that I was somehow to blame though I couldn't pin down why. Her pathetic and yet horrific body would now have been taken away by the police and be in the hands of the pathologist whose invasions of her most intimate secrets would at least be clinically impartial. How she would have shrunk from it all. I must find out when her funeral would be. I didn't know whether I could face going myself after my last experience, but I could at least send flowers.

Aunt Meg's little china clock pinged eleven. I had sat for over an hour, thinking, but I was no further forward. I took my breakfast things through into the kitchen. Tiger's dish looked up at me from in front of the catdoor. His uneaten breakfast was beginning to glaze and harden in the air. I thought back quickly. When had I last seen him? In the afternoon, before I went to Five Ways. I had been so tired last night I hadn't really missed him, but even when he spent most of the night out he would often arrive in the early hours, or in time for breakfast. I went first into the front and then the back garden and called into the frosty air, making my breath steam up with every cry.

Half an hour later I was close to panic. Tiger had become my lifeline. I must find him. Aunt Meg's own fear when he had been missing before was joined with mine. Then he had been trapped and injured, but had managed to find his way home. What if he had been caught again? If he was killed I couldn't bear it, not after Mary. Then there would be nothing left.

Could he be at Mary's? He was used to going to stay there sometimes. Perhaps he had gone visiting, not knowing she was no longer there to call on. It was a poor, thin, frayed hope, but I hung on to it. I put my coat on and set off up the path, calling as I went. The car was parked half on the pavement in front of the gate. I decided to leave it there and walk, looking fearfully in the gutter and the hedgesides for a battered ginger–and–white furred bundle.

My hand hesitated on the latch of the gate. Only too sharply I could see all the details of my last visit. Perhaps there would be a policeman on duty at the house who could tell me whether Tiger had been there without my having to go in. I went up the path towards the cottage that now seemed to squat under the brow of the hill as if hunched. There was no one outside and the door was shut. For a moment I stood there. Then I called, my voice sounding weak and high in the open air: 'Tiger, Tiger!' And then again.

When the front door was thrown suddenly open I was nearly sick with fright. A stranger stood there, not the uniformed bobby I had expected to see, or even the plain clothes detective. At once my own guilt and fear rushed back. Perhaps he was from some other branch of the police force, Scotland Yard even, and would see through me at once. At that moment Tiger appeared in the doorway beside him.

'You've got him!' My voice was a cross between relief and indignant accusation but he heard only the last.

'You could say he's got me.' Tiger ran forward, making his small chirp and then a series of comments as he shoved against my jeans. I picked him up. 'He seems to know you,' the man went on, 'unless he's completely promiscuous.'

It was a good voice that spoke in a tone both humorous and relaxed. I felt my own rumpled fur begin to settle as I cradled the purring Tiger and looked up at his kidnapper.

'I'm not actually given to napping cats. He came in when I opened the back door to look at the garden. He took me round the house.'

'He used to come and stay when Mary, Miss Dunscombe ... I mean—when my aunt went away. Sometimes he stayed and sometimes Mary went down to feed him in his own home.' Suddenly, for the first time since I had come to Scarborough, I found myself weeping. The tears began to run

160

down my face and drop into Tiger's coat. He put up a paw and touched my wet cheek, and that made them flow faster.

'You're making him all wet. Why don't you both come in and show me how to fill the teapot without burning my hand on the kettle?' My reluctance to enter the house must have shown, because he went on: 'I got here last night since when I've been cleaning up. I think you'll find it's alright now. He seemed to think so anyway. What's his name?'

'Tiger. I'm sorry to be such a fool. I thought I'd lost him, and it all seemed too much. Then I thought he might be here. I'm Paula Cockburn.'

'Hallo. I'm Tom Ferris. Come into the sitting room. Mary had a taste for a rather good dry sherry I find. It might do us more good than tea. Did you know her well? I'm a rather distant son of a cousin. I only met her once, at my christening which I don't remember with any great clarity. But no one else was free.'

'I've only met her recently.' Suddenly I didn't know how to begin the story. I could see her veined hand clenched round the handle of the teapot and the knitted blue cuff of her cardigan.

'There's an awful confusion about her will, it seems.' He came towards me, carrying two brimming glasses of pale straw–coloured wine. He had sensed that I was on the verge of tears again and was talking to soothe me. 'She left everything to a Dr Hackstead, some sort of quack who looked after her, I suppose and probably insinuated himself into her good books. Elderly ladies get into that kind of situation. Not that I mean they're necessarily more gullible than men; they just tend to live longer and therefore end up in a vulnerable position. Anyway, I shall have to try to trace this Dr Hackstead.'

'You can't,' I said, and this time I put my face in my hands and sobbed. Tom Ferris waited quietly for the spasm to pass. 'I'm sorry,' I said again when I could speak. 'I don't usually have to go around apologising all the time for being so wet. It's all been too much, I suppose: first my aunt; then Mary; then thinking I'd lost Tiger, and then being here again in this room. I had tea with her that afternoon. She saw me off at the gate.' I wept again.

'It's alright,' he said. 'I'm rather glad there's someone to cry about her. It just seems so hideous that it numbs one's responses. My father was very shocked, even though he hadn't seen her for years and didn't really know her in any personal way. That's why I offered to come.'

I tried to pull myself together. 'I ought to explain. My aunt is, was, Dr Hackstead. She and Mary were what we used to call at school best friends. She wasn't a doctor of medicine, she was ... a folklorist, a sort of anthropologist, you could say. She died a couple of weeks ago—that's why I'm here, like you, to sort things out. I don't know what happens now about the will. Probably it goes to the next of kin, perhaps your father. I think Mary was older than my aunt. I suppose she thought she would die first. Then, when my aunt did die so suddenly, Mary was too upset to get round to altering her will.'

Tom Ferris sighed. 'So that's it. I suppose Dad is the next of kin now. I'm rather sorry to have lost my villain. Somehow it made it easier to have someone specific to hate, not just a faceless nothing.'

'I don't quite understand.'

'Dr Hackstead was my number one suspect—the villainous doctor who preys on old ladies and then murders one of them. You sometimes get cases like it in the papers. It made some sort of sense. Now it doesn't again.'

'Didn't the police tell you?'

'Tell me what? I haven't seen them. They spoke to my father; sent somebody round from the local shop. He didn't know much and my father was too stunned to take it in. Judging by what I found, it must have been rather brutal and messy. Now I come to think of it, not at all a physicianly crime.'

'We have a local murderer; a maniac—he must be. There've been three, to my knowledge—murders, I mean. All women. Mary and I once talked about it. She warned me to be careful and said she was quite safe because he liked them young. That was what she said. "I'm quite safe: he likes them young." ' I felt the tears pricking my eyes again, but less urgently than before. It was such a relief to have someone to talk to and Tom Ferris was such a calm, rational presence. 'I'd better take Tiger home.' I stood up. 'If he goes astray again I'll know where to look first.'

Tom Ferris walked us both to the door. 'I'm grateful to him for bringing you. It's a doleful business on your own.'

'I'm afraid I wasn't very cheering. But if you need any practical help, I'll willingly come over. At the moment I'm rather a practised hand at sorting out.'

'I'd be very grateful, if you really mean it. The house has to be cleared and sold, I suppose. I tried opening a drawer or two, but I'm afraid I chickened out and shut them again. It seemed impertinent, almost.'

'I know.'

I gave him my telephone number and picked up Tiger. He lay purring in my arms, almost smiling, I thought, as we crossed the road and I carried him down the path. I felt calmer than I had done for days.

I don't know how *she* woke me that night, only that all at once I was staringly awake, as if my name had been called. Perhaps it had. I knew I had to get up and go to the window. *She* was there beyond the hedge, where I had seen her before, and where I now believed Aunt Meg's nocturnal visitor had stood. She was dressed in the long black gown she had worn to the funeral, with an evening cloak thrown over it, and she was waiting for me to dress and come down to her. I tried to keep some control by wondering why it was that sometimes she wore exactly the same clothes as I was wearing, and at others dressed quite differently. For a moment I even thought I might not go and then I knew I had no choice. If I refused, she would come up the path to the house and come inside to find me, and I didn't want her in there, didn't want to be alone indoors with her, Outdoors was less claustrophobic; even though last time she had taken me to Mary's bloodied cottage and the horror there ...

I pulled on jeans and a sweater over the shirt—like

nightdress I wear for sleeping in the Winter. As before, my actions seemed effortless. I sensed that if I had stuck a pin into my flesh I wouldn't have felt it. She had the ability at times to suspend my normal sensations as though my body were partly etherialised, its substance split between the two of us. I almost seemed to glide across the hall.

For a second I paused, with my hand on the doorcatch. I knew its metal was very cold, but my fingers were numbed, except for the one banded with jet, which was hot and throbbing. Then I felt her impatience like a live current flowing towards me and I opened the front door, stepped out and closed it behind. Even in that moment I was aware of Tiger, whom I had left asleep on my bed, and that it was important that he should be safely shut in.

A faint luminescence, a starshine, hung in the garden like that gauze they sometimes drop between set and audience in the theatre. I could see quite clearly even without a moon.

'Come on,' she said. 'You're so slow.' She reached out and took my hand, and immediately mine was joined to hers like those absurd advertisements for adhesive, where the join remains even when everything around is broken: I couldn't pull away. She led me round the side of the house, past the verandah and across the back garden lawn. This time, nothing heaved under my feet, for they barely touched it and anyway, I felt the creatures were all locked deep in a Winter trance as the earth hardened under the first frosts.

We passed through the back gate onto the cliff path. We were going down to the cove. Behind me was the dark wall of a yew hedge, and on either side the leafless spikes of the bushes that were cast in black iron, caging me in.

Her hand led me on to the rock–cut steps. My feet found the measure of them by instinct, for they were in shadow and in any case I couldn't look down or tumble for an edge with my toes because she drew me forward too quickly. Still I was aware of how slimy they had been before, and of my fear of slipping. Now that weeping damp might be frozen to black ice or silvered into frost crystals …

'Come on, Paula, I won't let you slip. It's all a matter of

confidence, like walking a tightrope.'

I knew she was right and that as long as her hand was fast to mine and I let her draw me effortlessly forward, I wouldn't stumble but the soles of my feet tingled with the danger. Then the steps were gone and we were on the open path with the bushes, too, fallen away. They had been like caged bars before, but now I missed their protection. Sea and sky were washed in black and silver—grey, and I could hear the sound of the waves against the cliffs. There was a rope banister here, I remembered, but she didn't give me time to clutch at it, only pulled me relentlessly on towards the rock shoulder that shut off the path and to the top of the last and steepest flight of steps, where she stopped and let fall my hand. The darkness below was full of shapes, breathing and rustling together with the occasional chink of metal on stone.

Suddenly a blue flame leapt, flared high and steadied into a bowl of fire burning on the jetty. Dark forms covered the strip of sand, where two boats were drawn up. In the blue light they lounged, half—sitting, half—lying on the beach, swaying their dark round heads. Their bodies were encased in long black skins that gleamed as they caught the light. They were open at the front and ended in a flat webbed tail behind. Webbed flippers hid their arms and legs like the wetsuits of frogmen.

The doors of the boathouse were open, and in front was a kind of dais on which another half—human, half—seal figure reclined on a long sofa. Behind stood the hooded shape that Aunt Meg had described and that I thought I had seen at Five Ways in a brief moment of consciousness in the tower room.

As if at some signal, the moving forms on the sand became still. A voice began to speak, loud enough to be audible on the strand within the high rock walls of the cove, but not beyond. Even from where I stood it was hard to make out the words clearly.

'You have come to be witnesses to the power, to and for the power. It must be renewed, or it will return to the depths of the sea and leave its people bereft.' There was a little groan from the listeners. 'Remember that what we do here is beyond the understanding of others and not to be spoken of. In and out of your skins, you are bound by the laws of our mystery and the second law is secrecy. You may not speak of our mystery or you will die; the power will seek you out wherever you hide and you will die. But if you are faithful and secret, you will know the power in you and our ecstasy.'

The shapes had partly raised themselves to listen. They swayed and groaned a little from time to time, as if they were trees bent and tossed by gusts of wind.

'You will bring out the old mistress, who can no longer renew the power. Her channel is faded and broken. The power grows faint and must have a fresh stream to flow through.'

A little procession came out of the boathouse behind the hooded figure and the black shape on the dais. The first was a woman, barefoot, in a dress of some dark thin material that was torn into long rags, barely covering the pale skin. Her hair was dishevelled and in the strange blue light her eyes stared from a white blank face. She was pushed forward by an upright form like the listeners on the beach. Then it stepped back and stood, an erect black phallus behind her. She seemed dazed or tranced and made no attempt to run away, struggle or raise an arm, as the hooded figure stepped in front of her, placed black—gloved hands round her throat and forced her to her knees. The watchers sighed and murmured.

'Let the blood flow to nourish both land and sea.'

I was frozen, dumb and alone at the top of the steps. *She* was no longer beside me, although in my concentration on the scene below I hadn't felt her go. I wanted to cry out, but I was as paralysed as the woman kneeling on the hard concrete of the jetty. I saw the blade in the headsman's right hand while he still held her throat with the left; saw it catch the blue fire as he brought it down; saw the black gush of blood, and the woman slump forward. The watchers groaned. The headsman picked her up, a limp rag dummy and carried her into the boathouse.

166

'You have seen. You have been witnesses. Blood renews the power. Now bring forward the new mistress. Let her be wedded to the lord of the sea!'

Even before she came out of the boathouse, I knew why *she* had left me at the top of the steps. She carried my body as I had never been able to, with a kind of erotic arrogance. Usually I drop my head a little. My mother has nagged me about it all my life. 'For heaven's sake Paul, have more confidence in yourself. Don't duck your head and look at the ground. It makes you seem furtive. How can you expect a man to notice you like that.'

She held her head up and looked about her as she came towards the dais. She made our body seem almost beautiful as the blue light flickered across the flowing lines of the black dress and cloak. It was all a trick, a hollow trick, an empty game I had refused to play, and now she was playing it for me. I hardly recognised myself as she stood in front of the dark seal shape lounging just as arrogantly before her. It stretched out a flippered arm.

She turned towards the watchers on the sand below and raised her left hand, where the jet band was black against the white ring finger.

'Be renewed,' the voice said. 'Renew the power in each other.'

There was a sigh like a faint hiss, and the dark forms began to move towards one another, slithering and writhing their bodies across the sand until they found another and then another, the whole mass entwining together like knotting serpents or great coupling slugs under the sinking blue light. Suddenly it was extinguished altogether. The beach was blotted out but I could still hear the grunts and groans of lust in the darkness. I heard my own voice cry aloud and then I turned and half–ran, half–stumbled up the path, not caring this time whether I fell, or was whirled from the cliff shoulder to dash to pieces below.

My breath came in great gasps as I struggled up the path and then the steps and onto the path again. I fumbled at the gate and staggered across the lawn to the back door. It was

167

locked. I went on round the house to the front, and stopped in horror. In my entranced preoccupation with her, I had forgotten to bring a key. I leant against the door and wept.

I don't know how long I stood there, but at last I became aware of the cold seeping into me, and then a new terror. Suppose someone should come after me? She might, or one of those featureless others, when they had finished the obscene rites I had left them at. Already they might be halfway up the cliff. In my mind I saw the blunt head silhouetted against the sky. The thought of it made me feel sick and I began to retch with fright. I must get away from the locked house. If only I had left the back door key where I had found it under the flowerpot, but I had felt too vulnerable at night with it there.

Then the idea came to me, bringing a wave of relief: I could go to Mary's. Tom Ferris would let me in and I could wait there until it was light. He would probably come back with me and help me break in to release Tiger.

But first I had to think of some plausible explanation for locking myself out of the bungalow in the early hours of the morning. The truth was out of the question, but some reason would have to be given. I turned towards the upward path, thinking hard.

By the time I reached Mary's gate I was frozen and exhausted. The influence which had kept me impervious to cold and effort had been withdrawn as soon as I had turned my back on the cove. Once again human time and care reasserted themselves. But I had decided on my tale.

It sounded a little weak, but it had an element of the truth in it. Tom Ferris looked down at me in sleepy unbelief.

'I've locked myself out,' I said at once. 'I wondered if you would let me sit in the warm in a chair until morning and then I can face trying to get in. Everything seems so much more difficult in the dark.' I shivered, not to gain sympathy, but quite simply because I couldn't help it.

'Of course. Come in. I'll open up the fire.' He led me into the sitting room and clanked open the little metal windows on Mary's all–night burner. The damped–down embers had been glowing behind them like a picture of London burning, seen through the mullions of St Paul's. 'Is it rude to ask how you locked yourself out?'

I stretched my hands out to the flames that were beginning already to lick up in little tongues as the draught sucked at them. 'I thought I heard something in the garden and I went out to see. In a daft moment I shut the door very carefully, so that Tiger wouldn't run out but I forgot to take the keys with me. I suppose I was half–asleep still. I'm very sorry to wake you, but the prospect of dying of exposure on the verandah or the doorstep was too much.'

'I'd have been very angry if you had.' He laughed. 'I think this time some proverbial British tea should be served. We can pretend we're in the shelter or something, seeing it through. Later we can try a chorus or two from Vera Lynn.'

For the first time for days I heard myself laugh. He was so solid, so easy to get on with: a bit like Martin. I was sorry I had had to half–lie to him. I wondered what he would say if I attempted to tell him the truth. He would think I was mad, and perhaps I was, but I didn't want him to think that. His good opinion seemed vital to me and I would do anything to keep it. I couldn't bear the uncertain look that would come into his eyes if I ever embarked on my story. Where would I begin? How would I phrase it? No, it couldn't be told.

A kind of despair took hold of me then. If I couldn't tell anyone, how could I ever be freed? Would she be with me all my life and where was she leading me? I tried not to let the tears overcome me, as I sat there waiting for Tom Ferris to come back with the British remedy for all ills, but one, I was afraid, that could do nothing for mine.

In the event I was wrong. The very banality of a brown pot of tea and the phrases that go with it are part of its soothing charm. I did feel better with my hands round a cup, and this was the tanned Indian brew of workmen and nursery. The memory of Leonard Wallace's disturbing tea ceremony stirred uneasily in me, but I looked across at Tom Ferris thrusting a poker into the flames to quicken them into fiercer life and was reassured.

'Did you find what you were looking for?'

'Sorry?'

'In the garden; whatever made the noise.'

'No, no, I didn't. Maybe there wasn't anything really and I just dreamt it.'

'Next time you really shouldn't go out looking. Given what's been happening in this town it's foolhardy, to say the least.'

'I know. I wasn't thinking. Half–asleep, I expect. That's why I forgot the key.' I would have to put up with his thinking me a fool because I couldn't tell him the truth.

'Would you please promise me not to do such a thing again but to ring me at any time you have an impulse to wander about the garden in the middle of the night?'

'What if I'm a sleepwalker?'

'Are you?'

'I don't know. Perhaps I'm a half–asleep–walker.' I knew that this must sound like the gibberings of an idiot, but there seemed nothing else I could say. He must think me the kind of girl who asked for trouble and would earn and deserve only his contempt. I didn't want Tom Ferris to despise me, but in his sane presence my other life appeared even more absurd and unreal. It was as if from time to time I fell through a hole in the everyday world and emerged on the other side in a different dimension that made sense while I was part of it, but total nonsense once I had stepped back through again into *real* time and place.

I yawned ostentatiously. Tom Ferris stood up. 'Look, there's a perfectly good second spare room. Why don't you sleep in that?'

'Could I? Don't bother to make the bed. For what's left of the night I can just stretch out under a couple of blankets. I'm suddenly very tired.' I smiled apologetically.

All concern, he ushered me upstairs. Fortunately Mary's house was three–bedroomed. I knew I couldn't have faced her own room, but I thought sheer fatigue would knock me out if I could just lie down. And I was absolutely right. When I woke again, it was to Tom Ferris bringing me in a fresh cup of tea. I sat up, feeling the usual sense of personal squalor that follows sleeping in one's day clothes, even though I was wearing my nightdress under them.

'You slept anyway.'

'Yes, like a log. What time is it?'

'Eight o'clock.'

'Are you usually an early riser?'

He laughed. 'Yes, I'm afraid so. I know it sounds very unattractive, but I usually get up about half—past seven and feel quite cheerful.'

'Why be afraid of that?'

'It doesn't seem very romantic, faintly boy—scoutish, or even schoolmasterly.'

'What do you do?' I sipped my tea.

'I work on the oilfields.'

'Oh, I know. You wear one of those rather fetching helmets and shout: "There she blows!" '

'That was for whales. The Greenland fishery.'

'But I thought the oilmen had taken it over.'

'I suppose we're the modern equivalent of the old whalers, especially in the North Sea. Less dashing, perhaps, but at least we don't have to stab animals to death for our oil.'

I liked that. 'I think it's just as dashing. I used to love American films about drilling for oil. They don't seem to make them any more.'

'That's because everyone's doing it now. It's no longer very unusual.'

I sighed. 'Nowadays you'd have to make one about the creature from the deep disturbed by an oilman who rises up to take his revenge and bites the legs off the platforms.'

'Don't! It's only too possible,' Tom Ferris said, but he was laughing.

I began to think it was time I got up. It suddenly struck me as a little odd to be sitting there in bed laughing with a man I barely knew. As if he had sensed it too, he turned towards the door. 'If you want any help with breaking and entering, let me know. I used to be quite good at it as a kid. No doubt it's like riding a bicycle, something you never forget.'

Tom Ferris insisted that we should have breakfast, before, as he put it, embarking on our new career as trainee burglars. I had to admit to myself that I rather enjoyed being made a fuss of. Perhaps I was more like my mother than I had ever acknowledged to myself.

As we began on the ritual of orange juice followed by cereal and toast, that filled the room with the nostalgic smell of childhood winter teas by the fire, he said, 'I'm sorry to ask you, but I need some advice. It's about Cousin Mary's funeral.'

'As I said to you yesterday, I'm an expert. What's the problem?'

'I don't know where to start. Presumably the police will release the body in the next few days. Then what?'

'Theale and Partners,' I told him.

'And the funeral itself?'

'Mary went to church, so that'll be easy. The vicar will help.'

'But which church? The town is full of them.'

'I only know it's got a lot of Pre—Raphaelite stuff in it. But there'll be a parish magazine somewhere among her things. That'll give you the name.'

'That's it. Sure to be. I knew you'd solve it for me.'

'One good turn ... ' I said, biting into a piece of toast.

'I feel a bit as if we're two orphans,' Tom Ferris said, as we retraced my steps of the night before. 'When you come to think of it, it's an unpromising way to meet, both in mourning, as it were. How long will you stay?'

'I can't decide what to do. My aunt left the house to me. Logically I should do as you're doing: put it up for sale and go back to London. But I keep putting it off. Where do you live?'

'Well, I've been up in Aberdeen for a few months, but my job's nearly finished, so they'll be sending me back to head office in London soon, while they decide what next to do with me.'

'It sounds a very mobile sort of life.'

'Yes. It's as well I'm by myself. I've seen a lot of marriages

172

crack under the strain.'

We had reached the gate and the path down. I led the way. As we turned the cliff shoulder and the two great bowls of sea and sky were laid before us, I heard him catch his breath behind me.

'I can see how you might want to hang onto this for when the streets get too narrow.'

'It's fantastic, isn't it? I'm sure that's why Aunt Meg lived here against all the well—meant advice of my family. And here's the bungalow we have to break into.'

'It's got a lot more charm than Cousin Mary's. I'd probably find it hard to part with too. Now we need a weapon. Let's reconnoitre just in case a window's open.' He went up to the front door and put his shoulder to it. 'Nothing doing there.'

In a way I was relieved. It would have been too humiliating if it had opened at a touch. I led the way round to the back.

'We might find a spade or something in the garden.'

'Not the ideal implement for forcible entry, but it'd do. What's in that box?' He pointed to the box under the verandah steps and moved towards it.

'Sticks for lighting the fire. I don't think they'd be heavy enough.'

Tom Ferris lifted the piece of sacking from the top. 'What about that? Just the job.'

The little axe looked up at him wickedly. For a moment I thought I was going to faint. It was quite clean, but as I looked, bright spots of blood blossomed on it and the air was full of cries and shouts. Tom Ferris's hand reached out towards it. I wanted to cry out too, but no sound would come. I couldn't bear to see Mary's blood stain his hand. He picked it up. The blood faded. The crying died away.

'This'll do fine. Now which shall I break, front or back?'

'Let's just go round to the front again.' I wanted to get away from the box.

'Are you alright? You're looking a bit rough.'

'I felt a bit sick suddenly.' That at least was the truth.

'My cooking, I expect.'

'It was only toast.'

'Ah—it's the thought that counts—or something.' I knew he was talking to give me time to recover as we went round the side of the house, and I was grateful. I clung on to the exchange of banalities, as if it was the rope banister against the cliff face. Even so in my overwrought state I almost cried out loud when I saw that the front garden was no longer empty but that Leonard Wallace was standing in front of the house in the green parka with the dark fur—lined hood Aunt Meg had described.

'Hallo, Paula. Having heard nothing from you since you came to tea and not getting an answer on the telephone this morning, I thought I'd come and see if you were quite well.'

I hardly knew how to answer. He looked at Tom Ferris, waiting for an introduction, and then at the little axe in his hand. His dark eyes were impenetrably opaque like wet slate. 'This is Tom Ferris, Mary Dunscombe's cousin. Leonard Wallace.'

'Hallo,' Tom said, waving the axe in greeting.

Leonard Wallace inclined his head. 'How do you do,' he said.

'I've locked myself out. Mr Ferris is helping me to break in.'

'Your aunt kept a spare key for such emergencies under a flowerpot in the back garden. Have you tried that?'

'Oh yes. I found that when I first came here. I'm afraid I never put it back.'

'It seems I'd better start on the window,' Tom said. I looked from one to the other and was struck by the contrast. Tom Ferris had commonplace blue—grey eyes and mousey hair, yet he too radiated a kind of energy as Wallace did. Suddenly the words of the evening collect we had used at school recited themselves in my head: *Lighten our darkness we beseech thee, O Lord* ...

'I've just remembered something,' I said. 'It's just a chance.' I turned to Tom. 'Did you bring Mary's keys with you?'

'I did indeed. I didn't want us to make the same mistake.'

Tom Ferris fished in his pocket and produced a sizeable assorted bunch.

'There's just a chance the keys to this house may be among them. I know Mary had a set.'

Tom handed them to me. 'They all look the same to me, but it's worth a try.' I began to work my way through the several versions of serrated edge. Mary must have kept every key she had ever possessed. At the third the lock turned and the door swung open.

'Hurray!' Tom Ferris set up a little mock cheer. 'I can postpone my career as a housebreaker. I'll just put this back.' He set off with the axe before I could stop him, leaving me alone with Leonard Wallace.

'Are you really alright, Paula? You look a little pale.'

'Yes, yes, thank you. I'm fine. I didn't get much sleep. I had to knock Tom Ferris up in the middle of the night and camp out there.'

'You said he was Mary Dunscombe's cousin. I wonder how effective he would have been with the axe.' His voice held a sneer, though I couldn't be precise about its implications. Now he looked down hard at me and the eyes were no longer flatly opaque. It was as if the shutters had been opened behind the camera lens and I could see myself deep far down drowning at the bottom of them—or rather, both my selves looking up and out of their darkness. He was saying something I couldn't quite hear. 'Goodbye then.' He raised his voice. Tom Ferris was coming back round the corner of the house. 'I'll telephone you tomorrow and fix something up. Goodbye.' He waved a hand at Tom in a kind of salute and turned back up the path.

'Can I offer you some coffee since you've come all this way?' I asked Tom. 'And then perhaps we should go back to Mary's and begin the sorting, once I've seen that Tiger's okay. He'll be wanting his breakfast.'

We spent the rest of the day in parcelling up the remains of Mary's life. At one point, Tom went off to see the vicar of St Martin's leaving me alone in the house amid piles of old cardigans, woolly vests and carefully darned and rolled

175

stockings; but I felt no qualms about being there by myself. Whatever evil had been done, the gentle spirit of Mary emanating from the very frailty of her old clothes dispelled it for me completely.

'The vicar says he'll take the lot with pleasure. I'm sorry to take up more of your time, but if we stuffed them into something we could run them over to the church hall. They're rather conveniently having a jumble sale on Saturday.'

'Black bags—that's the answer.' And then, as he looked puzzled, 'rubbish sacks. I expect she's got a drawer full somewhere.'

And she had. In the end we needed both our cars to take them all to St Martin's. 'I was going to ask you to have dinner with me in the town as a kind of thank you, but I'm wondering if you're too tired,' Tom said, when we had both drawn up beside his gate again.

'I am tired,' I admitted, 'but I'd love to. It would seem such a civilised thing to be doing.' I laughed. 'Does that sound absurd?'

'Not a bit. It'll do us both good. I'll be chauffeur. I'll pick you up at seven–thirty. I asked the vicar where was good to eat. He recommended the Golden Oriole or the Del Mare. Unless you prefer Indian or Chinese?'

'I think some nice fattening soothing pasta would suit me best. Let's go to the Del Mare.'

Scarborough bay had suddenly become the Bay of Naples. 'All it needs is Vesuvius,' Tom whispered, as the waiter went off to fetch the menu.

'I find Italian restaurant tat very comforting,' I said. 'I'm such a sucker for it that I feel myself transported as soon as I see the Chianti bottles in their straw jackets and smell the garlic. It's like being on instant holiday.'

We talked easily of places we had visited until the waiter came back, bowing over the menus and offering apéritifs. 'I'd like a Punt é Mes without ice but with lemon.'

'That sounds very authentic. Can I be a copycat?' Tom asked.

'Join the club. It isn't always easy to get them to leave the

176

ice out, but it's well worth it.'

'Mm.' Tom sipped at the spicy wine. 'Very good. Next time I have to take someone out on a business lunch, I shall stun them with my expertise.'

'What do you really do?'

'I'm a sort of consultant. I took a degree in marine biology and oceanography.'

'Oceanography always reminds me of Portuguese navigators and *The Lusiads*. Very romantic. I can see the oil companies would want to consult you about the North Sea. Who else?'

'Anyone who wants or needs to know. Not that I know much. No one does. We still have very little real information about what goes on down there. I know as much, that is as little, as anyone. Governments often need to know for defence and people laying cables—that sort of thing. And now commerce is getting interested in the idea of farming the seabed.'

'Nothing is to be left untouched by human hand.'

Tom Ferris sighed. 'No. It won't be left alone for long. That's why it's so important to see that whatever is done is done carefully and with proper concern for ecological factors; otherwise we'll end up with poisoned seas and a lot of dead plants and animals. We're quite capable of turning the whole ocean into a vast Dead Sea. I'm sorry—you must stop me, or I'll be off on my hobby–horse.'

'I imagine it as a big seahorse, with you perched on its back, like Tom in *The Water Babies*.'

'If I open my mouth again you must pop in a stone, like Mrs Whatsit'

'Bedonebyasyoudid.'

'That's it.'

'Have an olive instead. It has a stone in the middle.'

'And now you must tell me what you do,' he said, taking one. 'That's the rules of the game.'

'Have a guess.'

'Well, you're very imaginative. I'd guess you studied something like English.'

'Right first time.' I told him about the college, my year's sabbatical and class in Victorian fiction. Then we argued for a bit about snobbery in Dickens. She was far away and I had Tom Ferris all to myself.

'Tell me,' Tom said, 'did the police come to see you about Cousin Mary? I feel I ought to do something, at least check that they went through all the correct motions.'

'Yes, they did. Three of them. But there wasn't much I could tell them, except that I'd left her about five and she was alright then.' It wasn't quite a lie, more a sin of omission.

'You say Mary was the third?'

'Yes.' I stopped a forkful of spaghetti on its way to my mouth. It hung there in midair, dangling an entrail of pasta coated in tomato sauce. All the horror of the night before flooded over me. It had become an uneasy dream barely remembered during the day. Now I wondered if it had happened or not. How could I have pushed it all away and be calmly sitting here eating dinner if it was real? Surely that argued that I had dreamt it.

'Are you okay?' Tom Ferris was asking. 'Is there something wrong with that spaghetti?'

'No, no. It's fine.' I carried it to my lips. 'I'm sorry, I must be tired. I went off in a dream.'

'I'll take you home as soon as we've finished, and you must promise me to stay in bed until seven o'clock at least. No more nightwalking.'

'I promise.'

From then until the end of the meal he kept off anything in the least disturbing, guiding me into safe channels that I could almost see lying between sunlit banks. By the time we got into the car I felt totally relaxed.

He insisted on walking me down the path and watching while I opened the door. 'I'll ring you in the morning to make sure you didn't go for a midnight ramble.'

'I'm much too sleepy. Thank you for my delicious supper.' I yawned like a child up too late at a party. The next day we planned to try some of the antique shops in town to see if they would be interested in valuing Mary's furniture, though it might be weeks before its ownership was sorted out and the lawyers had had their ponderous way. With more huge yawns, I fed Tiger and switched on the television while he scoured his plate. They had reached the regional news and my mind was barely focused on the evenly–paced drone until the announcer said quite distinctly, '...Scarborough.'

I went forward and turned up the sound. Police were refusing to comment on the fourth in a series of brutal murders. It was hard to imagine an unbrutal one, my mind rambled. The body of a woman had been found on the South Cliff golf links. I switched it off and sat in front of the blank screen, trembling and sick.

So it was all true, and no dream. I could see the woman's tranced face uplifted for the fall of the blade. I knew that when I saw her photograph in the next day's paper I would recognise her. The headsman had carried her into the boathouse and then, by some means, to the golf course where the body had been left, and found.

All day I had thrust it out of my mind under the influence of Tom Ferris's commonsense, told myself it hadn't really happened. Now I knew I had been deceiving myself, as well as him. I didn't live in his real world, but in my own wraith–haunted twilight. I wept then, like a child seeing the party through the glass of the shut door. Inside, all was warmth, laughter, presents and the table laden with cake and jelly, while I stood outside in the grey chill of a Winter afternoon, forbidden to either give or receive. I should never come at reality, never put together my fragmented personality. The death she signalled was death in life.

Or was it? Thinking back to the rites I now knew I had really witnessed, it seemed as if each mistress reigned only for a short time and was then 'replaced'. I used that word to myself because I couldn't face the truth. Had all the other women except Mary been mistresses in their turn?

I got up from my chair in front of the television and began to search Aunt Meg's shelves for a book, or rather a series of volumes I was sure would be there somewhere. There they were: *The Golden Bough* by Sir James Frazer, all twelve volumes. I had, of course, known about them for years. Once I had even looked through them in search of background to the study of the poems of W.B. Yeats when I was a student, and I had been left with a residual memory of part of their contents that I was now trying to pin down.

Taking down the volume called *Adonis*, I carried it back to the fire and read the story of the young god who is sacrificed as a fertility priest–king, the lover of the goddess who must be renewed every year to nourish the earth. Where his blood fell anemones sprang up, purple and deep red from his rich veins. That had been in a society where a goddess was supreme. But in a society that worshipped the male principle, wouldn't the roles be reversed, and the woman, the mistress, become the fertility sacrifice just as I had seen on the jetty?

If that was so, then surely it was she who would die, not me. It was she, my other, my co–walker as the book had it, who had been proclaimed mistress, while I stood alone at the top of the steps. And if the headsman killed her, then wouldn't I be free or were we so intertwined that, like Siamese twins, one couldn't survive if the other died, unless they were physically sundered? My mind was blurred and heavy with trying to tease out an answer. I knew I had to sleep, as I had promised Tom Ferris I would; indeed, I knew I couldn't keep awake any longer. Tiger was off somewhere after his supper. I would leave the catdoor open for him. I got up and put the *Adonis* volume back among its siblings.

Even so, I was afraid to sleep, afraid to lie down, without Tiger's reassuring presence beside me. But I had no choice. My limbs were heavy as if I had been drugged and my mind seemed to be gradually revolving like a mobile in a draught of air, turning gently, the fish shapes swimming on the ends of their fine tethers as the current dictated. I climbed the stairs wearily, fumbled myself out of my clothes and into my nightdress, and fell into a deep sleep as soon as I had brought my chilled arm back under the bedclothes from putting out the bedside light.

Did I dream or was I 'broadwaking' when the incubus came to me? Moonlight lay in the room, making it a silver pool—moonlight so rare in that Autumn and early Winter that it seemed as if the sea itself threw up a mother of pearl reflection at the sky from the glinting of some great open oyster shell on the ocean bed. Even as I lay there, I sensed its approach—or so it seems to me now, with hindsight.

It was coming from the cove, mounting the steps and the path and then the steps again, the sea moonlight roiling on the wet, dark skin as the muscles flexed, heaving its bulk up towards me. I wanted to throw off the bedclothes and get out of bed and out of the house, but when I tried to move I became aware of her lying at full length through my body, weighting it down. I was the empty skin, and she was wrapped in me like a heavy–fleshed fruit.

'Lie still, Paula. It's no good your struggling. I have the strength and power. You're nothing but a husk.'

I heard the front door give below and a rubbery shuffling in the hall. I always slept with my door ajar, so I could hear it quite clearly bumping its way up the stairs, snorting and blowing. It was outside the door and still I couldn't move. She pinned me down, whispering to me, while the air seemed to be filled with a roaring and drumming. A wet, dark shoulder heaved the door open and it reared itself up inside the bedroom at the edge of my vision. A sharp reek of the sea filled the room. Unable even to turn my head, I half–saw the shadow moving towards the bed.

The strange light caught on wetly gleaming surfaces and on the brown, fleshy trails of weed in which it was decked for its wedding. It was from these that the strong ozone smell came.

'I am a man upon the land,
I am a silkie in the sea ...'

A wet, coldly–webbed dark hand drew back the bedclothes and I felt *her* press me harder down against the mattress. The same chill fingers pulled up my nightdress. I could hardly breathe and my heart pounded as if it would burst. The shape lowered itself towards me and laid its rank, cold rubbery skin to mine. The trails of weed rubbed against my breasts, the

181

hind flippers were thrust between my legs, forcing them apart.

And then I felt her begin to exult through our flesh as the cold probe prodded at me, thrusting hard, so that I cried out in pain while it reared up a little the better to thrust hard down again. A little strength came to me and I pushed against the slippery bulk, but my hands could get no purchase and I half–fell, and was half–pushed back.

I tried to cry out, but the sounds were choked back under the weight, although tears ran down my face. It rose and fell on me like the sea on the beach and my nose and mouth were filled with the smell of salt weed and decaying flesh at the tideline. She raised herself in me, thrusting up our thighs and looking up boldly, her own breath beginning to come fast, as it had done once before.

The anonymous round black head with the slit eyes, ray's baby mouth and round nostrils, was melting above me as she began to thrust against the cold limbs. First it became a mockery of Martin, a Martin sneering as he had never done as he tried to love me. Then it dissolved again into the dark, wolfish features of Leonard Wallace, bearing me down and whispering:

'You will come, Paula. I shall make you.'

And finally and most terrible, my father seemed to loom above me, thrusting hard into me, while she rose against him and I felt the cold fire beginning to spread from my bruised flesh into my thighs and belly, running along my veins as the creature grunted and bored, roaring and flinging itself on me. Faster and faster she drove us against it, until I heard my voice too begin to cry out, felt myself fighting against it for more and more, harder and harder, until I was drowned in a great wave of lust and flung panting and bruised on the shore, with the tide still sucking the last spasms from me before I lost consciousness.

182

Five

My mind had shut itself against ever waking but sometimes the body is stronger; its clocks go on ticking quietly away in the blood and the alarm eventually trips, jarring the brain into consciousness. When I woke, recovered my senses, whichever it was, my face, hair and the pillow were sodden with tears. For a few moments I lay there with the half–memory of my monstrous dream a dark shadow at the back of my mind, a shadow that as sleep receded didn't fade as dreams usually do, but lengthened into the foreground. Trying to shake it off, I pushed back the bedclothes, sat up shivering in the unheated room and reached for my dressing–gown. As I pulled it round me and fumbled for the tie, my eye focused on the stretch of floor between the bed and the door.

Almost indistinguishable at first against the brown boards, and to my tear–swollen eyes, lay a limp, rubbery frond of seaweed. Full remembrance flooded over me—but still shot through with disbelief. It must have been a dream, or rather nightmare that I had ridden. A sudden image of a picture I had once seen somewhere came to me, a grotesquely deformed creature squatting on a girl's bed while she slept; and then another of a demonic horsehead rearing over her. Was it the same girl? My mind caught at this question like a drowning hand clutching at air. The answer didn't matter;

183

only that for a moment I should be able to turn my eyes aside from a reality I couldn't face.

I knew that if I searched the bedclothes I might find further confirmation, but I shrank back from that. Instead, I pulled the top sheet up over the pillows, threw back the blankets and rolled up top and bottom sheets into a bundle without looking at them although as I did so my fingers flinched as if I was rolling up a nest of reptiles or insects. Then I carried them into the bathroom where Aunt Meg's Heath Robinson washing machine lived and thrust them behind the glass door, sprinkled a shower of blue soap powder over them and switched on, praying that whatever obscene relics there might be would be tumbled away into the suds.

Back in the bedroom I picked up the dank frond between finger and thumb and threw it out of the window. Shaking and with teeth chattering, I returned to the backroom, stripped and sank through a hot, scented foam into the cleansing waves of the bathwater. But the soft warm embrace reminded me of that other chill, dank covering and I couldn't look at the body that had betrayed me into her lust and jerked and cried out with pleasure. My thighs throbbed again and I could hardly breathe. I stood up shakily and wrapped myself up out of sight in a large towel.

In the mirror above the washbasin my eyes were hollowed out and my skin blotchy. I cleaned my teeth and spat as if I had sucked on poison. The telephone rang as I was finishing dressing, but I didn't try to answer it. I couldn't bear to speak to anyone. They might guess from my voice, or their eyes might somehow see through to my nakedness and shame. I crawled downstairs to the kitchen. I didn't feel like breakfast, but I made myself eat some muesli and milk.

It was Tiger who saved my sanity again by coming back from his night's travels. Perhaps he had been waiting outside until he heard me moving about in the kitchen. I picked him up and cradled him, and as he began to purr, the tears ran down my face once more and dripped into his fur, as they had done the other day on Tom Ferris's doorstep. How I longed for his sane presence and yet feared it. There was

184

nothing I could tell him. Whatever the truth of my experience, I could no more describe the obscene dream, if dream it was, than suggest that it had really happened. Both were unthinkable.

And then the thought came to me that it might come again. What was there to stop it? Night after night it could mount the stairs and lay its cold skin over me, until I was heavy with some monstrous birth. And I knew part of me would welcome it. Even at the thought, I felt my thighs begin to loosen and small flames flicker along them so that I could hardly stand. It even seemed wrong to be holding Tiger; I put him down as if he could sense my thoughts.

The telephone rang again. I would have to answer it sometime. I went through into the sitting room.

'Ah, Paula,' Leonard Wallace's voice said. 'I'm ringing to ask if you had a good night. I thought you looked a little pale and tired yesterday. I trust you feel better now.'

'Yes,' she said, and laughed. 'I had a very good night, thank you.'

'When can I expect you to come and see me again, to dinner perhaps? It's more grown up than tea.'

'I find your tea quite mature enough for my taste.'

'Good. Now when shall I see you?'

'I'll let you know. There's pleasure in anticipation.' She put down the receiver with another little laugh. Detaching herself from me, she went to sit in the armchair by the dead grate. 'You have Tom Ferris and I'll have Leonard Wallace. That way we're both happy. Only sometimes I might fancy a change, just to see what he's like.'

I wanted to protest, to cry out, but the doorbell was ringing. With a last look at her I turned towards the door. She smiled back at me. 'You'd better see who it is, Paula. They seem to want to come in.'

It was the young police inspector, but with only one accolyte this time.

'Miss Cockburn?'

'Yes.'

'I wonder if I might have a word with you.'

I held back the door. It was a politely worded request that seemed to offer the option of refusal, but I knew this was an illusion. 'Please come in.'

They came into the hall and I shut the door behind them and turned into the sitting room. Would she still be there? Would they see her? But the room was empty.

'Have you got time for a cup of coffee?'

'That would be very welcome. It's a cold morning.'

I hurried through making it, not liking to leave them alone too long. The unlettered spine of Aunt Meg's diary burned in my head. Suppose I hadn't put it back properly and it was sticking out from its camouflage?

When I carried the tray in, however, they were both sitting quietly staring at the ash in the hearth. 'I'm sorry it's so cold in here. I don't light the fire until afternoon.'

'The coffee will warm us up,' the inspector smiled, as he took a mug from the tray I held. I carried my own to an upright chair by the desk and perched on it. He took a sip and put down his mug on the carpet.

'As you may have heard, there's been another murder of a young woman.'

'I saw it on the news.'

'We haven't been idle since we last met, and now the scientific side have come up with some rather interesting results.'

I sat there sipping at my coffee and looking, I hoped, alert and interested like a good child.

'Analysis of material from the clothing of three of the victims indicates that they had been on the beach just before their deaths.'

'Three?'

'Not Miss Dunscombe. I was, if you remember, not convinced at the time that she was part of the same sequence.'

I said nothing, allowing him his moment of pride before I nodded.

'Now, the labs have compared the material with samples from along the whole foreshore and come up with a location.'

186

'How can they?'

'Apparently the currents and the nature of the rocks and so on make the stuff from North and South Bay sufficiently different under a microscope though not to the naked eye, of course.'

I nodded again. 'I see.'

'The upshot is that they've come down in favour of this stretch of coast, and we've put that together with ordnance survey maps and we're going over the ground again. Literally, this time. The constable is collecting samples for more precise analysis. The map seems to suggest that this cottage has its own bit of foreshore, with access.'

He made it sound like an estate agent's description of a desirable amenity. 'Yes, it does. There's a little cove with a jetty and boathouse. The path is very steep. I don't imagine my aunt used it much.'

'We'd like to see it, if we might.'

Again the request was polite, but not to be refused. I fought down my pedant's desire to correct his grammar. What right had I to feel superior to this young man whose patient work had brought him to the verge of my grotesque secret?

'Of course. I'll take you down there as soon as we've finished our coffee.' I wondered whether he could sense my disturbance. When the doorbell rang again I almost dropped my mug. 'Excuse me. I'll just see who it is.'

I could have hugged Tom Ferris's solid shape. 'I saw the police car by your gate and wondered if there were any developments. I hope you don't mind.'

'I'm so glad to see you.' I almost pulled him into the hall. 'Will you have some coffee? I led him into the sitting room. The inspector put down a map he had been studying and stood up.

'Inspector, this is Mr Ferris, Miss Dunscombe's cousin. He's staying in her cottage to sort things out.'

'How do you do, sir.'

'How do you do. I saw your car and wondered if there had been any new developments.'

'You're Miss Dunscombe's cousin, sir?'

'Well, my father is—was. I'm a second, I suppose. He's getting on a bit, so I said I'd come down. He was rather upset by it all, even though they didn't meet much.'

'It was an upsetting business even for us, and we're supposed to be used to it.'

'I'll just get Mr Ferris some coffee.'

I left them to it and went with relief into the kitchen. When I returned with the steaming mug, the two of them were looking at the map.

'Did you know you have a private beach, Paula?' Tom asked.

'Oh yes. I went down soon after I arrived; just followed the path to see where it went.'

'The inspector says that on old maps it's called Silky Cove. It seems an odd name for it. Perhaps the sand is very fine.'

I handed him the mug, or I might have dropped it. 'I think it means "seal cove",' I said as matter–of–factly as I could. 'It's the old word for seal. Norse, I think. The Vikings brought it.'

'Do seals come this far South? I always think of them in the Scottish islands.' The inspector looked up from his map.

'Oh, yes. They go down as far as the Wash, and anyway, it must have been all different when the cove was named. There were probably seals all round our coasts.'

'Yes, that's right.' Tom nodded. 'The inspector says he's even less satisfied that Mary's death was part of the same pattern. He thinks the others were killed on a beach somewhere and then dumped inland.'

'I know.' We looked at each other as if we were in some way conspirators hiding something but there was nothing for Tom Ferris to hide. I was the only guilty one.

'Well, sir, if you've finished, we'll go down and take a look.' The inspector folded his map and stood up. I collected my coat from the hall and led the way through the kitchen and out of the back door. I hoped Tiger wouldn't be driven away forever by the procession of trampling male feet. We crossed the lawn and went through the far gate onto the path.

188

Conversation became mercifully impossible as we were strung out down the face of the cliff, holding on to the rope rail. Whatever they might find at the bottom the affair was out of my hands. I was being carried along like an empty plastic bottle brought in on the tide and spewed out on the high water mark as it receded.

The constable looked a little green by the time we reached firm ground. The insepctor glanced at him. 'You alright, Marshall?'

'No head for heights, sir. I'll be OK now.'

'It'll be easier going up. Just keep looking at the person in front. Don't look back.'

I thought it might have been a recipe for life he was offering. 'That's the jetty with the boathouse, I take it. Is there a boat inside?'

'I don't think so.'

He moved towards it, and we followed. In the daylight the cove looked bleak and grey and it was hard to recreate it in the lurid dress of the other night. Perhaps they were the colours of a nightmare painting after all. But then the girl's face swam at me, a face I couldn't have seen elsewhere. If there was anything in the old stories, her blood ought to cry out from the concrete of the jetty. But instead there was only the mewing of gulls high above and the restless slap of waves on rock. We all followed the inspector up the few steps and across to the boathouse.

'Do you have a key to the padlock?' he asked conversationally. 'It looks quite new.'

'I've never seen one. There's nothing that would fit it on the ring with the other keys.' I pulled them out of my pocket and showed him.

'You've never seen anything among your aunt's things that could fit this?'

'She was fairly methodical; she'd have kept anything like that either with her other keys, or in her desk, or hanging up by the back door where it would be handy. I haven't looked for it, but I'm pretty sure it isn't in any of those places.'

He stared at the door. 'I suppose she could have let it to

someone for fishing or sailing. I'd like to see inside.' He moved to the stained window and tried to peer in as I had done. 'Would you give me your permission to break in if we can't find the key, Miss Cockburn?'

'Of course. There must be an exit to the sea at the back. If we had a boat we could try that way.'

'We could batter the padlock off with a stone,' Tom said, 'but it would take some time without a proper lever.'

'Perhaps Miss Cockburn could have a good hunt for the key; then, if she hasn't found it by tomorrow, we could bring along the right tools. I don't think there's much we can do here now, except for you to take a sample of the sand for analysis, Marshall.'

'Yes, sir.'

We waited while the constable gathered sand from different points on the foreshore into transparent envelopes and then formed our procession for climbing up, with Marshall tactfully manoeuvred into the middle of the line. The wind had grown stronger and specks of rain like ice darts stung our skin as we climbed.

'I'll ring you in the morning to see if you've had any luck with finding the key. If not, I'll ask you to accompany us to break in.'

'Can I come too, inspector?' asked Tom.

'I don't see why not, sir. Another witness is always useful.'

When they had gone, Tom Ferris and I stood in the hall, listening to the risen wind.

'Are you okay?' he asked, looking down at me.

'Yes. I didn't sleep very well.'

'I didn't sleep much either. I've got to go down into town to fix up a few things. Can I ring you when I get back?'

'Yes, please. I'd better start looking for that key.'

I saw him off up the path and went back into the house. I was almost sure there wasn't any key. After all, Meg hadn't put that padlock on. She had wanted to break into the boathouse herself to see what was in there, and if she'd lived she might have done so. No. There couldn't be any key to it in the house unless someone else had put one there since. I held on to the key and its whereabouts as an antidote to the horror that threatened to overwhelm me every time I had nothing else to occupy the surface of my mind, a horror that seemed to me equal, whether it was based on a real event or in an imagination so sick as to be able to conceive it. I would start by looking in the desk, just to say that I had tried.

She was sitting in the armchair again when I came through the doorway. 'I think Tom Ferris is falling in love with us,' she said, holding out her hand and thumbing the jet band, as a girl does to admire her engagement ring. 'And then there's the young inspector. Really Paul, I don't know what they see in you. I think I should let Leonard know they're taking an interest in the cove.' She reached for the telephone and dialled. I could do nothing but watch as she told him of the police visit. I could hear his voice quite distinctly, as if it was wired into my head.

'You did right to let me know.'

I wanted to snatch the receiver from her and slam it down on the rest, but I felt bodiless, drained of all power to act. She had taken my limbs and was moving them to her will. I had become an onlooker to my own actions. I heard her arrange to go to Five Ways tomorrow for supper, and then the telephone was silent as she replaced the black arm.

'What are you doing? I don't want to go to that house again.'

'But *I* do. I find it intriguing, exciting. It's my kind of place.'

'It frightens me.'

'Most things do. But I'm the mistress now. I have the power. Why should I be afraid?'

'That's what all those other women thought.'

'Local girls who didn't understand: waitresses and barmaids. Besides, you don't know that Leonard has anything to do with that. You didn't see him at the cove.'

'He could have been there. You couldn't tell who was behind the masks.'

'Why should he harm me, and in his own house? The inspector said all the women were killed on the beach.'

'Except Mary.'

'She was a silly old woman, just the sort of old woman you'll be if I don't take you in hand.' She stood up and came towards me. I knew that as she had that first time on the beach, she meant to suck me down inside her and I faced her across the room.

'I won't let you. Tom Ferris will ring me soon and you shan't have him too.'

'Who'll stop me, Paula?'

'I will. I can. I can hold you there. I can make you go away if I try. You're nothing. I'm the real Paula. See: you're growing fainter. I can see the room behind you, right through you. If I concentrate I can do it.'

She was shimmering and wavering before me like a gauze curtain shaken in a draught. While I stared her down her features were growing transparent as if painted on glass and only visible when the light strikes at a certain angle. I began to move towards her in my turn.

Suddenly the shrill of the telephone cut into the room. 'That will be Tom and I shall speak to him alone.' I reached out a hand to the receiver, passing it through the translucent shape. All substance had drained away from her until now there was just an outline on the air that, as I heard his voice, trembled around me and began to break and fade, leaving only the echo of where it had been, like an image held behind closed eyes.

His voice was cut off by a barrage of pips. He must be in a phone box. I heard him press in a coin and the pipping stopped.

'Paula?'

'Where are you?'

'I'm in a pub. I suddenly got very worried about you and felt I had to ring. You looked so tired this morning. Are you alright?'

I could hear the concern in his voice. It was a long time since I had heard that note of genuine caring from anyone. It almost made me cry. 'Yes, I'm fine. But I'm glad you rang. I was feeling a bit low.' It was near enough to the truth.

'Perhaps you should go back to bed. Did you have any luck with the key?'

'No, none at all.'

'I've found what I think is the same padlock in the hardware department of Boyes—that is, if my eye's right and I've remembered it correctly. I've bought one with its key. I thought we might anticipate our inspector friend and have a look in the boathouse ourselves. That's always supposing it is the same lock.'

I was silent. I would really have preferred to investigate alone. Who knew what we might find?

'Are you there, Paula?'

'Yes. I was just thinking how clever of you. Why don't you bring it here when you've finished in town and we can have a look together, if it isn't too dark.'

'Fine, I'll do that. Take care of yourself.'

She was right about one thing: Tom Ferris was falling in love with me. The moment would soon come when he would want to kiss me. Perhaps it already had. But soon he would try. How would I respond? Again, the memory of last night sucked at me. I had no right to take love from anyone, to encourage them to love someone who one minute was frigid, and the next conjured up such foully erotic phantoms.

It was two o'clock before Tom rang Aunt Meg's doorbell. The sky was a sheet of dull zinc, heavy with unshed rain or snow.

He came into the hall stamping and blowing like a horse back from a cold morning canter.

'That looks good,' he said, holding his hands out to the sitting room blaze. 'It's a nice room when the fire's roaring away up the chimney like that.'

'Do you believe houses have an atmosphere?'

'Yes, I do because I've felt it, but I can't account for it scientifically. Still, there's such a lot we don't know yet about physical laws. Energy, for instance. Even the old idea of an "aura" turns out to have an existence in terms of an electrical field that can be detected and measured. Perhaps the clue to the atmosphere in a house is there somewhere. Anyway, I think I know what you're getting at and, yes, this house does have a good atmosphere. There's nothing menacing or cold about it. In fact, I rather wish we didn't have to go down to the cove but could just stay here by the fire.'

'We don't *have* to go'.

'But we should, and if we didn't we'd kick ourselves after. Let's get it over with.'

'You don't think we could be accused of interfering with the course of a police investigation, do you?'

'Well, if we find anything, which I honestly think is unlikely, we won't touch it. Do you think it's irresponsible to go down there at all? Maybe it's just childish curiosity.'

He looked at me for a decision, and I was caught. I wanted to know, needed to know what was down there, and although I would have liked to search alone, I realised that this was impossible and that I would either have to go now with Tom or accompanied by the inspector as well tomorrow.

'No, I don't think so. As you say, if we find anything we won't touch it, and we *are* two of the people most concerned; Mary was your cousin and my aunt's best friend, and the cove is my property, even if I do find that a strange idea and very hard to get used to.'

'I think the inspector's right and Mary's murder *is* a different case although I think too that whoever killed her hoped it might be taken as all part of the same series.'

A chill of my old confusion went through me, even though I no longer believed I had killed her myself. In some way I still felt I was guilty but I wasn't sure how or whether it wasn't just part of the general burden of guilt I carried about with me.

'We'd better go before it gets any darker. Have you got a torch, Paula? It'll be quite dark in the boathouse.'

We shuffled ourselves into coats and I took the torch my methodical aunt had kept by her bed. The sky lay so heavy on the earth and sea that we seemed to be climbing down a dull metal funnel towards the beach. I led the way, very conscious of Tom's breathing and the scrabble of his feet behind me. If only we had been carrying a picnic down to the cove in the height of that mythical English summer that never comes but is part of our imaginings, instead of looking for murder clues in our bleak midwinter.

The sea unfurled along the little beach in long, slow, asphalt waves. We stood still for a moment, looking out across them to the horizon.

'Do you think there really were seals here?' Tom said, digging his hands deep into his pockets.

'I thought I saw one once, right out there.' I waved towards the leaden line where the two tones of grey met, almost expecting to see it broken by a black blob.

Tom set off towards the boathouse and I followed him, my eyes searching the ground for telltale signs, though I had no idea what form they might take. We went up the concrete steps of the jetty and over to the door. Tom fished in his pocket and pulled out the padlock with its key dangling from the hooped arm by a rubber band. He held it up against the one on the boathouse. They were a perfect match.

'You were clever to remember so clearly.' I knew that my own memory would have been blurred and useless.

'In we go,' he said, turning the little silver key in the lock and unhooking it from the catch. The door gave a groan as he pushed against it. 'You could tape that sound and sell it to the BBC for Mystery Playhouse,' he laughed. I knew he was trying to reassure me, and was grateful. I wished I knew him well enough to take his arm for comfort. Leonard Wallace would have taken mine, but Tom, I was instinctively sure, would think such a gesture impertinent. At the thought of Wallace my heart began to thud and panic threatened to choke me. What would we see inside? Would she be standing there and would Tom see her?

He disappeared into the wooden hut while I stood outside, unable to move. Then I heard his voice. 'Well, there's nothing here that I can see. A bit of a let—down really. Come and look.'

I moved at last, drawn by his call. At first I could hardly see anything except for the two squares of fainter grey which were the stained window and the open end of the boathouse.

Then I saw the little spotlight of the torch in Tom's hand. He played it over the walls and then onto the concrete slipway, divided by a narrow channel of water for a boat to come in and overhung by a Heath Robinson contraption of metal spars that I presumed were to lift a boat from the water.

The smell of seawater, fungus and weed was very strong. It seemed to envelop me and pour into my mouth and nostrils like a rank tide. I heard Tom's voice coming from a distance.

'There's plenty of this, but that's all.' He shone the torch onto a spot at his feet and bent forward to pick something up which he held out to me, letting the light fall on its slippery skin. It was a long, flat frond of brown weed, a leathery tentacle that dangled obscenely from his hand. I heard myself give a little cry and then I turned and stumbled to the door.

I leant against the outside of the hut and gulped at the air. Tom was beside me in a moment. 'What is it? Are you alright?'

'I'm sorry: I think it was the smell. I suppose I should have expected it, but it seemed so ... so fetid.' I was glad that he had dropped the thong of weed in his haste. In the torchlight it had almost seemed alive, a sea serpent that might writhe and strike, yet I knew that that wasn't what had made me cry out. It had been the memory of last night, and the brown plastic thing I had found on the bedroom floor in the morning.

'I'd better lock up again. I suppose there may be clues the forensic experts could sift out, but if he's looking for anything spectacular our inspector is going to be disappointed.'

I wondered what I had expected. The silkie throne? The sacrificial knife? It was almost dark now. We began to climb back up the cliff. I heard my own breathing and the thud of my heart. This was physical reality, not the effortless, tranced motion I knew when following her. All my life I had shunned reality, until now it was the only thing that held out a lifeline, a real rough, twisted rope that would bruise and blister my hands if I grasped it. And I would have to give up that other silken twine of illusion that I had always clung to with part of me, unable to confront the world without it. Now a choice

196

had to be made, but I didn't know whether I was strong enough. I had a sudden picture of myself as a series of snapshots spinning in dark water and being washed under. That was how Aunt Meg had seen me.

Instinctively I knew that if I stayed alone in the house my last night's visitor would come again tonight to further consummate its power, and that *she* would welcome it plunging me deeper into illusion. I had to get away from them both.

'You'll come in for a cup of tea before you go back?'

'Yes, please.'

I sat him down in the sitting room in front of the fire and went into the kitchen to make tea. Tiger came through his private entrance, ignored me and stalked out of the kitchen. In a few seconds I heard Tom's voice greeting him. By the time I went in with a dish of buttered crumpets, Tiger was sitting on Tom's knee, while he seemed to be reading to the purring cat.

'You don't know how honoured you are. Tiger's an anti–male chauvinist beast.'

'He knows that I know that any man who isn't a macho he–man caricature has a strong dash of the feminine in him.'

'Are you reading him a story?'

'In a way. I found this dictionary of fairies and I was just turning the pages and picking out unconsidered trifles. I hope you don't mind. If I see a bookcase when I'm left alone I have to take out a book or two. It's a very special form of kleptomania.'

'I think everyone who likes books finds themselves caught the same way. I know I do.'

'This one's quite extraordinary. I can't decide whether it's meant for adults or children.'

'Adults. My aunt was a folklorist. I expect she contributed to it. Tiger could probably tell us if he would.'

'There's no entry under "cats". I've looked.'

'Try "fairy animals".'

He turned the pages. 'Here we are: horses, dogs, bulls. Oh—look here's your silkie, but spelt with an 'e': "of

197

miscellaneous creatures, the most famous were the seal people, the selkies and roane." Cats come next as "almost fairies in themselves". What about that, young Tiger?' He rubbed the cat's neck. 'Let's look up these silkies and the—what was it? Roane.'

I felt my stomach begin to churn as he flipped through the pages, reading me the stories of seal maidens who laid aside their skins to dance on the sands; of the fisherman who plunged from a crag into the depths of the sea to cure a seal he had wounded; and finally of the amorous males who came ashore to bed mortal women, leaving them with children who had webbed hands and feet …

'People seem to have thought of them as humans, or even angels made to wear animal skins as punishment for some crime. Perhaps the males needed the love of a good woman to save them.'

'Tom,' I said suddenly, 'can I ask you a favour?'

'Of course.' He put down his plate on the hearth, with its half–eaten crumpet.

'I know it sounds rather wet, but I'm a bit afraid of being alone in this house at night. Would you mind if I came and occupied your spare bed again? Say if it isn't convenient, won't you?'

'It's perfectly convenient, and I'll be glad of a bit of company. Why don't I cook us some supper?'

'You don't have to do that.'

'I'm not a bad cook; not *cordon bleu* or even what mother makes, but a competent bachelor.'

'Thank you. Can I bring Tiger? I don't want him to feel deserted.'

As soon as Tom had gone, I began to have doubts about what I had done. Would he think I was angling for something, or was he emancipated enough to take my request at its face value? If only we could have just been friends without the added complication of sex and social conditioning. Yet was that what I really wanted? Again I cursed my own confusion that was indeed my curse I had to carry about with me.

Tom had made a mushroom quiche. 'I cheated and bought frozen pastry,' he said, as he carried it in proudly.

'That's not cheating, not for the workers.' I had brought the wine as my contribution. After we had eaten, we sat with the remains of the bottle between us, listening to records on Mary's player: Dowland and Wilkes pouring their very English sweet sadness into the air.

'Paula,' he said, as the last notes seemed to hang in the room, 'I think I'm falling a bit in love with you.'

'You mustn't. I'm not worth it. I'm no good at love.'

He leant forward and took my hand. 'I think it's too late for me to stop. But don't worry. I'm fairly civilised and well—behaved. I promise not to be a nuisance.'

'It's not that. It's me. I'm not worth loving.'

'I don't think you're the best judge of that.'

'I am. I am.' But even as I said it I knew that I wanted him to love me, even if I had no right to his love and would probably make him as unhappy as I had made Martin. When we stood up to go to bed he put his arms around me and bent his mouth to meet mine. As I kissed him, the memory of that other lover, phantom or real, rose in me with a flame like phosphorus in water, and I felt my lips pressing against his fiercely and my arms holding him close. In that moment I knew not only that I wanted him to love me, but also to make love to me. Yet as quickly as it flared, it was doused again by a familiar cold flood. He let me go.

'Sleep well,' he said, and turned away, although I had felt him trembling with desire and frustration as I had held him close.

Lying in Mary's narrow guestroom bed, I wondered if he too was awake, staring into the dark. And then I felt my thoughts climb down the cliff to the cove and the nocturnal thing that might even now be hauling itself up the steps. What would it do when it found the house empty or would she lie there in my bed, waiting to receive it? At last the wine had its way and I fell asleep.

Tom was cheerful and friendly in the morning. He saw me and Tiger off before going to visit Mary's vicar, who was to

199

take the funeral service the next day.

'What are you doing this evening?' he asked.

I was about to say 'Nothing,' but then I remembered. 'I have to go out to dinner. I don't want to, but I can't get out of it.'

His face fell and then he made an effort to recover himself. 'I'll ring you tomorrow. That's if you don't mind?'

'Please. Will you forgive me for not coming to the funeral? It's just that I don't feel well enough—I mean, strong enough—to face it. You do understand? It's not that I shan't be thinking and knowing how awful it is for you.'

'I know. I do understand it might be upsetting so close after, and I don't want that.'

'Perhaps you can come down to me for supper. Soon I suppose, we shall both have to make up our minds what we're going to do.'

'My holiday is over at the end of the week. I could take a bit more. I've got some days left to me, but I'll have to go soon. Anyway, we'll talk about that tomorrow. Have a nice dinner.' He smiled and kissed my cheek. 'I'll telephone in the morning, or you ring me at any time of day or night if you feel worried about anything.'

I went off along the road with Tiger in my arms, both wrapped in the comforting aura of Tom's reassurance and concern. But as I put him down to let us in, the ginger fur at the back of his neck rose in a harsh ruff that stretched the length of his spine. I knew then that it had been there and I had been right to spend the night at Mary's. Once inside, I crossed the hall to the foot of the stairs and stood looking up. The house was filled with the reek from the boathouse.

Slowly I began to climb the stairs as if I were being drawn up on a rope. On the landing I stood still. The smell was even stronger and the door of my bedroom was open before me. I walked forward and stood on the threshold.

The room was a wreck. Bedding and small furnishings were thrown about, and strewn among them were long fronds of thick, muscular, brown weed. Something thwarted of its expectation had raged and torn at the bed, tables and chairs

200

in a maniacal fury, wrenched at its own coverings and tossed them away among the fragments of china and glass and the ripped sheets. The savagery of it stunned me. I seemed to hear its howls and snarls and to have heard them before, mixed with an old woman's screams. Instinctively I realised that whatever it was that had ravaged my room, the same blind fury had destroyed Mary and would have torn me apart if I had resisted.

It seemed to be able to come and go at night at will. What should I do this time? Could I ask Tom Ferris for sanctuary again? And then I remembered my dinner engagement, pushed to the back of my mind by the confusion before me, and the grim joke of Hamlet's when they asked him where the murdered Polonius was: "At supper. Not where he eats but where 'a is eaten."

I was invited but was I to be the diner or the dish? For somehow all these happenings were connected, I was sure, even though I had no proof and no thread of explanation to lead me through the labyrinth. I could refuse to go, run to Tom Ferris, who would be only too glad to put sheltering arms around me; but it would solve nothing. My own nature was somehow locked into the pattern, a fingerprint key that caused the doors to open in Bluebeard's castle where the bodies of murdered women dangled from meathooks. I had to confront it, to confront myself, if I was ever to be whole again.

'We're very brave all of a sudden.'

She had come silently into the room and was lounging against the doorframe. 'It must be the manly presence of Prince Charming. I trust you had a good night.'

'You don't seem to have done so well.'

'You reduced me to nothing, remember. Now it's angry. Next time it'll tear you apart.'

'How do you know there'll be a next time?'

'I shall see to it. It's my beast. I shall call it up if it's sulking and doesn't come of its own accord. After all, it is my husband.' She waved a black–ringed hand at me. 'Meanwhile, you can take me to see Leonard this evening. I shan't be left

201

behind again, I promise you.' She turned and went out of the door.

Wearily, I began to straighten the room, leaving the gathering—up of the fronds of weeds until last. Then I took a deep breath and with a picture of Tom Ferris held firmly in my head, I began to bundle them together so that I could carry the whole evil—smelling heap downstairs and out into the back garden to Aunt Meg's compost heap. I would have liked to burn or bury it, but it was too fleshily moist for one and the ground was too frost—hard for the other. I went in and washed my hands again and again, as if in some cleansing religious ritual.

The day dragged on. Several times I thought of telephoning to see if Tom was back; several times I thought I heard the phone ring. When at last it did shrill through the house, I ran to pick it up.

'I hope you've not forgotten our dinner date,' Leonard Wallace's voice said.

I was so taken aback by the unexpectedness of hearing his voice when I had been sure I would hear Tom that I could hardly answer. 'No, no, of course not.' A faint hope flickered that he might be ringing to cancel. And died.

'Good. I'll expect you about seven.'

When I put the receiver down, *she* was there watching me and smiling. 'Now, what shall we wear for this evening? I can't have you disgracing us in your old jeans and sweater. Come upstairs and let's look in the cupboards. Perhaps there's something suitable that you didn't send to the jumble sale. Come along, Paul.' She reached out a hand to mine and drew me towards the stairs. 'You've never looked in the attic.'

'There isn't one. There can't be. This house is really only an overgrown bungalow.'

'There's a space above the bedroom ceiling. Don't you remember that little door on the landing?'

I saw it now; an opening big enough for a child or an adult on hands and knees, with a small door fastened by a butterfly button. I crouched down in front of it and pulled it open. The light from the landing fell into the gap.

202

'Go on.'

'I can't get in. It's too small, and there's nothing in there anyway.'

'Go on.'

I crawled forward and poked my head through. There was a kind of platform across the steepest part of the roof and I could make out one or two dark shapes resting on it. It was like being deep in the hold of a wooden sailing ship. For a moment my old illusionary way took me, and I could hear the creak of timber, the slap of water and dead sailors' cries. The reek of the boathouse was very strong in the confined space.

'It's too dark. I need a torch.'

'There's a light switch just inside the door.'

I pressed, and the space was lit by a bulb in a metal cage at the end of a trailing flex.

'Methodical Meg wouldn't have had a storage area she couldn't see into. Pick up the light and look in that trunk.'

The trunk stood surrounded by that array of domestic cast–offs every household accumulates: old oil fires, superceded but kept against the rainy day when everything else breaks down; a couple of scuffed suitcases, a table lamp, a chair. There was just room for me to stand bent double and lift the lid. The first layer was newspaper; the second yellowed tissue–paper, its faint papery odour suggesting a mummy's skin. Below were black soft folds of cloth.

'Lift it out.'

As I drew it up, leaves of tissue floated from between the layers and rustled to the floor. It was a long black dress. I knew at once it was the one I had seen her wearing at the funeral and on the jetty. I carried it into Meg's bedroom and laid it on the bed, before going back to put out the light and close the little door. Then I stood looking down at the swathe of black silk.

I knew that I had seen it before, and not just on her. There was a photograph in my mother's album of the three of them when young: John, Eileen and Meg, all dressed for a dance. My mother was wearing this dress with elbow–length black lace gloves; John was in a dinner jacket and black tie, Meg was looking uncomfortable in another similar dress that might have been any colour, but had been blackened by the photographer. They were sitting at a table with others in evening clothes and the caption read: *Claridges, 1946*.

For whatever reason Meg had kept my mother's dress for over thirty years, and apart from that same smell of age, it seemed as good as when she had put it carefully away.

'That'll do splendidly.'

'It smells.'

'You can disguise that with scent.'

'It may not fit me.'

'I'm sure it will.'

She was right. My protest had been a formality. My mother and I were of a size, however little I liked to recognise any close similarity between us. If it fitted both of them, it would fit me.

'You look terrible,' she said, 'haggard and old. You'd better get yourself some lunch and then have a sleep.'

'I don't feel like eating. I feel a bit sick.'

'Perhaps you're pregnant.' She laughed harshly, and then began to sing mockingly the words from the tape:

> *'And little ken I my bairn's father*
> *Far less the land that he dwells in …'*

'They'll be surprised at the hospital when you have a baby with webbed toes and fingers and green weed for hair. Whose baby will it be, Paul? Yours or mine? Who'll hold it to her breast, that little sea creature?'

The tears began to trickle down my face. I was being destroyed from within. Tom Ferris had come too late. Between them, she and Wallace would drown me in grief. I turned away, leaving her with a black fold of cloth in the hand that was already marked out by the black ring, and went downstairs into the kitchen. I cooked a little fish and the smell brought Tiger back to me.

For myself I made a cup of instant soup from a packet and carried it into the sitting room, where I raked out the hearth and lit the fire. The dictionary was still on the floor where Tom had put it down and I began to turn its pages, looking for help or comfort. Tiger came in, announcing that he had eaten his fish and, settling his back against me where I sat on the rug, began to wash. Throwing out his right leg, he bent his neck to lick along the muscular thigh, pausing from time to time to stare into the flames as if considering.

They were the thin flames of a newly–lit fire that waver and tongue out as they catch, but seem without warmth or substance—will o' the wisps that so easily sink and die. I watched them shooting up at the chimney and dropping back to reach out again. My eyes began to prick and blur and my ears were filled with a faint humming. I had slipped down on the rug with a cushion under my head and Tiger's back warm against me as he bent and washed and straightened to stare again into the flames that had lit now in his eyes and were flaring and dancing there.

I was on the landing at the top of the stairs, looking down. Two figures stood in the hall below me, face to face in front of the closed door: my aunt and Leonard Wallace. Their voices came to me quite clearly, but embedded in the kind of echo–chamber static of an indoor swimming bath.

The air flashed and crackled around them as if they were two electric pylons in a storm, confronting each other across a valley. The voices themselves were gritty and high–pitched.

'I can't sell it to you. I've told you, it goes with the house and it's useless without it.'

'Not to me. I don't want the house, just the cove. Alright. If you won't sell it, rent it to me.'

'But why? You really have to tell me what for first.'

'I don't see that. If I pay whatever rent we have agreed.'

'We *haven't* agreed. I hope that's quite clear. And we shan't, or at least *I* shan't, until you tell me what it's for.'

'It interests me. I've found an account in an old book that says the seals used to come ashore there.'

'Why should that make you want it? There must be lots of places where the seals came out. That was long ago, when there were more. Now they cull them to keep the fishermen happy.'

'Perhaps I want a place where they can be safe, that they can escape to.'

'No, Leonard, I'm sorry. The picture of you as a nature–lover joining the ecology party isn't convincing. You want the cove for some purpose of your own. Anyway, why bother to try to buy or rent it from me when you're already using it for nothing and keeping me away with that hooded figure beyond the hedge? He's there to stop me from going down to see what's happening, isn't he? I realise now. And of course, now that I do realise, it won't work, will it? What does go on there? What are you up to? You might as well tell me, because I shall go down and see for myself. And what have you got hidden in the boathouse with its new padlock I didn't put on and haven't got a key to? Tell me, or I shall break it off and look for myself.'

As she spoke the hall was lit by a kind of St Elmo's blue fire that played around her, while Wallace's black shape stood out against a faint red glow, like the night sky above a city street.

'You're making a mistake, Margaret, in trying to thwart me. I want the cove and I shall have it. I shall make you give it to me.'

'You've already tried and it doesn't work, because when I'm not so tired as I've been lately, my will is as strong as yours. You can't put me under as I'm sure you do other people. One in ten is a very bad subject for hypnosis, as I understand it, and I am that tenth.'

'You're very foolish, a silly old woman standing in the way of knowledge and power out of pride in your own strength. I can destroy you if I must.'

'No doubt you could destroy me physically. That's easily done. I'm an old woman, as you say. Whatever that hooded figure is that stands out there at night, no doubt it's capable of beating my brains out, and perhaps I wouldn't even resist. But you can't destroy me, and that's what really angers you and makes you so determined to have your way. I'm not touched by you—not really, not inside.'

'You were at first.'

'A little. You flattered an old woman's vanity; something I'm sure you're very practised in. But that quickly wore thin so that I could see through it. And then that day at your house, you tried to put me right under, to get control of my mind. For a few seconds you almost succeeded, but not for long enough. You see, you weren't very subtle: that cheap trick with the whisky in my tea like a poor conjuror who lets slip the card up his sleeve, so that even the children at the party can see.'

'Perhaps I was a little careless. I'm used to my tricks, as you call them, working. I have the power. Men's minds and especially women's weaker minds give themselves up to me. I couldn't see why yours didn't. Then I realised it was your vanity and your own wilfulness that wouldn't let you become a channel for the power to flow through. I made up my mind that you must bend, and you will. The cove is a place of power, one of the nodes where it can flow into the world and spread itself. Your refusal obstructs and blocks it. I shall go on pitching my will against yours until it is broken. We shall see who is strongest.'

She laughed then, and I saw him go rigid with anger. 'It's a delusion, Leonard; a game of bogles children play to frighten themselves with.'

'You think you can protect yourself by pretending not to believe, but the power is stronger than that. It will use you whether you acknowledge it or not.'

'What do you do with this power? What goes on in the cove? Why can't you answer that? Because it's something I wouldn't approve of, or would think silly, something you're ashamed of.'

'I exult in it. Their little minds and lives are thrown open. They are lifted out of their humdrum tepid thoughts into passion and imagination, into a new reality.'

'The sort of murkily farcical goings—on you read about in the Sunday papers from time to time. Am I supposed to be frightened of that kind of charlatan's mumbo—jumbo? Do you know, that's what I thought, that's the very word I put in my diary about the first time I saw you.'

'Show it to me. Show me this diary.'

'You've looked for it, haven't you? You've guessed it might be there, if only you could find it. But I have my tricks, my disguises too. There's a record of all your attempts to cajole and frighten me. I haven't decided yet how I shall use it, but I shall. Now go home. I'm getting tired of you.'

The blue fire had sunk to a flicker that played hesitantly about her. My aunt was tiring, her animal vitality failing in the struggle with Wallace under the force of his will and conviction.

'You see,' his figure seemed to grow taller as she shrank into herself. The red light glowed more strongly, and suddenly there were two of him, for his shadow was flung across my aunt by a fierce spurt of flame in the dark sitting room, where a dying ember had flared in the hearth. She cried out and clutched at her side. 'You see?' His voice rose. 'You are weaker! Admit it, admit it!'

He reached out long black arms and gripped her shoulders, shaking her like a sagging scarecrow whose stuffing has drained down to its rag legs through a long winter of frost and rain. I saw her begin to collapse, her body buckling and sinking in a kind of slow motion. He let go of her shoulders and she fell to the ground.

Leonard Wallace stepped back and stood for a moment, looking down at what now seemed a very small bundle on the floor. Then he stepped deliberately over it, opened the door and went out into the night, shutting the door behind him.

There was no blue flame now. I could still just see the hall from my vantage–point above, but the whole picture was fading. Then I too was sinking back, dwindling down into the body that lay abandoned beside the fire in a tranced sleep which was itself an echo of the death I had just witnessed. As I came to, I was aware of Tiger lying on my chest, kneading my sweater with his front paws as he purred into my face.

Leonard Wallace had killed her, or at least had brought about her death, but he hadn't conquered her will. Her heart had given out rather than give in. Frustrated, he had turned his power against her heir and had found in me a collusive victim. Tonight he would try to break me as he had tried to subdue her, and I was so weak by comparison with Meg that I might well turn to mush under his hand.

Yet to ring and say I wasn't coming, or even not to turn up, would solve nothing. He would merely come after me. I had to summon a courage I knew I didn't have, and with my black twin holding a dagger at my back. If only I could face her down again so that she would be left behind. It was time to get myself ready, to put on the dress she had chosen for me.

I went upstairs to where it was still lying on the bed. She was bending over it, picking at a minute speck of something, perhaps a fragment of tissue paper.

'Come here,' I said.

She straightened up. 'It's time for you to get dressed.'

'I know.' I walked towards the dressing–table and stood looking in the mirror.

'What are you doing?'

I didn't answer, but continued to face the glass. In a moment I felt her move towards me and then her face slid into the oval frame beside my own.

'You're not going with me tonight. I'm going by myself.'

'Yes, I am. I told you. I won't be left behind again.'

'Yes, you will. I have caught you, my likeness, in this glass and you will stay there. Feel it cold and flat and heavy on you, holding you down. You're just a tracing, a transfer between the glass and the silver back. You can't get out any more than a fish in an aquarium until I release you. You can't speak or move. You're just a trapped reflection of me I'm leaving behind.'

I turned and walked away from the dressing–table, not looking back in case in some way I should break the spell and set her free again. The telephone rang and I hurried downstairs.

'How's your day been?' Tom's voice asked. 'I thought I might just catch you to say hallo before you left.'

'I'm late. I'm not dressed or anything. I fell asleep.'

'You will drive carefully, won't you?'

I laughed with delight at his concern. 'I'm really quite a responsible driver.'

'I'll ring you in the morning to see when I can join the queue to take you out.'

I went upstairs again, picked up the dress, rummaged for my make–up case and tights and left the room without looking in the mirror to see if she was still frozen there. In the bathroom I washed and dressed. The clinging black folds fitted me perfectly. Now was the test. I should have to use a looking–glass to put on my make–up. Would it unlock her? I summoned Tom's voice and smile and began to trace my mouth with lipstick. My own image looked singly out at me as I concentrated on the practical gestures I had been making all my adult life. Suddenly I knew I was safe from her tonight. It had worked.

As I drove through the town, I told myself not to swing into an opposite state of over–confidence. If my aunt had had an Achilles' heel, that had been it. And I was no Abbess Hilda, as Leonard Wallace had called her. Inside, I was still the same Paula Cockburn who might crumble and liquefy at a touch. The first sight of the tower silhouetted against a faintly luminous night sky was enough to remind me how vulnerable I was.

I parked outside the high wall and left the ignition key dangling in its place and the driver's door unlocked. Car thieves were a hazard I had to accept in return for the chance to get away quickly. Taking a deep breath, and with a heart that threatened to deafen me, I got out and rang the bell beside the door in the wall. Its soundless opening, even though I was prepared for it, did nothing to reassure me. The garden beyond breathed all the starkness of Winter under the light from the hall door which slid open as I approached. Someone was monitoring my arrival from within the house.

Leonard Wallace came towards me as I entered, wearing the black velvet suit with a ruffled shirt that is part of Highland evening dress. He was smiling and holding out a hand to draw me in.

'Let me take your coat. Now, I think a small Malt to warm you up. What a charming dress.'

At once I knew I was a fool to think I could win against him, and yet I *had* to try. The first rule was not to drink too much; the second, not to let him see that I was resisting his influence for as long as I could. I must find some talisman to hold onto. And then I heard my aunt's voice say quite distinctly: '*I'm not touched by you, not inside.*' I sipped my drink carefully, casting around for a harmless topic of conversation but there was none.

'When is Mr Ferris leaving us?'

'Mary's funeral is tomorrow. He'll have to make up his mind after that.'

'I hope he goes soon: his presence is distracting.'

I couldn't think of an answer, and the silence grew between us. I was almost relieved when a buzzer sounded and Wallace stood up. 'Dinner is ready. You haven't seen my dining room I think. I wonder what you'll make of it.'

I felt his hand on my elbow, steering me towards the door. I hung back. 'You lead the way and I'll follow.'

He bowed ironically. 'We're having a touch of feminism this evening, are we?'

'It just seems so much more sensible to me when the woman doesn't know the way and the man does.'

He turned and led us out. It was a small victory but we both recognised it. I must try to be more careful not to show my hand. We were now descending one of the curved iron staircases into the basement. Leonard Wallace opened a door at the bottom.

The room was five—sided like the tower above, but with only high, narrow slit—windows, giving the sensation of being in a sugar sifter. A pentagonal table took up most of the space with its five dining chairs. But it was the walls that drew the eye, as they were meant to, rioting with every garishly painted image of lust and monstrousness man had imagined: coupling and prancing figures writhed in purple, viridian and blood up and down, in a devilish maypole dance whose centre was an erect Priapus.

211

'I see it's had its usual effect.' Wallace laughed. 'It's based on the decorative schemes for the houses of pleasure in classical times. We've become so mealy–mouthed about honest lust, I always think.'

'You don't find it makes the food rather indigestible?' My eye followed the two entwined lamias whose tails led to the offered buttocks of a young satyr or faun.

'It usually means there's no lack of dinner–table conversation.' He waved me to a seat opposite. There was a whirring noise and a hatch in the wall opened to show me an array of dishes, which he carried to the table and placed on a silver hot–plate. 'Let me give you some soup.'

He ladled out the thick green creme into two plates and then poured the wine. 'To your charming dress,' he said, raising his glass.

I lifted mine. 'I think I'm allowed to drink to that because it was actually my mother's, so it's her taste we're acknowledging.'

A shadow crossed his face. I almost bit my tongue, but it was too late. I was finding it very hard to disguise my hand. To make up for it, I said: 'It's a marvellous wine.'

'If you look deep into it, you'll see it's almost purple. Look, can you see? Look deep into the glass, Paula. Let your eyes go right down until you're resting on the bottom.'

There was nothing I could do. I *had* to look. I felt my head begin to swim. One bubble floated, turning gently, at the red heart of the glass. I narrowed my eyes against it and Mary's face smiled up at me out of the bloody depths.

'What do you see, Paula?'

'A face. I don't know whose. A face.'

'That's a good girl. Drink some more.'

Obediently I lifted the glass again, dulling my gaze as I looked up at him, but holding the image of Mary between us. Even so, I could see the touch of smugness about his mouth. The child was doing as it was told now.

'Now pass me your soup dish and you shall have some mushroom vol au vents. Remembering your curious squeamishness about flesh, I got Kasper to try his hand at

212

something special. Tell me more of Mr Ferris.'

'He's a marine biologist. He works on an oil rig.'

'One of the destroyers and polluters.'

'I think his job is actually trying to cut down on that.'

'You're defending him.'

'I'm trying to be fair.'

'Life isn't fair. It isn't meant to be. It's a conflict, a power struggle between those with imagination and the rest of the dead mass that tries to hold them back.'

He topped up my glass and held his own up, so that little sparkles caught on the cut edges. 'Look, Paula. This is a very good crystal. See how it takes the light.'

I had to look at him again and pretend that I wasn't pitting my will against the suck of his voice and eyes. The glass turned slowly in his hand.

'It's beautiful,' I heard myself say. 'The red is so deep I feel as if I'm drowning in it.' Behind the upheld glass a horned face simpered at a centaur nuzzling between a woman's thighs.

'After dinner I've prepared a little entertainment for you. Drink up, or I shall think you don't really like my wine in spite of your praises.'

The richness of the food and the rollicking figures on the walls were beginning to make me feel a little queasy. In normal circumstances I would have enjoyed the marrons and cream that appeared next, but today I could hardly swallow them. How soon would the real test come, and what form would it take? I didn't believe Leonard Wallace had invited me there just to appreciate his table and his cut glass. Even so, I was glad when he pushed back his chair saying that we would have our coffee elsewhere. He led me back to the drawing room and sat me down beside the fire.

'Coffee and a rather special liqueur to round it all off.' He was standing over me with a cup and a small glass of green liquid in his hands. 'You're not allowed to waste a drop of this.'

'What is it?'

'Something I bring back from California. An old Inca

recipe, they say.' He laughed.

'Do you often go to California. Is that where you brush up on your tan?'

'Yes, and further South. The Pentacle Press has a branch there I have to attend to.'

The green liqueur had a pungent, spicy flavour, almost like a sweet tobacco. Leonard Wallace kept his eyes on me as I sipped, lifting his own small glass in mock toasts that I was obliged to respond to. 'Now come with me.' He held out a hand.

His fingers were growing longer. They were the tentacles of an octopus, and a dead, drowned white. They swam towards me across the room as I tried to hold on to my talismen. When I stood up, my legs had become a fishtail that was quite numb. I looked down and conjured up a picture of Tiger winding himself about me until I could see my feet again.

'Your liqueur is very strong. I hope I'm going to be able to drive home.'

'Perhaps you won't have to. Come, Paula. You are waited for.' The white fingers took mine and we began to swim across a room whose air had become heavy as water, a room in a palace of a sunken city where bubbles streamed from us as we went and drifted up to bump against the ceiling. Wallace led me out and along the corridor I had travelled with him on my last visit. This time we didn't pause to go down to the print room, but kept on towards the black box ante–room of what he had called his study, the chamber of illusions. He drew me after him as effortlessly as she had. The door opened in front of us and closed behind.

His hand released mine. 'Wait there until you are called.'

I didn't see the far door open, but I knew I was alone. I had no choice but to wait. The black folds of airlessness began to press down on me. I tried to call up Aunt Meg's voice, but it seemed blurred and far away. Then, as before, a blue pentangle glowed in the wall.

'You may come in now, Paula,' Leonard Wallace's voice said. I moved towards it and the wall dissolved.

The whole chamber was on fire. Flames, its only light,

raced up the walls and danced on the floor, red and yellow, yet without heat. They were "the agony of flame that cannot singe a sleeve," demon fires that torment without consuming. At the far end, Leonard sat in one of two thrones, wearing a long black cloak fringed and flounced with fronds of brown weed. He stood up.

'You must come through the flames to take your place.'

My feet moved without my will. As I walked, red tongues licked up my skirt and flickered in my hair. The two thrones were set on a dais with four steps up. At the bottom I stood still.

'Come up, Paula.'

'Why should I?' I sounded childish and obstinate even in my own ears.

'Sit beside me. It's the best place to see the world from.'

'I don't know why you want me to.'

'Because you belong beside me.'

'How can I?' The small dregs of my courage were almost gone.

'We are two of a kind. My mind calls and yours answers. I knew it on the first day we met. You already wear my ring. You are the mistress and I am your master. I want you to marry me after the ceremonies of the outside world, even though we are already one after the rites of our own. I want us to be bound in that world, as in this.'

Tom Ferris' voice whispered: '*I'm ringing to see if you're alright.*'

'You don't really want me,' I said. 'You only want the cove for your obscene games.' I pulled at the black band on my finger and felt it move. I tugged more fiercely, not caring how much it hurt. With a sudden jerk it was off. I threw it at his feet. 'There's your ring. I'm not bound to you any more. Now let me go home.'

The air was filled with shrieking and high catcalls. Leonard Wallace strode down two steps and seized my arm, twisting it behind me so that I cried out in pain. 'Don't cross my will, Paula. You're not strong enough. Cross me, and the headsman shall have you, as he had the others. I only have to

215

summon him.'

His fingers bit into my flesh like the tearing claws of some carrion—eater, until I cried out once more with the pain. 'Come up,' he said fiercely, and dragged at me so that I was caught off balance and fell against his arm. For a moment I felt his grip slacken under the weight. I wrenched my own arm away and turned. Desperately I tried to remember where the second door had been last time. Was it worked by hand, or was it automatic like the doors in airports and the new trains?

'You know you can't get out. Come back where you belong.'

Why was he trying so hard to convince me if that was so? Was it because he knew I *could* escape? I ran to the nearest wall and began to move along it. The shrieking was louder now and the air full of flames and shadows that fell towards me and seemed to brush me like bat—wings. Mixed with the other sounds I could hear Leonard Wallace's voice calling me back. I reached the second length of wall whose upper tier was made of angled mirrors, where now devilish faces leered and threatened.

I was almost sure this was the wall that had held the door, and now suddenly I saw the pentacle that should mark it, not glowing as before, but a faint outline like a scorch where the blue light might have burnt. I moved towards it, willing an opening to appear. Leonard Wallace jumped down the last two steps and ran towards me at the same moment as the gap opened. I plunged through. It closed behind.

The trick that was meant for others had caught him for a moment but I must be quick. The door would open again in a second. I began to climb up the only way in front of me. The door opened below, letting out a bedlam of noise and the figure of Leonard Wallace. I ran on up the stairs.

'You can't get away, Paula. I can't let you go.'

At the top was a handled door. I turned the knob and was in the glass corridor between the leads. It was almost black after the light inside and the night sky pressed against me. The wind moaned behind the glass and I felt myself falling against it and its jagged splinters gashing through my skin to let the bright blood out. I crouched halfway along like a mesmerised rabbit.

Leonard Wallace wrenched open the door and flung it back. My eyes were accustoming themselves to the dark now, and I could see him silhouetted blackly against the night sky that streamed with washes of cloud on a starshine ground. 'Paula. Stop this nonsense. You can't escape me.' He moved forward a little hesitantly. I realised his eyes were less adjusted than my own and that he probably couldn't see me half–crouched down so that less of me was against the glass upper portion of the thin partition that threatened to crack and send me toppling down.

'Ah, there you are.' There was a note of triumph in his voice. 'You don't like heights, do you? I divined that that would be one of your pressure points the first time I met you and I was sure of it when we climbed up to Hilda's Abbey. You might fall, Paula, and go on spinning down like a leaf or a sycamore seed. But you're not light like them. You're heavy with human weight that bruises and crushes. Stay perfectly still until I reach you. You'll be safe with me.'

He began to creep forward, a black bulk that was nevertheless sinuous. The sea cloak rustled and whispered and the gallery was filled with the reek of the boathouse. He was very close now and raising himself above me. I heard a cry—mine—and I stood up, reaching out with both hands to push away the shape that was lowering itself onto me. I thrust blindly and fiercely. For a moment he seemed to waver and flung out a hand to steady himself. There was a crash of breaking glass. I turned and ran towards the far door, tore it open and began to run down the stairs.

In my mind's eye I saw him again as he staggered against the flimsy wall, saw the arm that was pierced by the shattering glass, the body following it, glass falling in glittering razor segments, the figure turning as it fell. I reached the door at the bottom and stared wildly about. Again I was in an ante–room. This time I could see a perfectly plain door. I tugged hard at it.

It was the kitchen. Across the room I could see what must be a back door leading into the garden, and on the right another door, partly ajar.

'Is that you, Leonard?' a man's voice asked.

I ran across the room and flung myself on the handle. At the edge of my vision a figure appeared, blue–denim clad, huge, with a white skin–domed head shining with sweat and grease. When it saw me it let out a roar, but I was through into the garden and running round the side of the house, blundering into the softness of flowerbeds and stumbling against shrubs. Several times I nearly fell. My ankle gave, but I struggled on against the pain. There at last was the wall. I must trace it to the gate. For once luck was with me. In a few steps I reached the flagged path and the high gate.

Fumbling at the catch, I expected every second to hear feet behind me and feel hands dragging me back. The catch clicked. I fell into the street, pulling open the car door and collapsed on the driving seat. I slammed and locked the door and switched on. The engine coughed, but didn't turn. I had forgotten the choke. I pulled it out.

Suddenly there was a hooded form in the gateway. I turned the ignition key again and the engine caught. Hands tore at the locked car door and beat at the windows as I let in the clutch. Sobbing for breath, I roared down the hill towards the lit part of the town. In the station yard I drew up, put my head down on the wheel and wept. Then, when my first reaction had subsided a little, I drove slowly on towards the cottage.

I longed to be able to pull up at Mary's and go in search of Tom Ferris's comforting presence, but my own complicity stopped me. My old problem of how to explain any of it to him hadn't gone away. I drove on and parked the car on the verge above Meg's house. As I went down the path I knew what I was going to do. I must make a bid now to free myself of them both.

Going into the kitchen, I took a hammer from among the tools my aunt had kept under the sink. I fetched a bath towel from the airing cupboard, climbed the stairs and, with it held

218

in front of me and my head slightly turned away, I went into Meg's bedroom, across to the dressing–table and threw the towel over the looking glass.

With the first blows of the hammer I felt something crack inside me as if the glass were an ice–shell about my own heart. I struck again and again, the splinters cracking behind the towel and shattering on the dark brown wooden top, to shower in fragments onto the floor as I alternately pounded the remains of the mirror in its frame and the larger pieces where they fell. With every crack of the hammer another piece of cold casing seemed to be torn away from inside me. A warm stream flowed from the back of my hand where a sliver had pierced the skin, and it was echoed by a warm gush that spread through my veins, as if the last ice river had been unlocked by the sun.

When I was sure *she* was pounded to fragments, I fetched a dustpan and brush and swept them up into an old newspaper. I would throw them into the sea and she would be gone forever. Even so, I didn't dare think of them settling down through the waves in a glittering silt in case her image should reform them on the seabed at the bottom of my mind.

In my concentration on smashing my mirror self, I had forgotten for a little what I had left behind, but now it came back to me, together with the realisation that I might be followed. I went downstairs and locked and bolted back and front doors. My legs began to tremble, not with fear but with delayed shock, and I was forced to lie down in front of the fire.

I must have fallen asleep, for I heard nothing more until something thudded against the front door, waking me with a violent start. Someone was smashing at it with great splintering blows. I remembered the axe under the verandah behind the house. I must try to see what was happening. I went upstairs to the spare room and peered down from behind the curtains.

A hooded shape was smashing at the door. Suddenly it stepped back and let out a howl of rage and frustration. Then it raised its weapon and ran at the door again. For a moment light had fallen on the axe blade. The air was full of screams and Mary's blood spurted over the kitchen walls until my nostrils were filled with the sickening sweetness of it.

There was nothing else for it. I had to get help. I dialled Mary's number.

'Oh, Tom!' I said, almost crying when I heard his voice. 'There's someone outside trying to break the front door down ...'

'Ring the police,' he said abruptly. 'I'm on my way.'

'Be careful. I think he's got an axe.'

'Don't worry. I'll bring a hammer or something.'

He slammed down the receiver, and I began dialling the emergency services.

'Someone's trying to break down my door with an axe. I think it could be the murderer. Please hurry.'

'Can you lock yourself in a bathroom or somewhere till we can get there? Anything to give us time.'

How much time did I have? The howling was almost continuous now, and so were the blows. I found myself begging Tom, out loud, to hurry; I could retreat to the bathroom if the door broke, but I couldn't bear to be shut in there any sooner than I had to be, not knowing whether he was in the house or not. The door panels were splintering now, but the bolt still held.

Suddenly the noise stopped. Then I heard shouting. I peered out again and saw the bobbing light of a torch. Tom was running down the path. As he came into my view I saw he too had a weapon that seemed in the uncertain light longer and frailer than the axe. I hoped it was enough.

The hooded shape left its attack on the door and turned to meet Tom with a snarl of rage. It was at least as tall, and much more heavily built. The round, hooded poll made it even more menacing. It lifted its weapon high. Tom backed and circled cautiously.

It was a dance of shadows, a contest with primitive weapons that was almost balletic in its movements as they each looked for advantage, swaying on their legs and hefting their arms. With a scream the headsman sprang forward. The

220

axe–blade caught the little light as it gashed at Tom's arm. I heard him half grunt, half cry out, but he didn't drop his own weapon. He circled again and then suddenly he too leapt, smashing down on the axe hand, so that the axe was sent spinning away. Then he leapt again, using the bar as a foil and jabbing at the throat.

The bulky figure in front of him staggered and put both hands to its neck. Then it turned and began to run. I too ran down the stairs to the battered front door, picking up Aunt Meg's walking stick as I passed the coat stand.

Drawing back the bolt, I hurried out into the night. I could hear shouts and feet pounding in front of me. Then a pause. I ran on faster. Ahead now I could make out what must be the back of Tom just on the top of the steps. Below him the other figure lumbered down, swinging from the rope banister. I saw Tom suddenly jump forward, bringing down his weapon as he did so. It cracked across the shoulder of the hand that held the rope. The figure let go, stumbled, missed its footing and pitched headlong, rolling over and over, scrabbling, howling until it hit a slight outcrop in the cliff face and was flung sideways off to crack down on the beach below. Behind me I heard the thudding of boots, and looking back I saw the jolting lights of torches as the police ran down the path towards us.

That was over a year ago, and now at last I have put it all down. I am doing what I should have done months before, because you want to marry me and you can't understand why although I say I love you, I still say I'm not worth loving. You will be here this weekend and I hope I shall have the courage to put this into your hands.

I'm afraid that the past is irrevocable, that what's done can't be undone—as my mother would say—and that there are some things in my nature I can't ask you to take on, including this too of having been for so long unable to tell you the truth. I am afraid that one morning when I wake beside you in bed, *she* may be standing by the window. I am afraid that when I am able to respond to your love–making, it's only the lust of that other beast that moves me. And most of all, I am afraid, because of all this, of losing you, of seeing you grow out of love and turn away from me.

I don't know fully what happened that night. I don't even know whether Leonard Wallace is alive or dead. I know that the murderer, the redcap, must have been Kasper, but because I pretended to the police and to you that I didn't know him, or why he should have attacked me, no one has ever been able to establish his identity or link him with Five Ways.

I could, I suppose, have tried ringing the house, or even driving past to see if it was for sale, but I didn't. There was no account in the papers of Wallace's body being found, but that might mean nothing. I feel, though, that he isn't dead, that he is still a presence in the world somewhere.

How can I ask you to take on all this mess that is me? At least now you will know how great it is, and it may be that it is too much, and that by the time you read this I have already lost you. And that breaks my heart, because I do truly love you. I see you sitting in front of the fire scratching Tiger's neck, and I yearn towards you. Please, if you still can, love me, help me, because I am afraid above all of being alone.

All Futura Books are available at your bookshop or
newsagent, or can be ordered from the following
address:
Futura Books, Cash Sales Department,
P.O. Box 11, Falmouth, Cornwall.

Please send cheque or postal order (no currency), and
allow 45p for postage and packing for the first book
plus 20p for the second book and 14p for each additional
book ordered up to a maximum charge of £1.63 in U.K.

Customers in Eire and B.F.P.O. please allow 45p for
the first book, 20p for the second book plus 14p per
copy for the next 7 books, thereafter 8p per book.

Overseas customers please allow 75p for postage and
packing for the first book and 21p per copy for each
additional book.